ALL THINGS RISE

All Things Rise

by

Missouri Vaun

2015

ALL THINGS RISE

ISBN 13: 978-1-62639-346-2

This Trade Paperback Original Is Published By
Bold Strokes Books, Inc.
P.O. Box 249
Valley Falls, NY 12185

First Edition: May 2015

Credits
Editor: Cindy Cresap
Production Design: Susan Ramundo
Cover Design By Sheri (graphicartist2020@hotmail.com)
Character Illustration By Paige Braddock

Acknowledgments

If you, kind reader, will indulge me, I'd like to take a few paragraphs to thank the people who helped make this book a reality.

I owe Radclyffe a big thank you for taking a chance on a new author. I'd also like to thank Radclyffe for creating a community of writers who are secure enough and talented enough that they graciously help others improve their craft. Everyone at Bold Strokes Books has been extremely kind, patient, and helpful. Sandy answered a million dumb questions, Ruth helped me talk through strategies and branding for my next books, Sheri did an amazing job on the cover design, and my editor, Cindy, is terrific to work with. I really can't say enough nice things about working with the entire BSB crew. You guys are all rock stars, you know, of the book world.

Carsen Taite, D. Jackson Leigh, and Kim Baldwin were incredibly generous with advice and encouragement when I was first working on my manuscript. VK Powell was kind enough to read an early draft and offer me some good constructive feedback. Actually, I've had great notes from several of my friends who agreed to beta read for me. My wife, Evelyn, Vanessa, Alena, Art, and Michelle, you guys offered thoughtful insights and lots of encouragement. Having friends willing to read the rough manuscript and give notes was invaluable. Thank you so much.

Celina de Leon, I could say thank you for being a beta reader also, but in reality you've contributed so much more to the online and social experience for my books, and soon, readers of those books.

Kathleen Knowles was nice enough to include me in a San Francisco Bay Area reading even before my book was out.

Deb Smith, weather scientist and friend, talked me through climate change and how it might affect the coastlines of the future. This comes into play even more in the second book in this series.

I'm sure the reason for writing is different for everyone who takes a seat in front of the keyboard. In my case, I feel that finding love in my own life made it easier for me to write a romance story. When I met Evelyn, it was basically love at first sight and now, six years later, every day is better than the one before. Evelyn, thank you for supporting this new adventure and for making me a believer in true love.

And lastly, I'd like to say thanks to the original Missouri Vaun, my great-grandmother. I want you to know I have your typewriter and I'm taking good care of it.

Dedication

For Evelyn, my true love.

Chapter One

Ava hesitated for an instant as the readout on the console flashed green. She held her breath as she hit the keystroke that would start the launch sequence. She adjusted the headset, placing the small receiver close to her lips so that she could speak quietly to the flight tower and still be heard. She received clearance for her flight plan and departure.

She wanted to escape.

As a commercial pilot, Ava was required to complete a one-week certification test every two years. She was scheduled to take the exam on the cloud city of Miami this week, but had decided instead to use this break in her regular work schedule as a ruse to get away from everyone—her mother, friends, Audrey…

She felt crowded in her own life and badly needed to be out of touch for a few days. She wanted to sleep late, have no responsibilities, think—especially think. She didn't know what the root of her discontent was, but lately she'd been feeling like her life wasn't her own. That something wasn't quite balanced. She was unsure what was causing her disquiet. Ava knew a few women who would be more than happy to console her, but they couldn't help her with this. This, whatever *this* was, was more about self than other. She needed to find a source of solace for her own soul. No other person could soothe the restless feeling that seemed to have settled deep in her chest.

"Ava, you might be a little crazy," she muttered to herself. She adjusted the straps across her flight jacket.

"Please repeat," came the monotone voice from the flight tower.

Great, my mic was on. "Sorry. I said, 'Ready for departure,'" Ava responded into her headset receiver.

She watched as the lights in the launch tube began to flicker at ever more rapid intervals in front of her craft indicating that a launch sequence was in progress. In a matter of seconds, the small, two-seater cruiser would be sent swiftly down the metallic tunnel and out into the blinding sunlight. Ava grabbed her visor for the inevitable solar glare that would envelop the cloudless afternoon sky.

As she began to feel more unsettled in her own life, she found herself requesting more and more flight hours, keeping her on the move and away from the confined spaces of the city. Flight made her feel free.

Ava banked the cruiser and circled above the floating cloud city now below. Glass towers reflected light from every angle as she circled. The open sea was gorgeous. Life on the densely populated cloud city of Easton did sometimes feel too close for comfort, but Ava could never complain about its view. Easton was made up of four floating platforms, each containing block after block of high-rise residential and commercial superstructures. Transit tubes connected each platform so that residents could travel easily between each quadrant.

Ava circled Easton once more before she assumed a lower altitude trajectory and headed toward the landmass that lay due west. As the sea passed beneath, her thoughts returned to Audrey.

It was her fault that things had almost gotten completely screwed up with Audrey. No, that wasn't entirely true. She and Audrey had been friends for years. Audrey knew what Ava was like and was equally to blame for the fact that the lines of friendship had almost been crossed. There had always been a slight sexual attraction between them. How could there not be? Audrey was gorgeous, beautiful in the classic sense of the word, the kind of voluptuous loveliness that painters through the centuries had tried to capture on canvas. So whose fault was it, really? Who was she kidding? It had been Ava's reckless libido and excessive alcohol to blame for nearly landing them in bed together. Sleeping with your best friend, such a cliché.

You're such an asshole. If she had allowed their relationship to transition from platonic to sexual, Ava would have ultimately hurt Audrey. What each of them wanted from a relationship was as far apart as night was to day. Ava knew Audrey wasn't a woman who engaged in casual sex. If they'd actually slept together, it would be impossible to go back to the way things were. A situation that would have no doubt been made worse by the fact that Ava bolted right after she and Audrey had kissed, before practically falling in bed together. Ava followed her abrupt exit from Audrey's residential cube by spending the day with her comm unit off and then scheduled an afternoon departure that would keep her away from the city for a few days. *When did you become such a fucking coward?*

The truth was, Ava wasn't the only one to blame for the near slip, but she also knew that if she'd really pushed, Audrey would have slept with her.

Yeah, space. Time alone. That was what Ava needed to get her head on straight. Maybe then she could return and face Audrey. Maybe. She was sure Audrey would agree that what had nearly happened between them would have been a mistake. Once that was settled then they could get back to normal, back to being friends. Friends, without benefits.

❖

A soft red color, low in the sky, began to appear just over Cole's left shoulder as she dug into the rich dark soil, unearthing the squirming bait. Cole pulled the worm loose from the dirt and studied its writhing complaint before she threaded it onto the hook and tossed it out into the pond.

The smell of moss and soggy earth hung in the warm evening air. Cole considered the worm's plight and then her own role in its demise. *The worm feeds on the earth, the fish on the worm, and me on the fish. Every creature exists to serve its own needs until the hand of God or some greater force of nature chooses to impose its will.*

The Earth, the ground beneath her feet, with its infinite spinning, was indifferent to those residing on its surface. Cole had heard all the stories. Stories that had been passed down through distant family of a time when there wasn't as much water. A time when the coastal regions extended farther and great cities perched on the shores of the seas. But those times were long gone.

According to Cole's great-grandmother, every doomsayer thought the end of everything would occur when peak oil occurred. But that just silenced all the machines and put everyone on foot. Everything really changed when the cities rose. The rich saw it coming and horded reserves for the construction of their own sky-bound life rafts. The working class was too distracted fighting day-to-day for basic needs like food and water to worry too much about what was happening with what little remained of the oil reserves. It's amazing what lengths some people will go to to save themselves. The elite clans definitely embraced the *us* versus *them* approach. Once their electromagnetic propulsion systems went online, they never looked down again.

Maybe those that remained are like the worm, playing their part in a much larger drama. Cole sat with her legs crossed in front of her, leaning against the grand cypress with its roots sunk in the wet soil at the edge of the water, its knees poking up through the pond's surface for air. Cole settled to wait for a fish to take the bait.

It was during these times of quietude that Cole reflected on herself as a part of the whole, of forces larger than herself, and wondered what the future held for her.

❖

Ava took note of the terrain passing beneath her as it transitioned gradually from a coastal landscape to the piedmont, and then rolling hills began on the horizon as she continued her westward trajectory. Low-altitude flights were frowned upon. Pilots were instructed not to create any distractions for the ground dwellers. Sometimes as she flew, Ava could spot beneath the clouds small clusters of buildings in organized grids surrounded by green landscapes. The cloud city cruisers flew silently with their hydrogen engines. Droplets of water were their only residue. Ava doubted any groundling ever noticed them pass overhead.

It had been more than one hundred years since planet Earth reached peak oil. With the end of oil reserves in sight, the pressure was on for the super wealthy to finally fund the research needed to perfect nuclear propulsion. Each city rested on several pressurized water reactors that ran perpetual turbines that kept them aloft and also provided all electrical power at deck level. One percent of the Earth's population, the wealthiest individuals of the world, literally rose above the chaos that erupted when the seas crested after oil's demise.

Once in the air, the huge hovercrafts moved out over the open sea where they'd have plenty of hydrogen power to draw from. The enormous cloud cities were constructed to insulate the elite from the collapse they had contributed to on the ground. New York, Toronto, London, Stockholm, Easton, Miami, Hong Kong, Monaco, Rome, and other metropolises now floated above it all, among the clouds. The lower classes lived on the land that was left. Their world was reminiscent of the nineteenth century. The benefits of cheap oil such as running water, central air and heat, electricity, cars, and supermarkets were now the stuff of folklore.

The late afternoon departure gave Ava a great sunset view of the mountains below as she turned north toward the cloud city of Toronto. It wasn't Ava's usual habit to leave so late in the day or to fly so low over the Blue Mountain ridges, but she felt like breaking the rules a little today. Besides, at this speed, Ava would pass overhead before any groundlings even had the notion to look skyward. As Ava turned north and recalculated her time and distance on the monitors, the horizon to the west began to turn pink. The sun was dipping. Then, unexpectedly, she felt a jolt and a quick drop in altitude.

"What the hell?"

Ava quickly looked at the gauges to her left. They were flashing red. *A power drain?*

Not good. Think, Ava. Think. Had she missed something on her preflight diagnostic? Was she so distracted with planning her escape that she'd overlooked something? Another jolt, sputter, and then a sharp drop in altitude. Considering her flight path was already low enough to afford a great view of the wooded hills, she didn't relish the thought of getting any closer to the treetops.

Ava spoke calmly and evenly into the small microphone mounted on her headset. "Easton Cloud City Tower, this is Jennings 5468."

Static. No response.

"Easton Cloud City Tower, this is J5468 reporting mechanical failure en route to Cloud City Toronto."

Static. No response.

Okay, the power cells are bottoming out, but the radio should be on a separate, self-sustained power grid. Ava threw the useless headset on the empty seat next to her and turned her focus back to the readout for the power grid. *Can I reroute something to gain a little altitude?*

Everything was happening too fast. In the simulators, it always felt like she had more time to fix a problem…and in the back of her mind she knew she wouldn't actually crash if she didn't figure it out. She'd reboot the simulator and try again.

Altitude alarms began to sing in unison with the flashing gauges.

"I know! I know!"

Ava was frantically trying to get the power back up to a normal level, but no matter what she tried, nothing was working. *Shit. I'm going down.* She reached back for her crash helmet and tightened the five-way strap across her chest. Ava grabbed the navigation handles with both hands. She had just enough power to adjust the pitch and roll. The craft shook as the bottom of the cruiser slid across the top of the tall trees below. The descent was happening faster than she'd expected. Tree limbs brushed the side of the cruiser. *Please, please, don't hit a tree full on.*

The cruiser rocked as it encountered thick forest but miraculously stayed fairly level. There was a hard jolt upon first impact with the ground, then a bone-jarring bounce. Another jolt and the cruiser dug a trough as it scraped a path across the ground, stopping no more than six feet from a massive old growth oak tree.

CHAPTER TWO

Cole looked over her shoulder to see that the red hue of the sky was shifting to purple as the sun dropped below the ridge. She picked up the basket and the cane pole and headed toward the house. The old roadbed still had some broken dark rock that used to fit together when it was a paved surface. But now it was just artifacts, with grass and trees breaking through. This was still the best route though. It was probably a deer trail long before it was a road, and now it had been reclaimed as a trail again. Cole turned off the lower roadbed and embarked on an elevated path. In patches where the mountain laurel was thick, it was very dark, but she knew the way by heart. Once the day sky converted to the night sky and she let her eyes adjust, the woods almost seemed translucent.

Cole sometimes spooked herself imagining she could see her ancestors walk among the trees. More than likely it was just the mist created from the day to night change in humidity, but she liked to imagine that sometimes her grandmother walked with her. A favorite tune of hers was "In the Garden," a real old-time classic. Sometimes Cole found herself humming it, and that made her wonder if her grandmother didn't put the idea of the song into her head as she passed Cole on the trail.

This evening, Cole was taking a shortcut, but a steeper route to the house. She'd stayed too long by the pond and the dark was catching up with her. She climbed out of a particularly thick patch of laurel when a light caught her eye. Something descended off to the right and was glowing below the ridge, just out of sight. *Did I spook myself with all my thoughts of ghosts? No, there's definitely something glowing over there.*

❖

Ava realized she'd been holding her breath during the whole landing ordeal and exhaled. She sat for a minute in stunned silence. The power in her cruiser had completely died. The warning signals had stopped, and the cockpit was dark before auxiliary battery power kicked on the emergency lights inside the small space. *Now what? This is not good.* She could see through the window of the cockpit door that the sun had just set. It was going to be dark soon, and she was on the ground in a dead aircraft.

Ava had never been on the ground before. Actually, no one she knew had ever been on the ground. Fantastical stories were spread among the cloud city elite regarding life on the ground. Gangs of desperate people striving to take what the urban sky dwellers worked so hard to create and keep were rumored to be everywhere. The realization that Ava was now alone on the unsafe ground sent panic charging through her. And then it dawned on her: none of her friends knew where she was. In her big hurry to get away from it all, she hadn't told anyone that she was going to the cloud city of Toronto. To top it off, Ava hadn't been able to signal a position before her radio went out and her cruiser went down. She had filed a flight plan, but it wasn't unheard of for small, personal aircraft to divert to a neighboring city once they were within tower range of that position. It would take some time for anyone to realize that Ava was not where she was supposed to be.

She removed her crash helmet and slumped forward, burying her face in her hands. *Keep it together.* She then pushed loose strands of her hair behind her ears and tried to steady herself. *I should take a look at the outside of the craft and see what kind of damage I'm going to have to deal with to get this thing airborne again. Maybe it will be as simple as a defective connection to the solar panels and several hours in the morning sun would solve the problem.*

Ava checked her supply kit. She had water and protein cubes. She'd be fine on the ground for a few hours. *Time alone to think was what I wanted, right?* She reached up to release the hatch. Nothing.

"You've got to be kidding." Ava applied more pressure to the hatch release. Frozen. *Okay, this is not happening.* She glimpsed a shadow coming over the rise to her right. Someone was coming this way. Her heart began to pound as fear crept over her. *Play dead, Ava. If you're lucky, they'll think you have nothing to offer and they'll leave you alone. No one down here has probably even seen a cruiser up close. They wouldn't be able to figure out how to open the hatch even if they wanted to.* Ava leaned back and tried to slow her heart from racing as the dark figure approached.

❖

Cole placed the basket and rod on the ground and walked slowly toward the ridge where she'd noticed the glowing object. Dry twigs snapped underfoot despite her best efforts. She didn't want to make too much noise, not knowing what to expect. And then Cole saw it clearly. It was a shiny capsule of some sort. The glow was coming from a glass window in the center of what looked like an oval door. Cole stared at the gleaming object. It was all slick metal and glass, the only modern thing for miles in any direction, and here it was, less than half a mile from her family's cabin.

Cole took a few steps closer and saw the dark shape of someone inside. The cruiser must have crashed, but it looked none the worse for wear. There was a pile of upturned dirt at the front of the vehicle. The crash landing had cut a ditch of sorts through the brush before it abruptly stopped right next to a giant oak. There were scratches all along its sides, probably from tree limbs, but no punctures were easily visible. Cole had never been this close to an aircraft, but had seen photos of various kinds in old books. She'd always wondered what it would be like to fly one, to get a bird's eye view from something higher than the old fire tower on Black Mountain.

There was a handle on the exterior of the vehicle that seemed like it would open the door. It was colored red as if to say, "Open here." Cole reached for it and then stopped her hand midair. She had a momentary thought that this felt like one of those times when you knew you were doing something that you couldn't take back. When you knew you were doing something that would change everything that came after this one action. Ignoring her fears, she pulled the release.

There was a whoosh as the hatch slowly opened. Condensation formed as the warm, summer evening air met the cool manufactured air of the cruiser's interior. This brief collision of climates blocked Cole's view of the pilot in the chair for a second or two. Then before she was able to get a good look, the person seated inside lunged forward and punched Cole right in the face. The blow caused Cole to fall backward and her nose to gush with blood. This didn't stop the pilot from leaping out of the cruiser to position herself for another swing.

"Geezus," Cole moaned. "That hurt like hell. You didn't have to swing at me. All I did was open the damn door."

When it was obvious that Cole wasn't taking any action to retaliate, the pilot relaxed her defensive stance.

"I...I'm sorry."

Cole jerked her arm as the pilot reached for it. "Well, that'll be the last time. You surprised me is all. I thought you were hurt. I was trying to be obliging." Cole was cupping her hand over her nose, but blood was all over her face as she got to her feet.

They were now eye-to-eye. Cole's first thought was that the pilot was strikingly attractive, despite being a little outside her element. She had the green eyes that gave her away as part of the elite. The exclusive synthetic food diet of the cloud city dwellers had changed the color of their eyes to green. Or so she'd been told. Cole had never seen anyone from the elite clan.

"Really, I'm sorry." The woman apologized again. "Let me...I mean, I've got a med kit. Hang on."

She rummaged through the small cockpit and came back with a white metal box. From it she took some white gauze and handed it to Cole.

"Thanks." Cole sat and put her head between her knees to avoid getting blood on her shirt.

"Where am I?"

"In the mountains," Cole said, her voice muffled by the gauze she was now holding over her nose.

"That much I know. I can see I'm in the mountains. I was hoping for something more specific."

"Maybe I'll tell you," Cole said, looking sideways at her from her seated position. "I haven't decided if I like you well enough to be very helpful."

The woman laughed. "You're right. I'm really sorry." She dropped to one knee beside Cole. "Listen, I've just heard too many scary stories about being on the ground. I had no idea what kind of person had opened the hatch. At the same time, I was also hoping *someone* would open the hatch because the air lock was jammed from inside. I could have been stuck in there for hours. Days even. So, thank you. Here, let me see the damage."

Cole moved her hand from her bleeding nose. The woman went back to the cruiser and returned with a canister of water and her last piece of clean gauze. She wet the sterile material and wiped Cole's face, causing her nose to bleed again.

"Lean back," she said as she put one hand behind Cole's neck for support and pinched the other over her nose with the clean gauze.

Cole felt very odd. Her heart fluttered in her chest as the woman put her hands on Cole's neck. Cole couldn't stop looking at the woman's face. She really was attractive. Cole realized she was having one of those fast-forward moments where you have a glimpse of something that hasn't happened yet, but you feel sure it will. A feeling like they had met before, or were meant to, she wasn't sure which yet.

"Why are you looking at me that way?"

"Um, what way?" replied Cole.

The woman gave Cole a puzzled smile.

The glow from the open cruiser had disguised the moonrise. Cole now looked around and realized it was fully dark.

"Will that thing fly?" Cole asked, gesturing toward the grounded cruiser.

"Not for a while. I think the cells ran down. It just died on me, thus my less than graceful emergency landing."

"Maybe you should come with me," said Cole as she slowly got to her feet. "No one will bother your vehicle up here. This is our property. No one really walks up here on the ridge because there's a roadbed down there that's much easier." Cole pointed downhill.

As she watched the pilot consider the invitation, Cole became aware of the fact that they were like two estranged civilizations, the only bridge for their cultural differences being a mostly common language. She knew they were seeing each other through a lens not of their own making.

Cole was struck by the rarity of their two worlds colliding. Those who resided in the cloud cities hovered above Earth, communicating and conducting commerce only between their urban counterparts, never touching down on the Earth's soil. Likewise, those on the ground had no means or desire to travel the skies or experience urban life. They resided on the ground only, living off the land, having evolved a system of barter for needed goods.

The pale glow from the cockpit shed some light on the scene. Cole and the pilot were now standing about three feet apart as they regarded each other, as if deciding what to do next. The pilot was wearing a sleek flight jacket with a cadet patch at the shoulder over a solid dark shirt made of thin material that clung to her slightly curvy, athletic body. The neck of the dark shirt dipped low enough for Cole to notice the slight swell of her firm breasts. She was not quite as tall as Cole and wore tight fitting pants made of a material Cole had never seen before. The fabric shimmered in the low light with the color of water reflecting a blue sky. Her hair was straight and hung just past her shoulders. Its dark color set off her green eyes in such a way that Cole couldn't stop looking at them. And she had an air about her. Was it arrogance, or just extreme confidence, or ego? Cole wasn't sure.

"Um, I'm Ruth Coleman George," said Cole as she offered her hand for a shake. "But everyone calls me Cole."

Chapter Three

Ava hesitated, trying to decide if Cole's hand was clean enough to shake. She finally accepted her offered hand. "I'm Ava. Ava Wynne."

Ava realized what she'd done. Not only was she on the ground, which in and of itself was unsafe, but she'd made physical contact with a ground dweller and had been in close contact with her blood. She'd simply reacted, without thinking of what the consequences might be. She had touched Cole first. Despite the fact that she knew she should be on high alert, Ava felt oddly drawn to the young woman standing in front of her.

Ava studied Cole. She was tall and lean with dark eyes and short, dark brown hair. She was wearing a button-down cotton shirt and cotton trousers with pockets up and down the sides of the legs. Cole nervously rolled up her sleeves against the warm, moist night revealing the edge of her tan. She had a boyish build with broad shoulders, small breasts, and narrow hips.

"Would you like to come to my house for supper?" Cole asked.

Ava realized that she was no longer afraid even though her brain was telling her she should be.

"Uh, yes. Actually, that would be very kind, under the circumstances," Ava said as she swung her fist in a mock punch. "You know, with the bloody nose and all."

Cole turned and began walking away from the grounded cruiser. "I need to pick up my things. I left them just over the rise," she said as Ava started to follow her.

"Oh, wait." Ava turned back to the cruiser and took out a bag with a long strap that she threw over her shoulder and across her chest. She used a remote device to close the hatch, and the light slowly dimmed to nothing. It took a minute for her eyes to adjust to the darkness and the moonlight.

While Cole retrieved her things, Ava began to study her surroundings. She realized she was standing in debris of some kind and that the trees that surrounded her were encased in rough bark. These were details she had never seen before from the cockpit of her cruiser, even flying at low altitudes. She scuffed her slick vinyl boots a little to see if she could figure out the ground covering. It looked like dead leaves from the trees, but the trees still had leaves, so maybe these were older leaves? She was still puzzling over this when Cole returned with her fishing rod.

"That was just a lucky punch, by the way."

"I'm sure," Ava said.

Ava felt surprisingly calm for someone who had just crashed her only form of transportation in the middle of nowhere and was now about to follow a total stranger into the inky woods. As they began walking, Ava brushed her fingers over the rough bark of several trees. She had the compulsion to touch every foreign texture she passed. The leaves of saplings, a dry branch, and the ferns that grew thick in patches close to the ground. A couple of times Ava noticed Cole looking back at her, she assumed to make sure she was still following her as the climb got steeper. At one point, Cole stopped on the rough path and looked at Ava.

"What?" Ava asked.

"Nothing," said Cole before she began walking again. As they topped the ridge and started down the backside, Ava could see the glow of a candle's light through the trees. She had a feeling of unease as they descended the path toward a rustic dwelling, not knowing what she would encounter once they arrived. Would everyone be as nice as Cole? She doubted it. But she realized she had no choice but to follow Cole down to the house.

❖

Cole saw her aunt Ida appear in the open doorway as they approached. She had a look of shock when she realized Cole wasn't alone. Cole was sure in the moonlight that Ava looked even more alien in her exotic, reflective clothing. They stopped at the edge of the porch so that Ida could get a better look at them in the glow from the open door. Ida opened her mouth, but no words came out.

"Aunt Ida, this is Ava. I invited her for supper." Cole extended an arm toward Ava. Ida was drying a dish with a worn, white towel. Wide-eyed, she looked from Cole to Ava and then back to Ava.

"Well, okay then. Please come in," said Ida, stepping back so they could enter and studying Ava closely as she passed her. "It was getting so dark I was about to send Vivian out to find you. I thought maybe you'd fallen in the pond or something." Ida turned and yelled toward the back of the house, "Vivian! Cole is back, and with a visitor!"

Cole's aunt Vivian appeared from the back room and stopped abruptly when she saw Ava.

Standing in the warm glow of the lantern light, Cole also became aware again of Ava's intense green eyes. Having fully separated from the ground, with no soil to grow their own food, cloud cities perfected food synthesis to be completely self-sufficient. Over time, scientists and biochemical companies eventually altered crops and seedlings genetically to such an extent that they became completely synthetic, with no molecular remnants of their former, natural states. Cole had read that the side effect of this synthetic diet was that all cloud city residents had green eyes.

Ava was unabashedly studying the interior of Cole's house.

Cole noticed the way Ava was settling her gaze on every feature of the cabin. She was sure she would have felt the same way if she'd found herself having dinner at Ava's place, floating in the clouds somewhere out over the open sea.

Cole handed the basket of fish to Vivian, which she took without saying a word.

"Ava," Cole said. "Would you like to sit down? Are you thirsty?"

"Good Lord. Where are my manners?" Ida chirped. "You'll have to forgive us. Our skills at hosting guests have gotten rusty. Please do sit down and make yourself comfortable. Cole, fetch her some water."

Suddenly back in control of her tongue, Ida began telling everyone what to do. "Viv, if you'll clean those fish I'll get them in the skillet and we'll have ourselves a nice dinner in no time. The squash and potatoes are nearly done. That fish will cook quick since the oven is already hot."

"Is that what smells so…interesting?" Ava asked as she hesitantly took a chair at the kitchen table before placing her bag on the floor.

Vivian stepped outside to clean the fish. Normally, Vivian would have tossed the basket of fish right back at Cole for her to clean, but tonight she let Cole have the night off.

Ida stirred the two pans on the stove before taking a closer look at Cole. As she brushed Cole's hair back from her forehead she asked with alarm, "Is that blood?"

"Oh, yeah, it's nothing." Cole tried to act cool. "Ava and I had a little misunderstanding when we first met."

Ava watched the interaction between Cole and her aunt with amusement.

"Well, please go wash up before coming to the table," said Ida.

"Yes, ma'am," Cole said as she left the room.

Cole walked to a basin on the table near the back door of the house. She poured water into the basin from the pitcher beside it before looking at herself in the mirror. She studied her reflection as she splashed water on her face, dispatching the last remnants of dry blood near her nose. Vivian walked up behind her to wait her turn to wash up. Lost in thought, it took Cole some time before she realized her aunt was standing near her, leaning against the doorframe watching her.

"I don't even know what to say, Cole," Vivian said as she playfully pushed her aside to wash up.

"Then don't say anything." Cole crossed her arms in front of her chest. "I'm as surprised as you are. I was just climbing up the ridge and there was her cruiser, resting under a tree."

"Resting?"

"It sort of crashed but not too badly. She wasn't hurt or anything."

"Well, she looks to be about your age, maybe a little older."

Knowing what Vivian was implying, Cole gave her a frowning look. Cole recognized the odds were against her in finding a mate.

Young adults made up smaller and smaller portions of the Earth's population, especially on the ground. Some regarded the drop in the Earth's population as nature's revenge against humanity's arrogant excesses. Humans had historically and systematically repressed any concern regarding the carrying capacity of Earth's habitat.

Now, hardly anyone had children. First, there was the problem of very few men being biologically able to father children because of increased levels of estrogen in the ground water. Then the national healthcare system collapsed, which had been offering fertility treatments to couples. Nowadays, babies had to happen the old-fashioned way or not at all. Given the shrunken landmass on the planet, that was probably for the best. But it also meant that if young adults wanted to couple, they had to travel far, and finding love was even harder than just finding a partner. Cole had turned twenty-two a couple of months ago, and she didn't even hold a glimmer of hope that she'd meet someone, let alone have someone interesting drop out of the sky less than half a mile from her homestead.

Cole peeked around the corner from the back of the house. Ava was standing near the oven watching Ida cook. Ava was holding her arms around her chest as if to keep herself small in the space. But she seemed curious about everything she was seeing.

"Do you think we're just some strange curiosity to her?" Cole asked Vivian, without turning to look at her. After Vivian dried her hands, she came to stand beside Cole.

"Probably," Vivian said nonchalantly before jokingly pushing Cole with her elbow as she walked past her toward the kitchen. "You should ask her."

❖

Ava felt overwhelmed by new information. The organic textures, fixtures, and scents of the rustic dwelling assaulted her senses as she stood near Ida watching her cook on the cast iron wood stove. Life as Ava experienced it was completely separate from nature. Up in the clouds, the major corporations that benefited from food synthesis had successfully convinced the general public that all things from the ground, planet Earth, were of lesser quality—and in many cases—

just plain toxic. As a result, everything was synthetic. But now she found her senses confronted with what she'd been taught since she was a child. Ava was standing in a non-sterile, wooden structure on the ground. And it felt good.

Ava watched Cole and her aunt as they entered the room and seated themselves around the table that Ida had just set with the steaming plates of food. Ava regarded them, attempting to take some social cue for what would come next. Cole's aunts, sitting at opposite ends of the table, each took one of Cole's hands. They then extended a hand to Ava. She hesitantly accepted the invitation. She put her hands in each of theirs. *More physical contact. It's too late now to worry about catching something from them, I suppose.* But in contrast to everything Ava had ever heard about life on the ground, these three women seemed healthy.

The three hosts bowed their heads, and Ava followed their lead, but Cole didn't close her eyes, so she didn't either. With heads bowed, Cole and Ava looked at each other across the table without blinking. There was some evocative quality in Cole's direct gaze that caused Ava's insides to stir. It was something Ava had not expected to experience, but felt she might want to explore. Ida's mealtime prayer interrupted Ava's thoughts.

"Dear Lord," Ida said. "We thank you for your gracious blessings on this household. We thank you for the opportunity to extend kindness to a stranger. Bless this food to the nourishment of our bodies and may our bodies glorify you. In your Holy name we pray. Amen."

They seemed devoted to their ritual and Christian teachings. Vivian and Cole both said "Amen." After a brief pause, Ava did also, which humored the others more than a little. Ava had no idea what "saying grace" before dinner meant, but there was a first time for everything. She had a feeling this night was the beginning of many firsts.

CHAPTER FOUR

Cole took a bite of food but then realized Ava wasn't eating.

"So, Cole said that your cruiser went down not too far from here. Was it badly damaged?" asked Vivian, no doubt hoping to get to the bottom of exactly how they ended up with a cloud city dinner guest.

"I'm not sure. I think the fuel cells just gave out. I thought I might have more luck figuring it out tomorrow," Ava replied. "I was very lucky that Cole found me. I might have been stranded in the cruiser for quite some time, as the internal release for the hatch was frozen."

Cole wasn't sure she knew what fuel cells were. She wasn't sure Vivian did either.

Cole tried to imagine how everything looked through Ava's eyes. Aunt Ida and her partner Vivian were opposites in both looks and temperaments. Aunt Ida was shorter and a bit on the plump side, proof that she sampled quite a bit while cooking, which was part of why her cooking was so good. Aunt Vivian was tall, fit, and muscular, with short black hair. Looking at her dark features, you could see the native Cherokee blood in her ancestry. She got very tan in the summer, almost brown, whereas Aunt Ida was of a fairer complexion, with blond, now mostly gray hair. Cole had come to live with them when her parents died. She was six years old. Ida started talking again, bringing Cole back to the present.

"So, Ava," she said. "Won't your people be worried about where you are?"

"My people? Oh, you mean like my family?"

Ida nodded. Cole knew full well that Ida and Vivian would be worried sick if she found herself stranded up in the clouds.

"Probably not for a little while. I didn't tell anyone I was leaving." Ava pushed her food around her plate, probably attempting to identify what she was eating.

"Is that right?" Ida asked.

"Um, I was supposed to be in a week-long recertification class that I never actually signed up for. So the flight instructor isn't expecting me, and no one else will be looking for me until the end of the week." Ava cleared her throat and took a sip of water. "I hope that doesn't make me sound like I'm hiding or on the run or something."

Ava became focused on the water in her glass as if she were studying it. She still hadn't touched the food on her plate.

Somehow Cole anticipated her silent question. "It's from an underground, spring-fed well. It's safe to drink." She took a gulp from her own glass.

Ava took a sip, followed by several large swigs. In a flash, the glass was empty. Vivian refilled it from the pitcher at the other end of the table.

"You don't seem like someone on the run," Vivian said. "Maybe you were just in search of some adventure. Everyone needs a little adventure every now and then. Right, Cole?" She bumped Cole's shoulder with her hand for emphasis, nearly causing Cole to drop the food from her fork.

Cole watched Ava's slow and deliberate motions as she ate. She had taken several tiny bites and seemed to be savoring each one more than the last.

"Is this a real potato?" asked Ava.

"What else would it be?" Cole replied.

"Synthetic," Ava responded. "I'm sorry if that seemed a strange thing to ask." She studied the soft piece of potato on her fork. "It just tastes so real."

"So where you live, is everything synthetic? I mean, all the food?" Cole asked. "Even the water?"

"All the food is synthetic, but the water is real," Ava said. "The water is desalinated seawater. That's why the cloud cities mostly stay out over the open sea. Well, partly for the water supply and partly for the open sky for the solar grids. Also, temperatures remain more constant when you aren't over the landmasses and we can be at an elevation above most weather patterns."

Ava looked up from her skewered potato wedge to see that they were all hanging on her every word. "It's pretty stunning to see a hurricane from above," she added. "And this is real fish?" Ava began studying a bit of white, flaky meat at the end of her fork. "I've never seen a fish before. The synthesizer just makes everything into a square…" Ava's voice trailed off.

Cole decided square food didn't sound very appealing, as she took in another mouthful of squash from her plate.

Ava seemed to be lost in thought, staring into the small flame of the flickering candle in the center of the table. "Even the light here is real…I'm sorry. I think I'm more tired than I realized."

Cole thought Ava did look tired, maybe exhausted even. Cole also recognized how lucky Ava was that Cole had found her when she did.

"Well, Ava, you'll stay with us tonight and that's all there is to it," Ida said as she stood from the table. "We have a spare bed and you are more than welcome to it." Ida then gently placed her hand on Ava's shoulder. "Come with me and I'll show you where you can freshen up, and I'll get some fresh sheets for the bed."

"I'm very grateful," Ava said. "Thank you."

Ava left the room with Ida, and Cole noticed that Vivian was watching her intently.

Cole studied the empty dishes. "Can you imagine never eating anything real?"

"It does sound very strange doesn't it?" said Vivian. "Depending on your perspective, some people believe those of us left on the ground got the worse end of the deal when everything collapsed. But I'm not so sure. We have enough and what we have is real. I'm not sure what more anyone could want."

Cole nodded in silent agreement.

Vivian took the plate from Cole's hand. "Why don't you go check and see how your new friend is settling in?" Vivian said with a wink.

❖

Ava heard a light knock on the door to the spare room.

"Come in."

Cole entered as Ava finished buttoning up one of Cole's shirts. Since she was not quite as tall as Cole, it fit her more like a nightshirt and clung more tightly over the rise of her breasts.

"I hope you don't mind," Ava said apologetically. "Your aunt Ida offered me one of your shirts to sleep in." She raised the sleeve and smelled it.

Cole stood awkwardly inside the room. She left the door slightly ajar, and she was now shifting her weight from one foot to the other.

"Um, I don't mind. Does it smell okay?" asked Cole. "I could find you another one if it doesn't."

"It smells good. It smells like fresh air." Ava sat on the side of the bed and reached over to run her fingers across the wall's wood siding. Then she leaned over and inhaled. "What kind of wood is this?"

"Heart pine."

"Heart pine," Ava repeated as she leaned back onto the bed. "Everything on the ground smells so different."

The candle on the small bedside table flickered and cast a warm radiance about the room. Ava's thoughts drifted. She had acted contrary to everything she had previously believed to be true. She had physically interacted with people on the ground and had eaten food from the earth. What did this say about her life?

Ava looked over at Cole, as she let the emotions of the day run through her. Ava had felt frightened on the ground, but contrary to what she had anticipated, she'd been met with only kindness. As she processed this realization, Ava felt her emotions rise into a knot in her throat. Her eyes moistened, and she thought she might actually cry.

"Everything is going to be okay," Cole said.

Ava smiled up at Cole, for the moment forgetting all she'd ever been told about life on the ground and the dangers one might encounter there. "Thank you."

"Ava, you can stay here a while if you want to…or need to," Cole said. "I know my aunts won't mind. We rarely have guests, and I think they enjoy the company."

"If you really don't think it will be a problem then I might accept your kind offer. I need to figure out an end game."

"End game?"

"End game, you know, master plan. I left without figuring out what my ultimate goal for this trip was. I think I just wanted to get away, and that's the only part I thought about. I wasn't planning for something this unexpected to happen."

"How old are you?" Cole asked. "I mean, if you don't mind my asking."

"I'm twenty-six. And you?"

"Twenty-two."

"Twenty-two." Ava smiled. "We're not so far apart are we?"

"No, I guess not. You seem, um, you seem more experienced so I just wondered," Cole said, fumbling her words a little.

"But only experienced in certain ways, right? I don't know anything about what it's like to be here, on the ground."

"I guess not."

Silence hung in the air between them for a few minutes. Cole put her hands in her pockets and looked around the room.

"Well, I should let you get some rest," Cole said finally.

"Okay," Ava said. "Maybe you're right."

Cole closed the door quietly behind her as Ava blew out the candle and the room went dark. Ava sat allowing her eyes to adjust. This was a darkness like she'd never experienced. Even in the deep of night in the cloud cities there were always lights of some kind. The only light she could see now was a bit of filtered moonlight through the partially open drapes. She shuddered, slid under the handmade quilt, and pulled the covers up to her chin. It was so dark and so quiet she wasn't sure she would be able to sleep.

Ava heard the sounds of night through the open window. A breeze caused the leaves of a tree close to the window to rustle. This was, according to the textbooks, her home world, yet everything seemed foreign: foreign, and yet somehow oddly familiar.

❖

Cole closed the door to the spare room and joined Ida and Vivian who were having tea in the kitchen. She could see they'd set a third cup out for her to join them.

"Well?" asked Ida.

Cole eased into a chair. "I told her she could stay for a little while if she wanted. Is that okay?"

"Of course it's okay. I'm just a little concerned that her family might be worried about her by the end of the week. We'll have to convince her to let them know where she is and that she's okay," Vivian said.

"She seems a little sad and lost to me," Cole said and then sipped her tea.

"I can only imagine that she's just now realizing she's on foreign soil and she's alone," said Ida. "She's lucky that you found her when you did."

"It's true. If I hadn't stuck around at the pond until it was almost dark I might not have noticed the light from her cruiser. I barely saw it as it was." Cole stared off into space as she re-imagined the scene.

"It's settled then. Ava can stay for a few days, and no doubt we'll find out more about our charming houseguest tomorrow. Tomorrow is a new day," said Ida as she stood and leaned over to kiss Cole's forehead. "Good night, sweet Cole."

"Sweet dreams," added Vivian with a wink.

Sweet dreams indeed. The day had been full of surprises for her, and now tomorrow looked to hold more of the same.

Cole blew out the candle and made her way to her room.

CHAPTER FIVE

Cole was up earlier than usual the next morning. It was her goal to get through all her daily chores and be freed up to spend time with Ava. Most of what she was doing she could do with her eyes closed so it was nice to let her mind wander while her hands were busy with familiar tasks.

Cole gathered the eggs from the small pen next to the cow shed. She then milked the cow and set her out in a small fenced area for some fresh grass. Cole put clean hay in her stall and fresh water in her trough. There were potatoes to dig, but that could wait until later in the day. Cole was coming out of the barn, propping the door wide open for fresh air, when she saw Ava standing on the porch of the house. Ava was still wearing Cole's shirt, which made Cole smile. Ida had obviously given Ava a wrap to ward off the morning chill and a mug of hot coffee that she was now holding close to her chest. Ava smiled as Cole walked toward the house.

"Good morning," Ava said over her steaming mug. Standing on the raised porch, Ava was at least two feet taller than Cole.

"Hey," said Cole. "I was trying to finish up things so I could have breakfast with you." The sun was now peaking causing Cole to have to squint to see Ava. She stepped up onto the porch and into the shade.

"Breakfast sounds good. I'm starved."

Ava followed Cole into the kitchen from the porch.

"Now, girls, I kept some biscuits warm on the stove for you," Ida said, motioning toward a black skillet covered with a towel. "If you want an egg you'll need to make that yourself, but there's sourwood honey in the jar for the biscuits. Vivian and I are headed out for blackberries. We'll be back soon and a blackberry pie will shortly follow our return. Make yourself at home, Ava," Ida said warmly as she picked up a woven wooden basket and placed a floppy sun hat on top of her head before heading out the door.

"Your aunt is very sweet," said Ava. "How are you related?"

"She and my father were brother and sister," Cole said as she licked a dollop of honey from her forefinger. "Have you ever had sourwood honey before?"

"It's made by bees, right? No, I've never had honey of any kind. We don't have insects in the cloud cities. Is it good?" Ava took the biscuit slathered with honey and fresh butter that Cole handed to her and took a bite. "Wow. That is *so* good. I have to admit that food has never held great interest for me until now, until right now." Ava took another bite of the biscuit. "Who in their right mind ever thought synthetic food was a good idea?"

"It started because they were trying to find a cheaper, more environmentally friendly way to create meat, right?" Cole asked, not sure if she was remembering her history correctly.

"I believe you're right. I was sort of asking a rhetorical question," said Ava. "I'm sorry. I didn't mean for that to sound sarcastic or condescending. Rhetorical just means you ask a question that you already know the answer to."

"It's not really a question then is it?" Cole responded with a slight smile.

Ava laughed. "No, I guess it isn't."

❖

Ava studied Cole from her side of the kitchen table as they finished their biscuits. "You're funny, Cole. Do you know that?"

And your boyish charm is adorable. Ava felt herself drawn to Cole, despite the fact that she usually found herself attracted to women with more feminine curves. There was honesty and an open way about Cole that Ava found herself responding to.

"Funny is good," said Cole, grinning behind her coffee mug. "I was thinking you might like to walk around and see more of where you landed. You know, since it was already dark when you got here. Do you feel up for a walk?"

"I would like that very much," said Ava. "Should I change?" She tugged at the front of her shirt for emphasis.

"You should wear my shirt just in case we run into anyone. We can't do anything about your eye color, but wearing local clothing will help a little."

Ava pulled her hair around her face, remembering her green eyes, which were a dead giveaway that she was not from the ground.

"Your eyes are beautiful, by the way," added Cole.

"Thank you."

It didn't take long for the two of them to be ready to head out for their walkabout. Cole gave Ava a large brimmed felt hat that shaded her eyes a little. She was wearing Cole's shirt still, but unfortunately, they didn't have any pants that would fit Ava. Cole was taller than she was, and Ava had slightly more curve at her hips. Cole picked up a long walking stick before they started out the door. She also had a linen satchel slung across her shoulder that hung down just past her waist.

"What's the stick for?" Ava asked as they headed up the hill toward the ridge.

"Snakes," Cole answered nonchalantly.

Ava stopped dead in her tracks.

"Snakes? Are you expecting to see many?"

"Sorry. I didn't mean to scare you. Sometimes they lie in the path to get warm in the sun. I just like to have a long stick so I can move them along," said Cole "Don't worry. They don't like us any more than we like them."

"Well, that's one thing to like about the city. No snakes!"

Ava followed Cole all over that morning. They climbed the ridge and then dropped down the hollow past Ava's cruiser. She took a moment to pop the solar panels up to make sure they were charging and to double check that all the connections between the panels and the ignition were in order. These were things she should have done but obviously hadn't. Then they headed down the path Cole had walked the night before. Past the pond and along the broken roadway that ran in front of an old stone building that was more of a shell than an actual building. No glass remained in the windows, and over time, locals had borrowed stone from the walls as needed. Some of the walls were only partially intact.

"That building is probably three hundred years old," Cole said.

"What was it?"

"It was a school a very long time ago. My great-grandmother went to school here when she was young. Now there just aren't that many kids. When I was of school age, we just met at Ms. Winston's place. She was trained as a teacher and gave lessons in her house. She had a very large collection of books, too."

Ava stepped into what rubble remained of the structure and ran her fingers across the stones of the still standing partial walls. She explored the stones and the mortar between them. Textures fascinated her.

They continued past the stone remnants and into a wide, open hayfield. They had walked partway across the field when Ava stopped. It took a moment for Cole to realize that Ava was no longer following her.

With arms outstretched, Ava began turning in a slow circle letting the tops of the tall grass brush her open palms. The sun was at about ten o'clock. The sky was a bright, cloudless blue. Her hair shifted around her cheekbones from her circular motion. Cole stood a few feet away, watching her silently.

"What is this?"

"The grass?"

Ava nodded.

"Hay."

"This is from a dream I had," said Ava as she turned to Cole and spoke with a far off look in her eyes. "I've had this reoccurring dream that I'm walking in a field of tall, golden grass just like this."

Ava dropped her hands at her sides and turned toward Cole. They were standing about ten feet apart, near the center of this giant field. "How is it possible that I saw this place when I didn't even know it existed?"

Cole shifted slightly to one side as something caught her eye just past Ava's shoulder. She leaned around Ava to get a better look. There was movement in the direction from where they had just walked. Cole could see three figures walking toward them from the roadbed.

"Someone is coming," Cole said. She walked over to Ava and stood in front of her. "Don't worry. I'll probably know who it is. I just can't tell from here. Let me do the talking, okay?"

Cole looked at Ava so that she could see by the look on Cole's face that she was serious, but not worried. Cole wasn't one to dwell on danger or what might happen, but it was always better to be prepared. Some people weren't as content with their lives on the ground as Cole and her aunts were. Some people had enough but wanted more. They could be dangerous if you had something they really wanted. And then there were those people that were just mean for no reason. She tried her best to stay out of their way and not provoke them. As the figures got closer, Cole could make out who they were: Margaret Tennyson, her brother Seth, and Jessica Walker.

"Do you know them?" Ava asked.

"Yeah, unfortunately."

Cole and Margaret had never really gotten along. Margaret had always wanted more from Cole than just friendship, and Cole was reluctant to respond in kind. There was something about Margaret that she didn't trust. Especially not with anything she really cared about, like her heart.

Cole and Ava stood quietly as the threesome approached.

Margaret started in on Cole right away.

"Well, look here. If it isn't the lanky and adorable Cole, and who's that with you?" She slid forward, closer to Cole than she liked. Cole took a step back and Ava echoed her backward motion.

Margaret was wearing a cotton dress that was loose at the shoulders. As she shifted her weight from one hip to the other, the drape of the dress slipped just enough to show ample cleavage. The material of the dress was thin and left little to the imagination.

Her brother couldn't have cared less about seeing them, or anyone for that matter. He always seemed impatient and in a bad mood to Cole. Jessica was quiet. Cole never could figure out why Jess was friends with Margaret. They didn't seem like a good fit to her at all. Jess was a nice person, sweet natured and friendly. Cole even thought of her as pretty in a girlish sort of way.

"This is Ava. She was just passing through and needed a place to stay for the night," Cole said.

Ava was shielding her eyes with the brim of the felt hat. She smiled but didn't respond verbally to Margaret.

"Well, she seems a little too shy for you, Cole," said Margaret as she plucked a piece of tall grass and twirled it around her fingers before stepping closer to Cole. "When are you gonna come by for that visit I offered? You never know, you might even like it."

"I've been busy."

Jess shifted her stance, seeming like she might be uncomfortable with Margaret's advances toward Cole.

"Let's go. I'm hot and I want a drink. We're still a half hour's walk from the house," whined Seth.

Margaret sighed and gave her brother a look of annoyance.

"All right, then, I guess we'll be on our way," said Margaret. She reached over and walked two fingers across Cole's chest from shoulder to shoulder. "Now you come see me, Ruth Coleman George. I won't wait forever, you know." With that, Margaret winked in Cole's direction, and the trio headed on across the open hay field.

"Bye, Cole." Jess waved as she passed and gave Cole a shy, sideways glance.

"Bye, Jess."

Cole stood still for a bit, watching them get smaller the farther they walked. Then Ava moved to stand beside her. Cole could see she was looking in the direction of their departure with a furrowed brow, as if she were studying on something.

"So, you and Margaret have never...you know, gotten together?"

"I hope that's a rhetorical question," Cole said, smiling.

Ava laughed and then raised the brim of her hat so that her green eyes caught the sunlight.

"Is it okay to lie down here in this tall grass?"

"Sure. It might be itchy," said Cole.

Smiling broadly, Ava spun slowly around and then lay down in the grass. Cole joined her. They lay side-by-side, invisible to the rest of the world in the tall hay.

"Is this a scary place to live?" Ava asked. "I've been so distracted by how everything feels, smells, and tastes. I didn't think to ask what it's really like here."

Cole listened with her arms folded behind her head, watching a small cloud pass overhead.

"We've always been told stories about how unsafe the ground is," Ava said then hesitated. "But I'm beginning to wonder if the stories are even true."

"Is anywhere truly safe?"

"I guess not."

"Here on the ground, there are those who don't have it so good. That's for sure. Sometimes you run into those people. You try and help when you can and you try to avoid the ones who just seem like they want to make trouble. We've been pretty lucky. If you can grow things, and make things, and have friends to barter with, then life is pretty good. People like Margaret, well, she's annoying, but harmless. She's just a local girl looking to couple."

"Is that what you call it, 'couple'?" Ava asked.

"What do you call it?"

"Partnering. Neither term sounds very romantic," said Ava as she rolled on her side to face Cole. "We need a better word."

"Hmmm. If I was going to come up with a better word what would that be?" Cole mused. She plucked a piece of dry grass and began to nibble the end of it. "Companion? No, that's no better. How do you find a single word that really captures how your heart feels about another person?"

"Margaret was right about one thing, Cole. You are lanky and adorable."

Cole blushed and looked in Ava's direction. She'd been lost in thought and hadn't realized Ava had been studying her this whole time. But Cole wanted to ask more about Ava's life. She rolled on her side to face her.

"So are you, um, are you partnered with anyone?" Cole used Ava's word, instead of the local word.

"No, not really. I mean, I go out with women, but nothing serious. Recently, I almost really screwed up with a close friend of mine, Audrey. So stupid."

"You and Audrey aren't a couple?"

"No. We're friends…at least I hope we're still friends."

Cole was puzzled by Ava's comments. She wasn't sure exactly what Ava was talking about.

"What do you mean by *go out*?"

"Oh, like date. Go out with women for dinner or drinks or sometimes we just you know…"

"You know what?"

"Have sex."

"Oh." Cole felt naïve for not understanding what Ava was talking about. Ava was obviously more experienced at some things. Cole's experience with women was more limited and definitely more provincial.

"Are you coupled with anyone, Cole?"

"I think you can tell I'm not."

"But not for want of some local girls trying to convince you otherwise," Ava teased her.

"Please," Cole said with sarcasm as she got to her feet. She extended a hand to help Ava up. "Do you want to see more before we go back to the house?"

"Yes. Absolutely."

CHAPTER SIX

Audrey stepped onto the pedestrian corridor and headed toward the transit station. If she didn't hurry she was going to be late, and that would be the second time this week. Audrey hated to be late. The med lab where she was doing her residency was only ten minutes away. If she caught the next transport she might just make it to work on time.

As Audrey joined a small group of people already gathered on the platform for the cross-town transport, she checked her comm unit again. Still no message from Ava. It wasn't as if they were normally in constant contact, but they hadn't parted on the best terms, and Ava hadn't responded to Audrey's earlier messages.

Audrey still couldn't believe that after being friends for so long they nearly had sex. What a disaster that would have been. And contrary to what Ava was likely thinking, it wasn't all her fault. Audrey was equally to blame for letting things get out of hand. Granted, Audrey had been the one to throw on the brakes, which no doubt embarrassed Ava, but Audrey was certain Ava now felt like that had been the right decision. But how would she find that out if Ava kept ignoring her messages? So typical of Ava to avoid even a remote chance of conflict rather than just communicate.

The transport doors opened and Audrey stepped inside, taking the first open seat. She was lost in thought and barely noticed the passengers seated and standing near her. One young man tried to catch her eye, and she smiled politely before looking down and pretending to look through messages on her comm device.

Audrey and Ava had been friends for a few years, and at some point she had entertained the idea of becoming romantically involved with Ava. But knowing Ava the way she did, Audrey had never believed they had a real future together. As much as she cared for Ava, she knew that they wanted different things. Audrey wanted true love. Blinding lightning bolts of take-your-breath-away-love. Audrey wanted forever. Ava wanted right now and maybe next week, but any real commitment seemed to send her into a tailspin.

Audrey smiled as she thought about the last night they'd spent together. Ava was definitely fun and adventurous and a good friend. But every time Audrey tried to broach any subject touching on "the future," Ava would log more flight hours and disappear. For some reason though, this time it felt different. Audrey was worried, and she couldn't put her finger on the exact source of her unease.

The doors slid open, and Audrey brushed past a couple lost in an intimate embrace as she stepped down onto the exit platform. She smiled to herself. *Don't give up. True love is a possibility.*

Audrey passed through the lobby and took the lift up to the third floor. She found James already looking over the active cases on a touch pad. When he saw her he glanced at his watch.

"Don't even look at your watch. I'm right on time," said Audrey. She reached around James for her duty roster.

He smiled. "Looks like a busy night ahead for us. Gregory called in sick and Marcia was needed at Med Lab North because they were shorthanded."

"I guess it's a good thing I had no plans for later then," Audrey said jokingly. She touched the screen she held and began scrolling through patients. "How about I start downstairs with post-op and you take this floor?"

"Sounds good. See you later for coffee?"

"Sure. I'm feeling like I'll need it in a couple of hours."

Audrey pulled the handheld comm unit from her pocket as she started back toward the lift. Still no messages. The uneasy feeling settled again into the pit of her stomach. *Ava, where are you?*

❖

Ava followed Cole back to the pond, and Cole found a snake for Ava to see. Ava was afraid of the creature and at the same time fascinated by how it moved. It was a water snake and was very happy to be released with a splash back into the pond. Ava knelt near the water's edge and dipped her fingers into the slightly murky water and then rubbed a bit of algae between her thumb and forefinger.

They walked up an old hunting trail to one of Cole's favorite spots: a large granite outcropping.

"When the leaves of the trees drop off during the autumn months this site offers a stunning view of the mountain ridges as far as you can see. In summer, like now, there is still a good view, just not as much of it," said Cole. She made a sweeping gesture toward the mountains in front of them before she settled onto the huge rock. She had a small jar of some type of liquid and a couple of biscuits that she'd brought. She pulled them out and shared each with Ava.

"What is this?" Ava asked. She studied the amber liquid.

"It's apple mash cider."

After taking a sip, Ava handed the jar back to Cole. "That's really good."

They sat side-by-side, nibbling at the biscuits and taking small sips from the jar of cider.

"This is one of my favorite places," Cole said, looking off into the distance. "I feel like if there's a problem I can't figure out that if I come up here and sit for a little while the answer always presents itself. Sometimes I just come up here to be alone and think."

"What do you think about?"

"I dunno. I guess the future mostly. Like, what am I supposed to do? Why am I here? Those sorts of things."

"The big questions. Yeah, I ask those questions, too. That's part of why I…part of why I left the city."

Ava turned in Cole's direction as she continued to talk. For some reason, in this foreign place, sitting with someone who held no expectations of her, who needed nothing from her, Ava felt like she could reveal more of herself. "Something is missing for me in the city," said Ava. "It's like this intangible thing that I can't quite put my finger on. A connection to something more…more real." She looked over at Cole. "I fully acknowledge that where I come from I have plenty, and yet, it's somehow not exactly what I want. I feel… restless."

"Everyone has moments in their life where they feel unsettled, adrift."

"Really? You don't seem unsettled or adrift. You seem grounded."

"That's a funny thing to say to someone who lives on the ground."

"That's not what I mean…"

"I know. I was joking with you."

"Good."

They were silent for a few moments as they passed the jar of cider back and forth. Cole leaned back on one elbow so that she was in a more reclined position on the large granite surface.

Ava found it hard to believe that no one had laid claim to Cole. There was an undeniable innocence and openness about Cole that she hadn't come across before among her urban friends.

"I still find it hard to believe that you're single, Cole."

"Really? Why?"

"Have you seen yourself? You've got this whole tall, lanky, charmingly unkempt, boyish thing going on. I'll bet you drive the girls crazy."

"What girls?" Cole took a sip of cider. "Margaret and Jess are pretty much it for the surrounding area." Cole sighed and leaned back on her elbows after handing the cider jar to Ava. "I'll probably be single forever."

Cole studied Ava's face, unable to read her expression. It surprised her that Ava was so curious about her personal life. The truth was, Cole hadn't been with many women. Well, there had been that one time at the fall harvest dance a year ago, when she'd danced with Marc's cousin, Alice. But she wasn't a local girl so she and Cole never got a chance to explore their feelings for each other. They did spend a few nights together during her visit. But then Alice left, and they hadn't made an effort to stay in touch. That time with Alice had been Cole's first sexual experience.

Cole wondered what it would be like to have a love interest. A girlfriend.

"You know, I could say the same thing to you, Ava. I'll bet you drive the girls crazy where you're from. I mean, look at you, and you're a pilot."

"I would say that getting dates is not my problem. Unlike you, I don't want to settle down with one woman, at least not at the moment anyway."

"And what makes you think that I do?"

"Call it an experienced hunch, but you strike me as the serious type. I'm not saying that's a bad thing either, just an observation."

"I would like to fall in love. I think I'm ready. I guess I'll just have to wait until the right girl comes along." Cole turned to Ava and smiled. "Or should I say, until the right girl falls out of the sky?"

"Too bad you aren't my type, Cole, otherwise, you'd be in serious trouble. And I dare say, so would I."

It was late afternoon, and Cole decided they should start their walk back to the house. She really liked Ava. It was nice to have a friend to talk with about these things. Her best friend, Marc, was already engaged, so he was blissfully oblivious to her plight. And her aunts were always trying to fix her up with Jessica. That wouldn't be the worst thing in the world, but at the same time, it didn't feel right to Cole. She was waiting for something. Cole hoped she'd recognize that *something* when it presented itself.

The sun was low in the afternoon sky. They could smell the smoke from the wood stove. Ida would be starting to cook soon. And Cole still had potatoes to dig and carry back to the springhouse for safekeeping.

"I have to do some things," Cole said as they neared the porch. "I'll be back before dark. Just make yourself at home, okay?"

Ava watched Cole walk away and then she turned and entered the house.

❖

Ava surprised herself by taking rustic life in stride. Cole had worried that the outhouse with the composting toilet would be what sent Ava running back to her cruiser, but it was just one more curious aspect of this new territory to experience. Ava was interested in everything, no matter how small the detail. She hovered around Ida, engrossed in her cooking. She also had no idea that potatoes grew underground. "They're a root vegetable," Ida explained and then laughed when Ava confessed how certain she'd been that they grew on trees.

Cole ran a bath for Ava in their big claw-foot tub. Ava now understood that they had a well for drinking water, but the pump took a lot of effort, so for household water they used a system attached to a cistern that collected rainwater. Cole added hot water from the kettle on the stove to the tub to warm things up then left Ava to enjoy a good soak.

"I'll go after you," Cole said and she pulled the door closed behind her.

Ava undressed and sank into the warm water. The steaming bath was a welcomed retreat after a day spent walking in the woods.

After a little while, Ava appeared in the front doorway, towel drying her hair. Cole and Vivian had been relaxing in chairs on the long wooden porch.

"The tub is all yours," Ava said. "That felt great. Thank you so much for letting me go first."

Ava took Cole's seat on the porch in a rocking chair next to Vivian.

"Did you two have a nice day?" Vivian asked.

"Yes. We did," Ava said. She now had the towel around her shoulders, over the shirt she'd borrowed from Cole the night before. "I got a tour and even met a few people."

"Really?" Vivian raised an eyebrow at the mention of locals.

"Let's see, um, what was her name? Margaret. Yes, that was it."

"White trash," said Vivian. "Do you know what that means?"

"I'm not sure, but it doesn't sound like a good thing," Ava responded with a chuckle.

"Cole needs to keep a safe distance from that one, believe you me."

Silence fell between them for a time before Ava spoke. "Do you mind if I ask you a question? I probably should ask Cole, but…"

"What's the question?"

"It's about Cole's parents." Ava hesitated. "What happened to them? Did you know them?"

"Oh, that's a sad story," Vivian started to speak, looking off into the distance as if it were showing her the past. "Ida and I met when Cole was about six years old. I knew her parents because they lived next door to Ida. Maybe Cole told you, but her grandparents owned about thirty acres that were eventually divided between her grandparents, her father, and Ida," Vivian explained. "Each child got a ten-acre plot. Ten acres is a good chunk of land—especially if it's not contaminated. You can grow and barter your own crops all the while never feeling like your neighbors are breathing down your neck, if you know what I mean?"

Ava had no idea how much ten acres was, but she nodded anyway. The average city apartment was only about eight hundred square feet. She had read about oil and chemical spills on the ground in her secondary school history books. Cloud cities were free of all that.

"Cole's parents died in a fire," Vivian said as she looked at Ava. "A bad storm was brewing. I could see it a few miles away, but lightning jumped ahead of the storm and hit the roof of Samuel's barn. Sam was Cole's father. He wasn't very nearby when the strike happened so by the time he got to the barn, the fire had spread and Rachel, Cole's mother, was inside trying to get the animals out."

Ava watched the expression on Vivian's face darken.

"I could see the smoke from where I was standing on Ida's porch. I got to the barn just before Samuel ran inside to help Rachel. Right about then, Cole ran up and tried to go in after her parents. I grabbed her and held her back. What with all the dry wood and hay, the fire was spreading like the place was tinder. You couldn't get near it."

Vivian reflected on her own words. "I couldn't help them."

Vivian was quiet for a few moments. Ava sat with her in silence.

"We'll never know exactly what happened," she continued. "I got the horse out, Rachel had gone back in for some things of value she didn't think we could do without. I can only imagine that she got trapped or something and Samuel wouldn't leave her."

Ava was prepared to hear that their deaths had been due to illness, or old age, or something else. This was not the story she expected to hear.

"It took Cole a long while to get past it. She was very angry for some time. From then on, Cole has lived with us."

"That may be the saddest story I've ever heard," said Ava.

"Stick around, Ava. The world is full of sadness," Vivian said, biting her lower lip and furrowing her brow. "Sorry. You're too young for thoughts like that." Vivian smiled at Ava.

"Thank you for telling me what happened," Ava said. She felt her heart expand from the sadness she felt for Cole. She couldn't begin to fully imagine what it must have been like for Cole to lose her parents so suddenly and so violently. Ava also realized that this sort of accident could possibly turn fatal in the city, but in urban spaces they had an emergency response infrastructure in place, unlike communities on the ground.

After sitting quietly for a time in the cool, night air, Ava stood up. "I think I'm going to go to bed now," she said. "Thank you again for talking with me."

Vivian smiled. "Sleep well."

❖

Audrey pushed through the double exit doors of the medical center. It had been a long day. Darkness had settled across the four city quadrants, and she'd considered going home and spending a quiet night reading, but then she'd gotten a message from Sara begging her to come out for a drink.

She stood silently contemplating her mood. Audrey did feel a bit too restless to go home just yet. Having spent a full day working, she was a little wound up. Maybe a drink would be just what she needed to take the edge off. Her next step was to assess her wardrobe. The silky fabric of her blouse had survived her day at the medical center, thanks to the white lab coat she'd kept on most of the day. And her dark dress pants would probably be nice enough for an early evening at the club. Audrey entered a message to Sara and hit send: *be there in 10.* She tucked her comm unit in her bag along with her white scrub jacket and started walking at a brisk pace toward the small bar that she and her friends were known to frequent.

Within fifteen minutes, she was nestled into a corner table with Sara and a brightly colored beverage. Audrey removed the synthetic fruit garnish resting on a skewer at the side of the glass and pulled a cherry off with her teeth. Audrey freed the small garnish from the skewer slowly, lost in thought. Sara spoke to her, snapping her out of her daydream.

"Be careful with that," said Sara. "That little move with your beverage accessories was so hot I just saw two women faint and collapse near the bar."

"Yeah, right. As if."

"I'm not kidding, and don't look now, but some attractive butch just stepped over their prone bodies and is walking this way," Sara said as she tried to nod subtly toward the approaching woman.

"What?"

But Sara didn't have time to respond. Audrey and Sara were seated at a tall table on chairs the height of barstools. So when the woman came to rest beside their perch she was at eye level with Audrey.

"Hello, can I buy you a drink?"

"Thank you, but I have a drink." Audrey took a few seconds to catalog the woman's features—short blond hair, well dressed in dark shirt and slacks, stocky in an athletic way. She also had a slight cockiness to the tilt of her head as she leaned an arm on the table, angling her body away from Sara so that she was facing Audrey.

"Maybe you'd like something other than a drink then?" The edge of her mouth curved up slightly.

"Thank you, but I think I'll just sit here with my friend."

Obviously, not used to rejection, the woman pushed further. "My name is Mac. What's your name, beautiful?"

"Hi, Mac. Listen, thank you for the kind offer to buy me a drink and whatever else you were offering, but please allow my friend and me to get back to our conversation." Audrey took the fruit spear again in her hand and slowly pulled off another delicate edible decoration with her teeth.

"Maybe another time." Mac squared her shoulders and attempted to save face. She turned slowly and walked back toward the bar.

"Ouch," was all that Sara said. "You could at least have gotten a free drink out of that."

"That drink would not have been free. Why tease her when I could tell already there was nothing between us?"

"Just like that?"

"Just like that."

"I thought she was kinda cute in a *jock* sort of way," said Sara.

Audrey scanned the room to see where Mac had wondered off. She finally saw her leaning against the bar, whispering to another woman, both of them risking glances in their direction.

"She wasn't my type, but I could get her number for you if you like."

"No, thanks. Evidently, *I'm* not her type."

"Now, where were we?" asked Audrey, sipping her drink.

"Talking about how hard it is to meet someone interesting," said Sara, rolling her eyes.

"Oh yeah."

They both laughed.

"I'm holding out for that lightning bolt," said Audrey.

They toasted each other, clinking their glasses together lightly.

"To lightning bolts," said Sara.

❖

After bathing, Cole walked through the now quiet house. Ida had retired her sewing project she'd been working on and she and Vivian were in their room for the night.

Cole got a drink of water from the pitcher in the kitchen. She could see that Ava was already in the spare room and the door was closed. *Should I knock and say good night?* Cole stood outside Ava's door. When she didn't hear any sounds and saw no candlelight coming from under the door, she figured Ava was asleep and walked toward her own room, leaving her door half open. For some reason, Cole could never sleep in a room with a closed door. Between the darkness and the closed door, it made her feel too shut in.

Cole was halfway under the covers, propped up on her pillow, reflecting on the day, when she heard the creak of a floorboard from just outside her door. Cole had blown the candle out earlier, but there was enough moonlight streaming in for her to see Ava step around the door.

"Cole?" Ava whispered, "Are you awake?"

"Yeah, I'm awake. I thought you were asleep already," she whispered back.

Ava stepped inside and pulled the door closed behind her. She leaned against the closed door, no doubt giving her eyes a moment to adjust to the moonlit room.

Cole became aware that she was in bed and got up to stand beside the bed.

Ava walked over and stood very close. "Something is happening outside."

"What do you mean?"

Ava grabbed Cole's arm and pulled her quietly through the darkened house and out to the front porch. They stood for a few minutes in silence.

"What am I looking for out here?" Cole asked.

"There!" Ava pointed toward the edge of the yard, to the dark spaces between the trees. "See that flickering light? And there…there it is again!" Ava whispered excitedly.

"That's a firefly."

"A fly on fire?"

"No, it's a bug that signals by lighting its tail up. It's called a firefly."

"Unbelievable."

"Ava, you scared me. I thought you'd seen a bear or something."

"Well, excuse me for getting excited, but I've never seen anything like that."

They sat near each other on the porch steps in the cool evening air for some time before they headed off to bed. As she closed the door to her room, Ava felt a little sad. She knew she would be leaving as soon as her cruiser was fully charged. She would return to the cloud city and Cole would remain here. And she'd have to forget about life on the ground because it wasn't an option for her. Ava's life was in the city, no matter how intrigued she was by all the things she'd seen and felt during her brief time on the ground.

Ava settled under the covers but lay awake for some time, listening to the sounds of night and trying to identify why she still carried a dull ache in her chest.

Chapter Seven

As the sun began to streak through her bedroom window, Cole pulled on clothes and shoes to begin her morning routine. Ava's door was closed as she headed outside to start her chores.

The early morning light cast a pinkish hue on every surface it touched. Cole was thinking of all the things that had happened in the past day and all the things she and Ava had talked about, which distracted her from first noticing the cowshed door was open. Cole was sure she'd shut it the night before. When she stepped inside to inspect the shed, she found the cow in her stall. Good, she thought to herself. But wait. The pail of potatoes she had left inside the door the night before was tipped over, and at least half the tubers were missing. Damn raccoons. Cole righted the bucket and pulled the door of the cowshed closed as she walked back toward the house to finish her chores.

Then she heard a noise behind her. Someone had opened the cowshed door again. Cole turned to find a gaunt figure stumbling toward her. Panic gripped the pit of her stomach. She'd been walking around in such a fog she'd obviously missed some detail that would have alerted her to this person's presence in the barn. Cole backed slowly toward the house. Trying not to sound overly alarmed, she called for Vivian. She saw now that the person approaching her was holding a buck knife with a six-inch blade. Cole had nothing at hand to ward off this stranger. She looked around for a fire log or some other object with which to defend herself, but there was nothing nearby she could grab.

"Vivian," she called just a little louder as she managed to get closer to the house. The stranger holding the knife was a woman who looked to be of middle age, very thin, with matted hair. She had a strange look on her face, like she might not be in the best mental state.

"Vivian!" Cole called out for the third time, this time yelling. But it was Ava who responded.

"Cole? Who is—"

"Get Vivian!" She didn't want to take her eyes off the woman, so she spoke without looking in Ava's direction.

Cole held her hands out in front of her, palms open, to show the woman that she was unarmed and could do her no harm.

"No one's gonna hurt you. See," said Cole. "Why don't you put the knife down? Are you hungry? I could get you some food."

The woman's face showed no recognition of what Cole was saying. She had the look of a wild animal as she darted her head slightly from side to side as Cole spoke. The stranger stepped closer and closer to Cole, forcing Cole to back up against the raised boards of the porch.

And then two rapid strikes! The woman plunged the knife into Cole's torso before Cole could climb out of her way. Cole fell backward onto the rough boards of the porch. She pressed her right hand onto the dark redness that quickly spread across her white undershirt. Cole had on one of her long-sleeved, button-down shirts over her white cotton undershirt, but the overshirt was now open at the front. Cole looked down in disbelief as she lifted her hand and saw blood.

"Cole!" Ava cried.

Ava reached out, and Cole felt hands pulling her backward and up onto the porch.

Vivian barreled onto the porch with her crossbow cocked and ready to go. Ida stood in shock in the doorway with her hands over her mouth.

"Back away, lady!" yelled Vivian. She aimed the weapon at the intruder. "I mean it! Step away now or relish your final moments on this earth."

The woman had an empty, angry look on her face as she held the bloodied knife and looked from Cole to Vivian and back to Cole. She took a half step toward Vivian. Her foot didn't even touch the ground before Vivian pulled the trigger and the woman was knocked back several feet by a direct hit to her chest. Blood splattered everywhere from the wound. The woman's hands, covered with her own blood, twitched at her side, and then she was still. Her eyes remained open and staring. The knife, no longer a threat, lay in the grass near her elbow.

Cole coughed and groaned. Ida had gotten a towel and was applying pressure to the wound.

❖

Ava looked at Vivian. "This is not good. She's losing too much blood too fast." She bent down and pressed her palm to Cole's forehead.

"We've got to get her to my cruiser," said Ava. "Hang on, Cole."

"What?" asked Ida.

"She's right," said Vivian. "The cloud cities have surgeons. We'll never get her to a healer down here in time."

The cities had medical schools and, as a result, surgeons. There was no opportunity for such advanced medical training on the ground.

"If you can help me get her to the cruiser, I can get her to a critical care unit in about forty minutes," said Ava, realizing Cole's towel was now soaked through with blood. "We need to hurry."

"I think I can carry her," Vivian said as she scooped Cole up in her arms. Cole was conscious, but just barely. The movement caused her to moan.

Ava ran inside and came back with her flight bag.

"Wait!" yelled Ida as she disappeared into the house before coming back outside with Cole's linen satchel. "Take this. She'll want it when she wakes up."

They hurried up the ridge as fast as they could and ran down the other side to the cruiser. Ava opened the hatch, and Vivian placed Cole in the passenger seat. Ava punched the solar panels back in place. They were only partially charged but had just enough to get them back to a medical crisis unit on Easton.

Ava looked at Cole's aunts. "She'll be okay. I promise."

Ida gave Ava a quick but fervent embrace.

"We are in your debt, Ava. Take care of our Cole."

Ava gave them one last look before she closed the hatch and charged the cylinders. The aircraft began to rise as the hydrogen boosters kicked in, leaving behind the soil the cruiser had unearthed during its crash landing. The solar grid booted back online as Ava looked down at Ida and Vivian before rotating the cruiser toward a clear exit from the trees.

Ava punched the accelerator. It would be forty minutes to Easton; thirty-five if she was lucky. She entered her GPS coordinates as she flew the craft fast over the Blue Mountains. The valleys below were still softened by the early morning fog.

"Hold on, Cole." She looked over at Cole in the seat beside her. Cole looked very pale. Her eyes began to oscillate, but she didn't make any noise except for a slight moan. Cole was still losing so much blood. Ava attempted to keep pressure on the wound with one hand while flying with the other.

Chapter Eight

Ava could see the cloud city of Easton in the distance. It had been thirty-five minutes. The longest thirty-five minutes of her life. She announced her approach vector and alerted the tower that she was in need of immediate medical assistance. Ava landed the craft, and the medlift arrived at the side of her cruiser by the time she had the hatch open. Three emergency personnel lifted Cole onto a gurney and into the medlift. Ava climbed in with them, afraid to let Cole out of her sight.

When they got to the surgical lab, Ava had to wait while they rushed Cole to the emergency wing. The tower had alerted Ava's mother, as next of kin, thinking it was Ava who needed medical attention. Before Ava remembered she was covered in Cole's blood, Ava's mother screamed in horror as she ran to be with her.

"I'm fine, Mother. It's not my blood," Ava said.

Her mother released her embrace and held Ava at arm's length. Ava had thrown her flight jacket over the cotton shirt she'd borrowed from Cole, and now two bags were slung across her chest. Her own vinyl bag and Cole's linen satchel were now covered with blotches of red. Ava realized that standing in the unforgiving florescent lighting of the waiting room, she must have looked like a creature from another world. But what mattered most now was that whatever happened next, Cole was safe. She would be okay. Ava repeated this to herself as she waited for news from the surgical team.

❖

Cole was in surgery for two hours and then placed in the recovery unit. Knowing she would not be awake for a few hours, Ava made a quick trip to her residential cube for fresh clothes. Ava's mother promised to stay with Cole until Ava returned to the medical lab.

The surgeon had been very pleased with the outcome. He'd spoken with Ava before she left about recovery time and what to expect. All internal injuries had been repaired. Ava's quick actions had saved Cole's life.

Ava was seated at the bedside, holding one of Cole's hands as she stroked Cole's head with the other. Cole began to stir finally. Her eyes fluttered, once, twice…then she squinted at the artificial light in the room. Ava reached over and dimmed the light. Cole tried to talk. Her mouth was so dry that she couldn't speak easily and she had a confused look in her eyes.

"I'm here, Cole," Ava said as she stood and leaned over Cole so that Cole could see her without raising herself up.

"So…so thirsty," Cole said.

Ava put a straw to Cole's lips so she could take a small sip of water.

"Where am I? I feel so weird. I hurt…"

"Cole, do you remember the woman with the knife? She stabbed you twice."

Ava waited to see some recognition of the ordeal on Cole's face.

"I had to bring you to a medical emergency clinic in the cloud city of Easton. You've been in surgery, and now you'll be here in the recovery room for a few hours."

Moisture gathered at the corners of Cole's eyes, and a tear slowly ran down her cheek. "Ava?"

"Yes, Cole. I'm here." Ava placed a soothing palm on Cole's forehead. "You're going to be fine now. Just rest."

"Okay." Cole faced Ava and blinked slowly. "Okay." And with that, she drifted off to sleep again.

Ava stroked Cole's head and tucked the hand she'd been holding under the sheet. She slumped into a chair a few feet from where her mother was seated on the other side of the room. She turned to look at her mother, who was studying her as if she were some stranger she was meeting for the first time.

"I suppose I owe you an explanation," Ava said.

"I would appreciate that. I feel like you left two days ago and returned as someone I don't even know," Ava's mother said.

"I didn't go to the training center."

"I guessed that much."

"Just don't be angry until you hear the entire story, because obviously, I'm fine. There's nothing to worry about."

Ava told her mother about her unexpected landing in the mountains. She described how Cole had discovered her trapped in the cruiser and then had invited her back to her house for food and rest. As Ava described her adventures, her mother studied her with wide eyes.

"But clearly there is something going on between you and this young woman," said her mother. "Whatever you may have experienced, groundlings are still very different people from us. They live different lives. Their values are not the same as ours. Not like you and Audrey."

Having just spent two days on the ground discovering that things were very unlike what she had been led to believe, her mother's words were like a slap in the face. *We're so arrogant*. Ava decided there was no point in softening the blow she was about to deliver to her mother. "Mother, Audrey and I are never going to be a couple."

"I'm not even sure what you mean about that."

"What I mean is that I shouldn't have let you continue to think there was something more than friendship between Audrey and me, because there isn't." Spending time on the ground where everything was *real* had made an impact on Ava. She wanted to be real for a change.

"But there is something between you and this…this person?"

"Her name is Cole and I owe her. She saved my life and now I'm saving hers."

"What about Audrey? I think she'll feel very hurt that you brought this…Cole back with you," her mother said. "I'm fairly certain that she believes her friendship with you will lead to a permanent partnering. You and Audrey are equals. I know you think I'm being harsh about this groundling, but if you told me you'd fallen for a transit operator I'd have the same reservations."

Ava was becoming impatient. This was a boundary she had never crossed with her mother, and she was surprised by her mother's class-based arguments. However, in fairness, she might have carried within her the same unconscious views had she not just spent two days on the ground having those perceptions shattered by the reality of life on Earth.

"I'm not in a relationship with Cole. She's a friend, the same way Audrey and I are friends. Audrey and I want different things from relationships. You need to deal with the reality that we will never be a couple," said Ava. "Look, Mother, I don't really want to get into all of this with you right now." Ava was angry with herself for letting the ruse about a relationship with Audrey go on for so long, but it kept her parents off her back. As long as they thought there was a glimmer of hope with Audrey they didn't hassle her about settling down.

Her mother frowned. Audrey was her mother's choice for Ava. Audrey was beautiful, smart, and kind. She had a degree in medicine and came from a very good family in the cloud city of London. Her parents had died when she was a child but had left her with quite a secure financial future. Ava's mother and father felt like the match was good. They had pushed Ava to court Audrey, and Ava, in an attempt to keep her parents happy, had played along. Now she was regretting the deception because her mother was not letting go of the idea that they would be together.

"Audrey and I definitely need to talk. But not right now."

"You may not have the luxury of choosing your own timing for a conversation." Her mother was looking past Ava's shoulder and out the glass window toward the outside corridor.

Ava turned to see Audrey standing at the window. She rose and shut the door behind her as she stepped into the corridor to speak with Audrey, who had a rather stricken look on her face.

"I was so worried," Audrey said as she reached out to embrace Ava. They held each other for a long, reassuring moment.

"I'm fine," said Ava. She pulled back from the embrace, keeping her hands on Audrey's arms.

"Your mother left me a message when she thought you had been injured. Sorry. This is as soon as I could get here. The trauma unit was swamped with injuries from another bombing near a transit center. Damn radicals. Lots of innocent people got hurt," said Audrey. "Anyway, I just got the message a half hour ago."

Ava was struck by how awkward things might have been if Audrey had been on call at this medical clinic when she'd arrived with Cole. Audrey wasn't a surgeon, but she could easily have been working in this trauma unit when they arrived.

Ava frowned at her mother through the glass. She turned back to Audrey. "There was a mix-up when I landed. They contacted Mother because they thought I had been injured. I'm sorry I frightened you. I should have called you when I got back. Everything just happened so fast."

"Where have you been the past two days?" Audrey asked. "I know you didn't go south to the cloud city of Miami for flight training. I tried to reach you there. They didn't even have you registered. Where did you go? You disappeared and didn't respond to my messages."

Ava heard the hurt and concern in Audrey's voice. "Don't be upset with me," Ava pleaded. "I was headed to Toronto. I just needed to get away for a few days. My cruiser lost power and I had to set it down in the Blue Mountains."

Audrey stared at Ava in disbelief. Then she pulled Ava into another embrace. "You could have been hurt—killed even. Damn you!" She released Ava and held her in front of her.

"Audrey," Ava said, "I'm really sorry for how I acted the other night. You were right to stop me from crossing the line."

"Listen, we were both equally to blame for things getting out of hand. It just scared me the way you made yourself scarce. The only way to fix things is to talk them out, not run away from them." It was then that Audrey noticed Cole sleeping on the other side of the glass wall.

"I don't really want to talk about it right now if that's okay," Ava said and made a motion toward the room behind them. "That's Cole, and she'll be in recovery until at least tomorrow. Can we talk when I get home?"

Audrey reluctantly agreed. After Audrey left, Ava returned to sit next to her mother.

"I'm sorry," said her mother. "I wouldn't have called her if I'd known. I thought I was doing the right thing."

"I know. It's okay." Ava pinched the bridge of her nose to ward off a headache that had started to develop. She realized she needed to eat. "Will you stay here while I go get something to eat from downstairs?"

"Of course."

"I don't want Cole to wake up alone. Do you want me to get anything for you? A coffee maybe?" she asked.

"I'm fine. Just get some food for yourself. Take your time," her mother said with faux compassion in her voice. "Your friend will probably sleep for quite some time."

"Her name is Cole," Ava said, with no particular inflection.

"Well, did *Cole* instruct you on how she would pay for this surgery?"

"Of course not! Everything was so sudden. It was an emergency situation, Mother!"

"Huh, how convenient. The sooner Cole can get back to the ground the better we all will be—including Cole. I'll pay for her bill myself. No need to tell her of this."

Ava didn't know whether to thank her mother or scream with rage. She left the room not saying a word.

❖

Ava found the food service center and walked up to a large food unit that contained multiple kiosks and slots offering a range of different foods and beverages. She entered credits for a cheese sandwich. She felt like that might be all she could handle. She waited for the synthesis unit to recognize the order and then the processed food appeared in the slot for retrieval. After eating real food for two days on the ground, this square, sterile food substance was even less appealing than usual. *I'm ruined.* She sniffed the sandwich square and nibbled at its corner.

The comfort of Cole's home came rushing back to her as she sat quietly eating; the smells, the sensations, the warmth of the candlelight, the claw-foot tub filled with rainwater. It never rained at this altitude. She felt sad to her core. The cities had risen from the sinking shores more than a century ago, but at what cost to the quality of their lives? But without this floating city of modernity, Cole might be dead. Reflecting on that frightening thought, she figured she should try to get a message to Ida and Vivian to let them know that Cole was okay. Even though there seemed to be no communications grid on the ground, it seemed plausible that if she had the GPS coordinates she should be able to send a message droid from the city down to their location. She figured it was at least worth a try. Ava doubted Cole would be able to leave Easton for a few days. It would be best for her to stay close to advanced medical care in case she experienced any health complications. On the brighter side, Ava would get to share a little part of her world with Cole.

Ava walked to the clinic's communications center and sat at one of the stations to prepare a dispatch for Ida and Vivian. It was possible to get a communication droid anywhere if you knew the GPS coordinates. Hopefully, this would work. She entered a simple message into the digital interface:

"Cole is in recovery. Surgery went well. Cole should stay here until fully recovered in case of complications. Thank you for…"

Ava paused. Thank you for what? Thank you for showing me a way of life outside my own? Thank you for sheltering a stranger, who until now had a pretty skewed view of who you were? There was so much to say. Too much. So, instead she ended with:

"I will bring her home soon. (End Trans)."

CHAPTER NINE

Cole was weak and unstable on her feet as Ava took her back to her residential cube to rest. It was now Cole's turn to notice all the differences between her world and Ava's. Every surface seemed slick and reflective. All the lights had a strange, artificial blue tint. Cole couldn't stop rubbing her hands across every smooth, machined surface. Cole knew two things for sure. She was ready to be rid of the hospital recovery gown, and she could use a good soak.

"Um, do you have a tub?" Cole asked, steadying herself on a nearby counter at the edge of Ava's small kitchen space. There were small machines and appliances throughout the cubby that Cole didn't recognize. "I feel like I really need a bath."

"Have you ever taken a shower?" Ava said. "That's what everyone uses in the city."

"A shower? Like a rain shower?" asked Cole, her head was foggy from the pain meds.

"Sort of." Ava smiled. "Come this way. I'll help you." She motioned for Cole to follow her to the back of the living space.

There was a small, tiled space set against the back wall, lit by a glass covered, square window that connected to the outside. Ava helped Cole slip out of her post-op garb. A waterproof bandage had been placed over the repaired wounds. Cole began to undress slowly, but then stopped. She didn't feel comfortable being completely nude in front of Ava.

"I'll let you have some privacy," Ava said. Before she exited, she turned on the water and showed Cole how to adjust the temperature.

Cole stepped into the spray and placed her hands on the cool tile of the shower space to brace herself. She closed her eyes and let the water run over her frail body. She felt sore and emotionally raw from the experiences of the past two days.

After showering and putting on only a shirt, Cole climbed gingerly into Ava's bed, with Ava's assistance. She had to be careful not to rely on her stomach muscles for stability or strength just yet. Cole collapsed into the pillows with a sigh. Within moments, she was sound asleep.

❖

Ava watched Cole's restful breathing. She didn't want to disturb Cole, and she didn't feel sleepy just yet. As she dimmed the bedside light, Cole's linen satchel caught her eye. *What had Ida said about the bag? That Cole would want it when she woke up.*

Cole had not yet asked about the satchel, but Ava placed it on the floor next to the bed. She backed out of the room, leaving the door ajar so that Cole could call out if she needed anything during the night. Ava settled herself into blankets on the sofa and began scrolling through the digital mail she'd missed while she'd been off the grid for two days.

CHAPTER TEN

Cole blinked at the sun streaming in across her pillow. She had no idea what time it was and was confused about her surroundings. She realized she was in Ava's apartment. Cole moved slightly to test how she was feeling. There was stiffness, and she was still sore, but she felt like she could get out of bed without assistance if she was careful. She rolled on her uninjured side and slowly pushed up with her right arm, swinging her legs over the edge of the bed. She rested for a minute, giving herself a moment to shake the fog of sleep.

Cole noticed her bag on the floor near the bed. A small bit of home. She heard a noise coming from the other room and made her way toward the door after she gingerly pulled on her cleaned cotton trousers and her shoes, which she slipped into but didn't bother to tighten the laces.

"Hey, good morning," said Ava.

"Someone is having a good morning, somewhere, but it might not be me." Cole grimaced. She settled herself onto a high chair by the counter.

"Feeling that well, huh?" Ava pressed a button on one of the strange devices mounted near her kitchen cabinets and produced a hot cup of coffee for Cole.

"Don't expect it to be as good as what you have on the ground," said Ava. "Now that I've tasted the real thing, it'll be hard to enjoy the synthetic version."

Cole sipped the cup curiously. It was no doubt the flavor of coffee, but it had a flat taste.

"I don't understand why everything has to be synthetic here. If we can have real food, why can't you?"

"Where would we grow it? There's no earth up here. Plus, the cloud cities have much larger populations. And I'm sure long ago the powers that be broke off ties with the ground to ensure that they could protect the way of life up here. Our standard of living."

Ava made herself a cup of coffee and turned to prepare some food. She entered what appeared to be codes into a different device mounted among the kitchen cabinets. A minute later, Ava handed Cole a glass of thick green liquid.

"It's a protein drink," said Ava. "It actually has synthetic vegetable mass and an immune booster. Oh, and I added some protein to help you get your strength back."

Cole looked suspiciously at the glass.

"Trust me. It tastes much better than it looks. Maybe not as good as Ida's biscuits, but it will help you heal."

Cole scowled as the thick beverage crossed her tongue. After taking a couple more tortured sips, Cole turned to take in Ava's living space. It was mostly cast in tones of soft gray. Cushions on the sofa had a slightly darker hue, but there were no patterns and no splashes of color. Maybe under other circumstances the neutral coloring might have been soothing, but the sameness of it all made Cole feel strangely uneasy.

"How are you feeling? Does your side hurt?"

"Only when I move," said Cole. "Or breathe." She smiled and slowly adjusted her position on the stool. Cole was using mostly her right hand, as moving her left would affect the muscles on the side of her injury.

"You seem so calm about the whole experience. Are you angry?"

"I don't feel angry," said Cole. "What's there to be angry about? That woman was not in her right mind. She was half starved to death." She took another sip of her green drink. "I actually feel lucky. She's dead and I'm alive."

"An obviously unstable woman punctured your abdomen twice with a six-inch blade for no apparent reason and you feel lucky?"

"Yeah, lucky. Think about it. You show up out of nowhere, I miraculously stumble across your downed cruiser two days before some woman stabs me, and you're able to bring me to the city right away for surgery. I'd say that's pretty damn lucky."

"I guess that's one way to see things…"

"It was like it was meant to be," Cole said earnestly.

Ava puzzled over the notion that something was "meant to be." *What did that mean exactly? That they were meant to meet? That Cole was meant to be injured?* That seemed like an extreme interpretation to Ava, but before she could ask Cole to explain further, the comm box beside the door gave a low buzz. Ava and Cole looked in the direction of the sound, and Ava walked over to hit the receiver button.

"Hello?" Ava said into the small white box.

"Ava," Audrey's voice came through the speaker. "It's Audrey. Can I come up?"

Ava hesitated. She hadn't even had a chance to explain to Cole about who Audrey was. And she and Audrey hadn't had a chance to talk. Should she try to deflect a visit? She decided to buzz Audrey up.

"Sure," Ava spoke into the speaker. "Come up."

Cole was watching intensely when Audrey arrived and hugged Ava upon entering the living space. As Audrey released Ava, she realized Cole was seated at the counter.

"Oh," Audrey said. "I'm sorry. I didn't realize you had a guest."

"It's okay. I wanted you two to meet," said Ava. "Audrey, this is Cole. Ruth Coleman George. Cole, this is Audrey Jameson."

Cole extended her right hand to Audrey. Audrey observed Cole with a puzzled expression. Cole held Audrey's hand, meeting her eyes with a direct gaze.

Audrey found herself unexpectedly captivated by the dark-eyed stranger. She felt a strange surge of warmth from Cole's touch and registered its absence when she pulled her hand away.

"Hi," said Audrey. She quickly looked back at Ava.

"Let me get you a drink, Audrey," said Ava. "Audrey stopped by the medical unit yesterday while you were still in recovery," she said to Cole.

Cole changed her position on the stool a little and visibly winced as she turned.

Audrey got her first chance to study Cole. *Tall and boyishly good-looking. Brown eyes, not green!* Cole was wearing a soft fabric shirt with buttons up the front and trousers with pockets of various sizes up the outside of each leg. She had on worn leather shoes. Audrey became aware that Cole and Ava had noticed her looking Cole up and down.

"Sorry," Audrey said as she accepted a cup of coffee from Ava. "I didn't mean to stare. I've just never seen leather shoes before."

"Oh," said Cole.

Cole did look rather out of place in this aseptic environment. She was the only "color" in the room. "I guess I do dress, um, differently. These are made from deer hide."

"Deer hide? As in deer skin?" asked Audrey.

"You have a very interesting way of speaking," said Cole, ignoring Audrey's question.

"Audrey is from the cloud city of London," Ava said. "She has a British accent."

"Oh," said Cole. "I like it."

Audrey found herself inexplicably blushing at Cole's interest in her. She tried to regain her composure. Audrey had expected Ava to be alone, and then finding that she wasn't, well, Audrey hadn't expected to be so unnerved by the attractive stranger.

"Ava, is there a way to let my aunts know I'm okay? I thought of it last night, but I forgot to ask," Cole said. "I figure they'll be plenty worried until they get word I'm okay."

Audrey couldn't take her eyes off Cole. She was fascinated by her manner of speech. The cadence and choice of words she used was so different.

"I should have told you," said Ava. "I sent them a communication droid yesterday afternoon."

"A what?" asked Cole.

"It's a digital box with a readout like this." She pointed at one of the synthesizers that had digital text scrolling across a small screen near the machine that had produced the coffee.

"Can they even read?" asked Audrey.

Ava visibly bristled at the question.

"I'm sorry. Did that sound rude? I just meant…"

Cole smiled good-naturedly. "It's okay. It's a fair question. Not everyone on the ground can read because there aren't as many schools as there used to be. And some families can't afford to spare their children for school because every hand is needed to farm or do other tasks that contribute to their family's well-being." Cole sipped her drink again. "Lucky for me, my aunts feel that the ability to read is important. In fact, Vivian is famous for quoting a twentieth century writer, C.S. Lewis who said: 'We read to know we are not alone.'"

Cole watched their reactions to her. She took in details about Audrey. When she had first arrived, Cole thought she was pretty. Now that she'd spent a few minutes in close proximity to Audrey, Cole found herself unsettled by the very sight of her. She was a natural beauty with long, wavy auburn hair that fell slightly below her shoulders. She had a feminine figure, round hips, and full breasts. Her green eyes were offset by her smooth, fair complexion. She was wearing a fitted skirt that showed off her shapely legs. Cole had never met anyone as beautiful, and she had a hard time redirecting her gaze so as to not make Audrey uncomfortable. She felt like she needed to leave the room. Cole shifted off the stool to stand. She straightened slowly and winced at the movement, placing her hand over her injured side.

"I'm sorry, but I don't feel so good. If you don't mind, I'm going to rest a bit more," Cole said, looking at Ava as she spoke. "It was nice to meet you, Audrey."

"I'll help you get into bed." Ava moved quickly to Cole's side and kept a gentle hand at the small of her back and on her arm to stabilize her slow movement to the bedroom.

Audrey registered the tender way Ava dealt with Cole. She wasn't sure if she was feeling jealous about Ava paying such close attention to Cole or if she was wishing she were in Ava's position helping Cole into bed. She shook her head to dislodge her crazy thoughts.

After a few minutes, Ava returned and Audrey quickly made an excuse to leave. "I should really get going. I have to be at the terminal point by ten a.m. if I'm going to make it over to city center by ten thirty."

"Oh, okay."

"Yeah, I'm sorry. I'll call you later or tomorrow." Audrey leaned in and brushed Ava's cheek with a kiss.

Once Audrey was in the corridor, she let out a shuddering sigh. *What was that about?* She entered the elevator lift and pushed the button for street level. Audrey felt like someone had just knocked the wind out of her. She had planned to talk with Ava about what had happened between them, assuring Ava that everything was okay, only to have her agenda completely derailed by the very distracting Cole. It had been a while since Audrey had been physically intimate with anyone, and she ached from the loss of intimacy in her life. Audrey couldn't understand her physical reaction to Cole when they shook hands. The brief encounter had left Audrey off balance and unsure of herself.

She tried to calm down and pull herself together as she exited the lift and joined the crowded street. Everyone was in a hurry. She turned left and headed toward the transportation terminal.

Chapter Eleven

Another day passed, and Cole was regaining her strength. Ava had hardly left her residential cube except once or twice to run an errand. At which point she usually left Cole to nap until her return.

Cole and Ava were both becoming restless. Cole, used to living more in the outdoors, especially wanted to get outside and walk around a little. Ava decided if they were going to finally venture out into the city that Cole would need some new clothes. She explained to Cole that everything would be much easier if Cole could blend in a little. They decided they would go shopping and then walk around the city, maybe even have lunch out somewhere.

As they rode the lift down to street level, Cole was nervous about not knowing what to expect. They stepped off the lift into a crowded street. Sleekly dressed individuals passed by, not noticing or making eye contact with either of them. The sun was blinding. Cole squinted and waited for her eyes to adjust.

"Oh, here," said Ava, "Wear these." She handed Cole her dark lenses to block the sun a bit. "We should pick up a pair for you. You'll need them. The sun can be very intense, as we're at a higher altitude."

Cole gratefully accepted the sunglasses. "Much better. Thank you. Wow." Now it was Cole's turn to marvel at her surroundings.

"Come on," Ava said. "Let's get you some new clothes."

They walked no more than a block to a store that Ava was familiar with. As they entered the retail space, Cole lifted the dark glasses to better see the interior. Racks of clothing, mostly muted colors of grays, blacks, and blues, hung in rows on steel frames. Ava went to a section of the store where the clothing seemed more androgynous. She began to sift through the items and pulled out a couple of shirts and some pants for Cole to try, guessing at her size. Cole stood silently nearby, taking it all in. As Ava picked items out for Cole, a sales clerk walked over to them.

"Can I help you find anything specific?" she asked. She was a slim, regal woman, probably in her forties. Even though she was speaking to Ava, her eyes remained focused on Cole.

Cole turned to say hello. The woman involuntarily took a step back. Ava stepped to Cole's side.

"No, we're fine, thanks," said Ava. "We'd like to try on these items if you don't mind."

The sales associate was speechless as she showed them to a fitting room. She couldn't stop staring at Cole. Cole stared back at her, more out of curiosity than malice. Ava gently pushed Cole into a fitting room and handed her the items she'd selected.

"Pick two shirts and two pairs of pants, okay?" Ava said before waiting outside the fitting room. "I also think you should get that jacket if it fits."

"Okay," said Cole.

Cole dressed and undressed slowly, not wanting to make any quick movements for fear of feeling the injury at her side. After a few moments, Ava knocked softly on the door. "How does everything fit? I was guessing at your size."

Cole opened the door and stepped out. She was wearing a fitted black T-shirt and gray, straight-cut slacks that hung low on her hips.

"How does this look?" asked Cole, holding her hands out at her sides.

"Wow. You look *good*," Ava and the sales clerk said in unison. Ava looked over at the woman and frowned.

"Sorry, but she does," said the clerk, shrugging.

After Ava paid for the clothing, they took Cole's new threads back to Ava's residential cube. They then struck back out again for a brief tour of the city.

As they returned to street level, Ava took Cole's arm. "Let's walk this way. I'll take you to one of the observation points so you can get a better look at your surroundings."

The view was stunning. There were observation decks at various points all over the city that offered a view of the vast ocean below, the sky above, and the city's skyline ahead. Cole tried to get her bearings, taking in each new, breathtaking view. There were small clouds moving overhead, but there were also clouds moving underneath the floating urban center. Their altitude was much higher than Cole had realized. Looking east, she could see the faint, dark line of the coast on the distant horizon. The sheer scale of it all made her dizzy. Cole leaned against the railing of the observation deck and exhaled.

"Are you okay?"

"Yeah, I'm fine," said Cole as she steadied herself. "I just felt dizzy. I didn't think I was afraid of heights, but I've never been this high before."

"I guess I hadn't thought of that," mused Ava. "Let's get you some food. That'll help ground you a little. Also, drinking lots of water will help you adjust to the altitude."

"I guess I've been on so many pain meds since the surgery that it blocked the sensation of the altitude."

Ava put her arm through Cole's and steered them toward one of her favorite spots for lunch. The trip to the restaurant took longer than Ava expected because everything along the way, particularly small details, caught Cole's attention. Window displays, mechanical street sweepers, small maglev transports, people of different races, strange clothing, and electronic newsstands. There was a lot to absorb.

At one point, Cole stepped out of the flow of pedestrian traffic and braced her arm against a building façade. Ava circled back quickly and stepped beside her.

"Are you okay?"

"It's just…I had to close my eyes for a moment. There are so many people, so close, all moving."

"Just take as much time as you need. We're not in a hurry."

"I'm okay," said Cole. She let out a long, slow exhale. "I think all the movement was just making me motion sick. But I'm feeling better."

"I didn't really think about it, but it is much more crowded here. It's like a sea of humanity."

"Where no one looks at you."

"What?"

"No one ever looks up or looks anyone in the face. No one makes eye contact," Cole observed. "It's like being alone only you're in a crowd."

"I guess I hadn't noticed."

Everything was more personal and immediate on the ground. There were no comm devices to scroll there. The social structure on the ground was homogenous so there was no class separation, and food was a communal activity—not something made by a machine.

They continued walking for a few more minutes and then Ava stopped in front of a café that was partially enclosed but also had a raised deck area with tables on an outdoor platform hovering just above their heads. "Want to sit outside?"

"Sure," said Cole.

People reacted to Cole as they moved through the café. Ava was glad that she'd given Cole her dark lenses because they covered her true eye color. Cole was getting enough stares as it was as they maneuvered carefully between the closely arranged tables.

Cole's manner stood out. For one thing, she looked at people as she passed them. Random patrons expressed surprise as they made visual contact with Cole. Cole also occasionally smiled and said hello to complete strangers, which caused several women to pause, fork in midair, to offer a stunned salutation in return.

Ava smiled to herself. *Ruth Coleman George, what a charmer you are and you don't even know it.*

They climbed the short set of stairs to the café's outdoor deck.

"Ava?"

Ava heard her name and turned to see Audrey and her friend Sara seated at a table near the deck railing. Ava's stomach sank. She wasn't ready to explain her visitor, but there was no way to avoid that now. Cole raised a hand in Audrey's direction. Sara stopped whatever she was saying, mid-sentence, and stared at them as they approached.

Audrey spoke first. "I'm so surprised to see you. Please join us."

"Hi, Audrey," said Ava as she leaned over and brushed Audrey's cheek with a friendly kiss. She then stretched across the table and did the same for Sara. "Sara, this is Cole."

Sara's mouth hung partially open. "Uh…Hi…"

Cole responded to them both, smiling. "Hello." She felt her pulse speed up slightly at the sight of Audrey. She didn't want to admit it, but she was very pleased to see her again and under better circumstances. Cole felt like she might not have made the greatest first impression when they'd met at Ava's apartment a few days earlier.

There was an awkward silence for a moment as Ava and Cole settled into their seats, luckily broken by a young woman who stopped by to ask for orders from Cole and Ava. Cole pushed the dark lenses to the top of her head so she could make eye contact with the waitress. The young woman almost dropped the menus as she looked at Cole.

Ava broke the silence. "Cole, why don't I order something for both of us since I'm more familiar with the menu here?"

Cole nodded, slightly relieved by the intervention. She'd never been to a restaurant and wasn't sure of the protocol.

As soon as the waitress left to place the order, Ava launched in. She could see by the look on Sara's face that a million questions were hovering just below the surface. This also let her know that Audrey had not spoken with anyone about Cole. Ava was silently grateful to Audrey for her discretion.

"I guess I have a story to tell you, Sara." Ava smiled in her direction.

"You think?" Sara laughed.

Ava spoke in a matter-of-fact way about how she'd met Cole and the circumstances of bringing her to the cloud city.

Sara responded first with shock, followed by disbelief, and then concern. "Ava, are you seriously telling me you spent two days in the mountains, on the ground, and nothing bad happened to you?"

"Yes, it was unplanned. But that's what happened."

"And, Cole, you're okay now?" Sara said as she looked in her direction. Cole nodded. "I'm in shock, Ava. I don't really know what to say."

The waitress returned with the food and drinks that Ava had ordered.

"This is Cole's first experience in the city. She hasn't been well enough to leave my residential cube."

Cole sat quietly watching them at the table. She realized that there was a social nuance at work here that she didn't fully understand. Ava seemed on edge and maybe a little defensive. Sara and Audrey offered some resistance to Ava's story—some *healthy skepticism*. It seemed like both women were sincerely shocked at Ava's story. Mostly that life on the ground wasn't so bad after all. It might even be great for some folks. Cole decided a simple question might help change the direction of the slightly uncomfortable conversation.

"So, what do you two do here in the city?" asked Cole before sipping the purple beverage that Ava had ordered on her behalf. After one sip she winced and looked down at the glass. She half smiled at Ava.

"Sorry. I wasn't sure which you would like. Why don't we trade because I'll drink either one." Ava handed Cole a glass filled with a bright orange liquid. Cole tasted the drink.

"Yeah, that's better, thanks."

Returning to Cole's original question, Sara responded, "I'm a teacher." She paused for a brief moment as if she were unsettled by Cole's unwavering gaze. "Um, I teach mathematics."

Ava then responded on Audrey's behalf. "Audrey is a doctor."

Audrey was a little annoyed that Ava had answered for her.

"What do you do, Cole?" Audrey asked. She noticed that Cole had been quite transformed since last she'd seen her. Audrey was acutely aware that Cole was very attractive. She felt her cheeks involuntarily flush. *What is happening to me?*

"Um, what do I do?" Cole pondered the question. "I guess I help run a farm. Does that make me a farmer? We, my two aunts and I, we have a homestead in the mountains where we have a cow, some chickens, and quite a large year-round garden. You know, tomatoes in the summer, and then root vegetables in the fall. There's also a pond nearby that's swarming with catfish and…" Cole trailed off as she realized Audrey and Sara were staring at her with mouths slightly ajar.

Cole was also aware that even the patrons seated closest to them at neighboring tables had stopped their conversations to hang on her every word. Cole rotated slightly in her seat and offered them a smile.

She leaned closer to Ava and quietly asked, "Was I talking too loud?"

Ava smiled. "No, Cole. It's fine."

Cole looked around and nodded to the women seated around them who now slowly began returning to their respective conversations.

"It's probably just because no one has heard anyone talk about the things you are talking about, probably ever," said Ava.

"Listen, you guys, I was there. I can tell you it's not like what we've been told. It's…It's rather magical. I had *real* food. It tasted amazing. And, well, everything smells so good. It's all very hard to describe."

Hearing Ava talk about her two days in the mountains gave Cole just the slightest twinge of homesickness.

Audrey's reaction was tentative, with just the slightest hint of disappointment. "Wow. It sounds to me as if you'd go back to the ground, given the option," said Audrey, curious if her assessment was true. But before Ava responded, Cole directed a question to Audrey. There's that unnerving intense gaze again, Audrey thought.

"So what kind of healing do you do?" Cole asked.

Audrey returned Cole's piercing gaze and didn't immediately answer.

Ava offered a response instead. "Audrey does general medicine. She's a terrific doctor. Her patients love her."

Finding her voice finally, Audrey asked, "What do you think of the cloud city of Easton so far, Cole?"

Cole smiled and responded directly to Audrey without breaking her gaze. "It's, well, it's definitely different. Ask me again after I've walked around a bit more."

Is Cole trying to make a connection with me? Am I trying to connect with her? Some strange energy was starting to develop between them, and Audrey's internal response to Cole's unwavering eye contact made her uncomfortable. She became aware that her proximity to Cole was beginning to make her feel aroused. Audrey felt that she should make her exit, but she had the simultaneous urge to linger in Cole's presence.

Sara ended up announcing her departure before Audrey could make up her mind.

"Well, I should get to work," said Sara. "Cole, it was very nice meeting you. I hope I see you again. Everyone is going to the club tomorrow night for Katherine's birthday. You two should come out."

Ava looked up at Sara from her seated position. "Thanks, Sara. That would be fun. I've been so out of touch that I completely forgot about Kate's big day."

Sara left. Audrey thought Cole was beginning to show signs of fatigue. The doctor in her couldn't help but ask, "Cole, how are you feeling?"

"To be honest, at the moment, I'm not feeling very well. I'm just tired I guess."

Ava looked a little disappointed. "Really? I was kind of hoping we could make a few more stops before heading back to my place."

Before really thinking it through, Audrey said, "I could take Cole back to your place if you have things you need to do." Audrey's heart began to race at just the suggestion of being alone with Cole.

"Really? You wouldn't mind?" Ava sounded grateful.

Audrey figured Ava was in need of some alone time, and the thought of Cole having to suffer further fatigue following Ava around the city caused her concern.

"I wouldn't mind. I have the rest of the afternoon off." Audrey paused and looked at Cole. "I mean, if Cole is okay with this plan?"

"I'd be grateful. I know I've been keeping Ava tethered more than she probably likes." Cole smiled at Ava good-naturedly.

"I love this plan. Thank you so much, Audrey." Ava stood and left credits on the table for the bill. "I'll see you later, Cole. Get some rest." And with that, she was off, leaving Audrey and Cole to themselves.

A moment of silence passed between them while Audrey riffled in her bag for credits to add to what Ava had left on the table. She consciously attempted not to look up at Cole.

"Well, should we go? We can get an auto lift near the corner, and that way you won't have to walk."

"Not walking sounds very appealing."

Cole stood, a bit shaky on her feet. Audrey instinctively reached for her arm to steady her. She felt heat rush to the pale skin on her neck and cheeks from the physical contact. Cole just smiled at her.

"Thank you, Audrey."

"It's really my pleasure."

Audrey kept her hand on the small of Cole's back as they navigated through the café's interior and down to street level. The contact that Audrey had previously been so jealous of Ava for. They walked to the corner and Audrey used a credit card to release the auto taxi from its station bracket. The door slid upward and Audrey helped Cole step inside. The two-seated vehicle was a bit intimate for two people who hardly knew each other. They sat across from each other in the coach, their knees touching in the tight space. Audrey leaned forward and entered the destination address, and the taxi began to rotate and slip into the lane set aside for non-pedestrian traffic.

"How does this work? I mean, it's not even touching the ground," said Cole.

"It uses maglev technology. Which I'm not sure I can adequately explain, but basically, there's a metal strip imbedded in the concrete, almost like a train track, except it's not raised. The magnet is in the undercarriage and follows the rail. It will autopilot to the address I just entered."

"That's really something."

Cole relaxed more into the seat back. Her legs were long, so in the small space between the seats that faced each other their knees kept brushing against each other. Audrey registered the physical contact immediately. Cole's body seemed like an electric charge for Audrey's system. She felt herself blush again and made a feeble attempt to look out the window. When she looked back she noticed that Cole had her head back and her eyes closed, which allowed Audrey to study her for a few minutes without discovery. Cole had an easy manner about her, slouched in the opposite chair, her hair loosely disheveled. Audrey had the urge to reach over and brush her fingers through the hair falling across her forehead.

Does she feel it too? Audrey had a hard time reading Cole's expressions.

After another ten minutes, the taxi slowed and stopped in front of Ava's building. Cole didn't seem to register that the vehicle had stopped so Audrey gently put her hand on Cole's leg.

"Cole," Audrey said, "we're here."

"Oh, I'm so sorry. I didn't mean to drift off on you."

They exited and rode the lift in silence to Ava's apartment. Cole seemed to be shaking her head to dislodge the fog of her quick nap in the taxi. Audrey punched the code that allowed them entrance to Ava's place, and Cole settled onto the sofa in the main living area. Audrey dropped her bag on a chair near the kitchen and brought a glass of water back for Cole.

"This is very kind of you. Helping me get back here. Thank you."

"It's no problem, really."

Audrey noticed a linen satchel resting on the upholstered chair near the sofa. It looked so foreign in the context of Ava's modern décor. "Is that yours?"

"The bag? Yes."

Audrey lifted it and studied the outside for a moment with a frown on her face.

"It's actually a nice satchel," said Cole.

"Oh, sorry. It's not that. But there's blood on it. That's so typical of Ava not to notice. It looks as if this material is washable." Audrey turned toward Cole as she was holding the bag. "Why don't I put this in the machine to wash for you?"

"Yeah. If you have such a thing, that'd be great."

"Just give me a minute." Audrey opened the bag and gently placed each of the odd objects from its interior on the small low table in front of the sofa. After a few minutes, she returned from her task. "It's in the wash. Good as new, shortly."

Cole smiled at Audrey as she took a seat next to Cole on the sofa. They were both quiet for a moment as Audrey began to study the items she'd placed on the table. "Cole, can I ask you about these things?"

"Sure."

There was a small round object with numbers and a circular, and cracked, glass surface cover. Audrey recognized the object from photos she had seen. It was an analog timepiece.

"May I pick this up?"

"Please, be my guest."

Audrey held the watch in her hand for a moment and then replaced it and picked up an oddly shaped object with a rough, porous surface. It had ridges and was completely white. It looked like a shell from the sea. Audrey placed the white, organic shape next to the other object and reached for the next object. It appeared to have been carved out of some smooth, well-worn wood. The object was shaped like the letter Y with narrow pieces of rubber affixed to each side at the top of the Y shape. The two rubber straps were joined in the center by a small, square piece of leather. Audrey had no idea what this was. She placed it carefully on the table surface.

Audrey picked up the last item, a small, frayed, leather-bound book. Faded letters on the book's black cover read "Holy Bible." She carefully opened the book. Pages seemed to flip over of their own accord from having been much used. It fell open to one passage in the book that had been marked in the margin. Audrey read the passage silently to herself:

"But Ruth said, do not urge me to leave you or turn back from following you; for where you go, I will go, and where you lodge, I will lodge. Your people shall be my people, and your God, my God. Where you die, I will die, and there I will be buried. Thus may the Lord do to me and worse, if anything but death parts you and me."

Audrey gently closed the book as she turned to see Cole watching her intently.

"Would you tell me what these things are?" asked Audrey. "I mean, I know what most of them are. I just wanted to know more about why you have them."

"Sure." Cole raised her head slightly so she could see the items spread out on top of the table. She pointed at the analog timepiece with the cracked face. "That's a pocket watch that belonged to my father, and his father before him. Unfortunately, it doesn't work, and I've been unable to get parts for it. That was the only thing I got from my father after he died."

Audrey made a note to herself to ask more about Cole's parents later.

Audrey reached for one of the other objects. "What is this?"

Cole smiled. "A slingshot. Have you never seen one before?"

"No. What's it for?"

"It can be a weapon if you have a small stone handy." Cole took the slingshot and demonstrated its use. "You put the stone in here and pull it back like this." She pulled up short and winced when her left arm pulled at her wounded side.

"Careful," said Audrey. "Sorry. I didn't mean to make you move so much. I'm just so curious. And what's this?" Audrey held up the small-leather bound book.

"You don't know what that is either?" asked Cole with some genuine surprise. "That's a Bible."

"I've heard of the Bible, but I don't know anyone who has one," said Audrey. "It's an interesting book. It's small, and the pages are extremely thin. I didn't mean to intrude, but I did read one passage marked in the book."

"That's okay."

"When I opened it, the book fell open to a page in the chapter named 'Ruth,'" said Audrey. "The passage was one woman talking about never leaving another woman. It sounded intense. Is that where your first name came from, Ruth Coleman George?"

"I assume so, but I never asked," mused Cole. "Ruth is an interesting book in the Bible. It's about kinship and ultimately loyalty. Ruth isn't part of the Jewish tribe, the group that the book is about, but ultimately she becomes the great-grandmother of their king, David. Not only was she a foreigner who was fully assimilated into their tribe, but ultimately Ruth became God's instrument for some higher good.

"Basically it's a lesson in universality versus tribalism. You know, it's about inclusion. About not being closed off and insulated but being open to others who might be outside your group and what they might contribute to the greater good."

Audrey had never heard anyone speak the way Cole was speaking. "Wow. How did you learn about this?"

Audrey had never had any interest in philosophy or the study of ancient religions, although she did feel some pull toward spiritual pursuits. Her interests in college had always been focused on biology and anatomy.

"People don't practice religion here?"

"Not really. Some people do meditation, not many people, but I've known a few. But no one ever talks about God as if God is real."

In the cities, only science and commerce were considered worthy of study. Religion had long been abandoned as a salve for the underprivileged masses, something to give them hope for the future, or if not a better future, then a better afterlife.

"So, you don't believe there's something, some force, larger than yourself at work in the world?"

"I'm not sure. I think institutionalized religion can be dangerous in the wrong hands. Historically, religion has caused more problems than it's solved. I think in some ways we're better off without it."

"Interesting," said Cole. "Well, that Bible belonged to my great-great-grandmother. I find comfort in the words I read there. I guess it's hard to understand how comforting faith can be if you've never experienced it firsthand."

Audrey reached for the last item. "And this?"

"It's a seashell," said Cole. She took the object from Audrey and rubbed her fingers across the ridges. "It's to remind me that there are things on the Earth older than me. Once, water was everywhere, and then there was dry land, and now the water is rising again. We are small, while the forces around us are epic." Cole paused. "Perspective can be life-altering."

Audrey was taken by surprise at this complex explanation of a simple shell. As they'd been talking, they had somehow unconsciously moved closer to each other on the sofa. Audrey rubbed her fingers lightly across the ridges of the shell that Cole held in her open palm. She had found the entire exchange intimate, bordering on erotic. She lifted her eyes from the shell to see that Cole was watching her with that unwavering gaze.

"Audrey, you are so beautiful," Cole whispered.

Audrey didn't know how to respond. She thought Cole was beautiful too. Not just because of the way she looked but because of the way her mind worked. Audrey was unnerved. Cole had closed her fingers around Audrey's hand as they still held the seashell between them. She wanted to lean into Cole, tucking her head into the hollow space in Cole's shoulder. She had to remind herself that Cole wasn't well. She shifted slightly on the sofa to put more space between them. Audrey felt like she needed breathing space to sort out her feelings, and being physically close to Cole was making that impossible.

Cole wasn't sure how to interpret Audrey's shift in position away from her.

"I'm sorry. I didn't mean to offend you."

"You didn't…not at all. I just…" Audrey paused as if unsure of what she wanted to say. "I just thought maybe I should help you lie down. I didn't mean to keep you from resting."

Audrey stood and offered her hand to Cole.

"I'll help you get tucked in."

Cole wasn't ready for Audrey to leave. She wanted to be close to Audrey and talk with her more, but she wasn't sure if that was what Audrey wanted. There seemed to be some sort of shared attraction. Cole registered heat whenever Audrey touched her, but she wasn't sure if Audrey was also feeling their connection. She took Audrey's hand and gingerly rose off the sofa. Her side still ached from the surgery but was definitely feeling better. However, as she stood, a wave of dizziness washed over her. She swayed slightly, and Audrey put an arm around her waist to stabilize her.

"That's the second time you've kept me from toppling," said Cole. Audrey's face was very close to hers. Her breath stirred soft auburn strands near Audrey's forehead, and she closed her eyes, allowing herself to briefly lean into Audrey before taking a step back.

"I think you just need a little rest." Audrey smiled at Cole.

Cole thought Audrey had the most beautiful smile she'd ever seen. She allowed Audrey to lead her to the bedroom, and she sat on the side of the bed as Audrey helped her lift her legs so that she was fully reclined. Then Cole watched with surprise as Audrey gently untied her shoes and removed them. Cole wanted to ask Audrey to stay, but she knew she was only moments from falling asleep. She'd taken a pain pill with lunch, and it was beginning to kick in. Cole was granted a tantalizing view of Audrey's slightly exposed cleavage as she leaned across Cole to adjust the pillow behind her head.

"Why are you being so sweet to me?" Cole asked sincerely.

Audrey smiled down at her. "I'm not sure yet. Do you mind it?"

"No. To be truthful, I'd like more of it."

Audrey blushed. "Just rest, Cole." She placed her soft palm on Cole's forehead. "Just rest."

Audrey lingered by the bed until she was sure Cole was asleep. She allowed herself the luxury of trailing her fingers across the back of Cole's hand. Then she brought her fingertips to her lips. Audrey shuddered with the knowledge that she was now fully captivated by this outlander.

She quietly left the room, leaving the door slightly ajar, and let herself out of Ava's apartment. Audrey assumed that Ava would return shortly, and she didn't relish having Ava as an audience. Ava would surely pick up on the growing attraction that Audrey felt for Cole, and Audrey wasn't sure she was quite ready to go public with that revelation.

Chapter Twelve

Audrey gave herself one more glance in the mirror. She was pleased with the way the fabric of the dress hugged her every curve. The opening at the neck was just low enough to offer a tempting view of the cleavage of her breasts, without offering too much. *Not bad.* She had decided to make a splash at Kate's party.

Audrey picked up a small shoulder bag for keys and lipstick and left her residential unit for Club Six. It was Kate's twenty-fifth birthday. It was a short commute to Club Six, and during the transit ride Audrey couldn't keep her mind from returning to thoughts of Cole. She hoped to see her at the club tonight, in which case the red dress would hopefully not go unnoticed or unappreciated. She climbed the few steps into the club and scanned the room for her friends. Audrey spotted Sara and a small group of familiar faces at the far end of the bar and headed that way.

Sara saw Audrey and choked on her festive, umbrella-garnished drink, coughing and smiling as Audrey walked up. Audrey took the drink from her hand and helped herself to a long sip from the straw.

"Holy shit, Audrey." Sara gave Audrey a full body scan. "Who is the intended recipient of this red hot message?"

"Not you, so you can relax," said Audrey playfully as she handed the drink back to Sara. "I can see from your reaction that I picked the right outfit for tonight though. Thanks for the endorsement."

Audrey smiled and waved in Kate's direction. Kate was surrounded by several friends: Aesha, Naomi, Ty, Sandra, Sara's ex Candice, and others. It was a regular sorority reunion.

The music was loud and thumping. Audrey had to lean close to Sara's ear to be heard.

"Ava and I still haven't talked about what almost happened over a week ago. I feel like she's avoiding me," said Audrey.

"I got that impression at lunch yesterday," replied Sara sympathetically. "I guess she's had a big distraction named Cole. You guys will work it out."

"Yeah." Audrey saw Ava and Cole approach them through the crowd. Audrey didn't fail to notice Ava's eyes widen slightly when she caught sight of Audrey in the tight-fitting, red dress. *Well, at least that's something.* Cole seemed intrigued by her surroundings. Audrey was doubtful that a place such as this existed anywhere near where Cole was from. She almost felt a pang of sympathy for how overwhelming all of this must be for someone in her situation.

Cole didn't seem intimidated though. She seemed calm and observant. Ava had undoubtedly done some shopping on Cole's behalf. She was wearing dark gray, straight-cut pants that hung just at the right spot on her narrow hips, with a tailored dark-collared shirt, left untucked. *Not bad.*

"Hi," said Ava as they approached Sara and Audrey. "Um, you look amazing, Audrey."

"Thank you," said Audrey. Cole didn't even pretend not to stare at Audrey. There was something refreshing about Cole's complete lack of pretense.

Ava turned to Cole. "I'm going to go say hi to Kate and get us drinks. Are you okay here?"

Cole nodded without taking her eyes off Audrey.

First Ava and then Sara moved to the bar to join Kate's small celebratory circle, leaving Cole and Audrey standing near each other. Audrey thought about attempting to make some sort of small talk with Cole, but before words escaped her lips they were joined by a third party. Mac, the woman who'd made an attempt to buy her a drink on a previous night out, walked up. Mac was standing on Audrey's other side, opposite Cole. It was loud so she had to lean to speak to Audrey.

"How about that rain check you owe me?" said Mac, oozing self-confidence.

"Did I owe you a rain check?" Audrey was being polite, but she shot a sideways anxious glance in Cole's direction.

Cole swiftly moved in between Audrey and Mac. Audrey felt Cole's arm around her waist and her hand resting lightly at the small of Audrey's back. The action was so quick and smooth that it surprised both Audrey and Mac.

"Sorry, friend, but we were in the middle of something here," Cole said in a friendly but firm tone to Mac.

Mac looked at Audrey for confirmation, and when Audrey tucked her head closer to Cole's chest, Mac got the hint to move along. Cole and Mac gave each other parting glances, as if to say *this isn't over* before Cole turned to face Audrey. She moved her hand so that it came to rest on Audrey's hip. Audrey didn't really need protection from someone like Mac, but she appreciated the chivalrous gesture.

"Were we?" asked Audrey, tilting her head up to meet Cole's eyes. She allowed her hand to rest gently on Cole's torso; the electricity building between them as a result of their proximity sent a tingle up Audrey's spine.

"Excuse me?"

"Were we in the middle of something?"

"I'd like to be." Cole's lips were dangerously close to Audrey's.

"Dance with me."

Audrey took Cole's hand and began pulling her toward the dance floor. She steered them through the densely populated area around the dance floor, looking for an opening. Audrey found a barely open space and pulled Cole in next to her. Cole seemed at a complete loss. She remained motionless while women all around her were coupled and moving to the beat of the music. The haze of sexual energy was palpable all around her.

Cole said something that Audrey couldn't make out.

"I'm sorry, what did you say?"

Placing her mouth close to Audrey's ear, Cole repeated, "I don't really dance."

Audrey felt herself react to the touch of Cole's lips on the edge of her ear.

"It's okay," said Audrey. "I do. Just relax."

But Audrey wasn't sure why she said that last part because Cole was relaxed. Cole seemed to feel no pressure to try to mimic the movements around her. *What are you doing, Audrey? You got her on the dance floor, now what?* Audrey felt a little silly, like an adolescent schoolgirl. She hadn't been able to stop thinking about Cole since she'd escorted her back to Ava's, and now she had pulled her on the dance floor almost immediately. So much for playing it cool.

As a new song cranked up, the dance floor became even more crowded, and Audrey was pressed closer to Cole. Audrey moved rhythmically close to her, at some moments brushing up against Cole with her breasts or her hips. As the crowd closed in around them, Audrey found herself almost entirely pressed against Cole, who still remained standing with her relaxed arms hanging at her sides. At one point, Audrey placed her hands on Cole's shoulders to keep from falling into her as a woman near them encroached into their space on the dance floor. She let her open palms drift slowly down Cole's chest. She felt Cole's firmly erect nipples under the surface of the thin, dark shirt. The sensation sent a rush of heat through Audrey's core. She let her hands remain on Cole's small, firm breasts and continued to slowly move to the music, as if the tempo was her own and not directed by the pounding bass that surrounded them. It was clear from Cole's physical reaction that the red dress had delivered its message. Audrey was getting the response she'd hoped for.

Near the bar, Ava returned to the spot where she'd left Cole. She turned to Sara. "Do you know where Cole is?"

Sara pointed toward the dance floor. "She's with Audrey, getting a dance lesson."

"Seriously?" Ava was holding two drinks and could scarcely hide her surprise. A twinge of jealousy rose in her chest. *What is that about?* The dance floor was completely packed. She could just barely spot the tops of Cole's and Audrey's heads in the center of the crowd. But before she could move in their direction, Kate was at her side, pulling her into a friendly embrace, causing her to slosh one of her drinks in Sara's direction.

❖

In the center of the pulsing revelers, Audrey could no longer remember why she first thought pulling Cole onto the dance floor was a good idea. She became aware that she was incredibly physically close to Cole and that she couldn't stop looking at Cole's mouth. Audrey caressed Cole's lower, full lip with her thumb. She slipped her thumb in between Cole's lips causing Cole to open her mouth just enough to place a kiss on Audrey's thumb. That was all the invitation Audrey needed to press closer with open mouth, tongue searching.

At first, Audrey was kissing Cole.

Cole passively accepted the kiss, but then something about the connection shifted, and Cole began to kiss Audrey back with force and passion. In surprise, Audrey attempted to pull back, but Cole put one hand at the back of Audrey's neck, the other on Audrey's hip and pulled her closer so that the kiss could deepen.

For a moment, Audrey forgot where she was. She forgot that she hardly knew Cole. She forgot everything but Cole's mouth and the feel of her strong body pressed against her. The intensity of the connection between them washed over her. She wrapped her arms around Cole's neck and gave herself over to the moment. Then, as quickly as the embrace had happened, it was over. Breathless, Audrey pulled away and gave Cole a confused look, before pushing her way through the crowded dance floor toward the back of the club.

Cole stood alone in the midst of the throbbing crowd, with her face flushed and her heart pounding. She had watched as the crowd closed and concealed Audrey's exit.

Fresh air. That's what I need, fresh air. She pushed through the teeming room and through a dark opening that she hoped would lead her outside. She stepped onto the outdoor deck to find that Audrey had taken the same route. Audrey was leaning up against the railing, facing forward, as Cole stepped through the door into the crisp night air. Without speaking, Cole stepped over and leaned against Audrey.

Cole was looking at her with an intensity that she hoped conveyed at least some of what she was feeling. Audrey reached up and removed a smudge of her lipstick from Cole's mouth.

Cole leaned in and kissed Audrey again, this time slower, sweeter. As she luxuriated against Audrey's lips, she allowed her hands to drift up Audrey's ribs, brushing the outer curve of her breasts beneath the sheer fabric. Cole felt Audrey shudder slightly against her.

"You have to stop doing that," whispered Audrey.

"Doing what?"

"Moving your hands like that. I'm…what are you doing to me?"

"I don't know. What are you doing to me?" Cole tilted her head to catch Audrey's eye. "Audrey, you're like this beautiful warm light and I'm the moth."

"The cutest damn moth I've ever seen."

"And I'm about to burn up for you. Please kiss me again."

The outdoor deck where they stood was mostly dark, and in the dim, pulsing light from the open door, Audrey kissed Cole again. Cole felt the crush of Audrey's breasts against her chest as Audrey draped her arms around Cole's neck and explored her mouth with her tongue. Cole was on fire; she pressed harder into Audrey allowing her hands to drift down to the full curve of Audrey's hips. Cole realized something big was happening between them. Her heart was pounding; she felt her stomach upend and dive. Cole was losing herself in this kiss.

Audrey felt wetness spreading between her legs as Cole pulled them tightly together. She knew that she was getting close to the edge. She either had to leave now and take Cole to bed or they had to stop. Audrey forced herself to pull away. She needed to regain her bearings and stop thinking with her libido.

Audrey pushed away from Cole, her face flushed. She rested her forehead on Cole's shoulder.

"We have to stop."

She was taking a step away from Cole just as Sara stepped out onto the deck with Ava trailing close behind her.

Ava didn't seem to be aware of the blanket of sexual tension that was hanging in the air, but Audrey could tell that Sara picked up on it right away.

"There you are," said Ava as she wrapped an arm around Cole's shoulder. "Come back in. I really want you to have a chance to meet Kate."

Without offering a verbal response or a glance back at Audrey, Cole allowed herself to be led by the arm back into the bar's dark, noisy interior. Audrey watched intently, leaving her gaze on the door after they had already passed through it.

"Audrey?" Sara said.

Audrey turned in her direction.

"What's going on?" Sara asked.

"Nothing," Audrey said without looking at Sara.

"I think Ava is too oblivious to notice, but I'm not. I could feel the sexual energy between you two the minute I walked out here. I'm surprised Ava didn't get a static discharge when she touched Cole's arm. Geez, Audrey, what the hell?"

"We kissed on the dance floor. And then again out here."

"What?"

"I know. I don't know how it happened."

"I know how it happened," said Sara. "That red dress, that cleavage, oh, and I've seen you dance. I know exactly how it happened. The question is, now what?"

"I have no idea," answered Audrey, and it was the truth. No one had been more surprised than her at the passion that had erupted between her and Cole. "Oh, Sara, what am I going to do? I'm in serious trouble I think."

❖

Later that night, Ava and Cole took the train back to Ava's place. Cole had been very quiet for most of the night. She didn't say much when she was introduced to Kate or any of Ava's other friends. Granted, it was hard to have a decent conversation over the noise, but Cole didn't even make an effort. Audrey had been oddly distant from Ava also, which made Ava wonder what might have transpired between Cole and Audrey earlier in the night on the dance floor.

Cole was watching the scenery speed by the window. It was a short, fifteen-minute transit ride back to Ava's residential cube.

"Hey, Cole?" she said. "What's going on? You seem quiet. Did something happen at the club?"

Cole fell into the sofa, seated so that she was facing Ava.

"Was the scene at the bar too much? I know you probably hadn't been in a place like that before."

"Audrey and I kissed."

That was the last thing Ava had expected Cole to say. After a moment, Ava responded as if she were unsure she'd heard Cole correctly. "What?"

"We kissed…a few times."

Ava decided she needed to sit down. She dropped into an overstuffed chair that faced the loveseat. She didn't know how to respond to this revelation.

"That's okay, right?" asked Cole. "I mean, you and Audrey are just friends, right?"

"Yeah, Audrey and I are just friends." Ava studied Cole. "I'm, well, I'm just surprised. I think Audrey's an amazing person. I can see why you're attracted to her."

"I don't know how to explain it, Ava. But it's more than just an attraction."

"Wow. When did you figure this out?"

"I think it started yesterday when she brought me back to your place." Cole paused as she reflected back. "No, if I was honest about it, I felt something the very first time I shook her hand. Like a heat reaction."

Ava sat silently, watching Cole.

"Hey, I'm sorry. I didn't mean to start a heavy conversation so late. I think I'm just really tired." Cole glanced up to see Ava watching her, a stone expression on her face. "Why don't I take the sofa tonight so you can have your room back?"

"No, I'm fine out here. Seriously."

Cole stood and began to move toward the bedroom. As she passed Ava in the chair, she let her hand rest on Ava's shoulder for a moment. "You're a true friend, Ava. Good night."

Cole peeled off her clothes and lay on her back in bed with her eyes closed. It was not her intention to do anything to create tension with Ava, but the kiss had done just that. Cole wasn't sure exactly why. The emotional divide that had arisen between them felt just the same as if they were miles apart. Cole felt tired, confused, and homesick for candlelight, quiet, trees, grass, and space to think. She drifted off to sleep thinking of Audrey.

CHAPTER THIRTEEN

The next morning, Cole and Ava were having coffee, when Ava received an active flight notice on her phone. "Sorry," Ava said. "I need to call in about this."

Ava returned to the room shortly.

"That was my flight supervisor. It looks like I'm going to have to do a goods transfer to the cloud city of Stockholm. The good news is that it's just up and back. The bad news is it's a long day. Maybe sixteen or eighteen hours total travel time."

"Uh, okay. What should I do?"

"Stay here, of course," said Ava. "It won't hurt for you to take it easy for another day, right? There's plenty of food here. You can make yourself at home. The good thing about a long shift is that I'll get two days off when I'm back. Time to fly you home if you're fully mended by then."

Ava thought maybe a few hours apart would be good for them. She needed to deal with her feelings about what had happened between Cole and Audrey and regroup. She didn't want to admit it, but the revelation that Audrey had kissed Cole had shaken her up. It was true that she and Audrey weren't in a relationship, so why did it bother her so much that Audrey and Cole had kissed? Ava couldn't figure it out and so her usual solution was to leave. She'd have plenty of time to think and sort out her confusing feelings during the long flight.

Ava left the room to change into her flight gear, the same slightly reflective jacket Cole had first seen her wear. She packed a small bag with a few items just in case they had to overnight for some reason and then jotted down some info for Cole.

"This is the passcode for my apartment. And this is the number for my comm unit in case you need to reach me."

Ava didn't write down Audrey's number, and Cole obviously sensed it was best not to ask for it.

"I'll be fine, thanks. And fly safe this time, okay?" Cole said.

Ava smiled. "Yeah, that's my plan."

❖

About four hours after Ava left, Cole decided she needed to see the sky and feel the sun. She rode the lift down to the pedestrian level and idled for a moment, deciding which direction to walk. She sauntered toward the east, keeping to the edge of the seething sea of pedestrians so that she could keep her slower pace. She had her bag with her so she thought she might find a place to sit in the sun and maybe read the small book she always had with her. The language and stories in the book would likely remind her of things she felt homesick for: family, tradition, history, and faith.

A half hour later, Cole stumbled across a small green space with a few benches. She chose a sunny bench next to the exterior wall of a building. She took a seat, leaned back against the building wall, and soaked up the sun's warmth. Cole had been reclining there for no more than ten minutes when she heard a voice with a familiar British accent.

"Cole?"

Cole squinted up into the sun, the figure speaking to her silhouetted against the bright light.

"Audrey?"

"What are you doing here by yourself?" asked Audrey.

"What are you, the leisure patrol?" asked Cole teasingly.

Audrey laughed. "Sorry. I don't think I meant that the way it sounded."

Audrey took a seat next to Cole. As she sat close to Cole, their thighs touched, and Cole felt her heart rate speed up.

"Ava is doing a cargo flight to Stockholm so I'm left to my own devices," said Cole. "It seems I'm not very ambitious, as my first endeavor has been to lounge in the sun."

"I see," said Audrey as she studied Cole's face.

Cole felt butterflies in her stomach as she looked at Audrey's lips and remembered their kiss from the previous night. She wondered if Audrey was having the same reaction. Before she could figure it out, Audrey asked, "Have you had lunch?"

"Um, not yet."

"Good. Then I think you should come with me."

Audrey stood and extended a hand to Cole.

"Really?" Cole said doubtfully. She was uncertain that time with Audrey would be such a good idea. She wasn't sure she fully trusted herself with Audrey, who was looking just as lovely in the light of day as she had at the club the night before.

"Come with me," Audrey said.

"Okay." It seemed not within Cole's power to refuse the invitation. Audrey hooked her arm through Cole's and they walked together in silence.

After several minutes, they stepped into the ground floor lift of Audrey's building and rode upward to the twenty-seventh floor. Cole leaned against the interior wall of the lift and smiled at Audrey. It was interesting that they had walked the entire time in comfortable silence, but now that Cole realized they were not going to a café but rather to Audrey's home, she felt unsettled inside. She was unable to read Audrey and whether she was feeling the same unsettled feeling in the pit of her stomach that Cole was feeling.

Audrey was wearing a skirt of some lightweight material, not unlike the dress she'd worn the previous night that hugged the curve of her hips. She was also wearing a tailored shirt with buttons that strained ever so slightly over her ample breasts. The shirt was light blue, untucked, slightly wrinkled, and her sleeves were rolled up at the elbows. As they exited the lift, she stood quietly by while Audrey entered the door code and then followed her inside.

Audrey's place was similar in size and layout to Ava's, but there was a softness and coziness that seemed to smooth the edges of the metallic and sleek space. There were splashes of warm colors here and there and the kitchen looked much more lived in.

Audrey dropped the small bag she'd been carrying into a nearby chair and turned to look at Cole. Audrey stepped over to stand near

Cole. She stood for a moment, very close to Cole, studying her face. Cole thought Audrey might initiate another kiss, but instead, Audrey took a step back and asked, "May I see the site of your surgery?"

"Um…okay," Cole responded. Momentarily, she'd forgotten that Audrey was a doctor.

Audrey started to slowly unbutton Cole's shirt from the bottom up. She unfastened the bottom three buttons and then lifted the shirt so that she could see the two puncture wounds. They were now just two red, slightly raised marks where the blade had entered. They had been expertly closed in surgery. Audrey bent to get a closer look and placed an open palm over the site of injury. Cole's stomach muscles shuddered slightly at Audrey's touch.

She is so gorgeous, thought Cole.

There was something in the way Audrey was studying Cole's face. Was it sympathy? Or worry, or something else? Cole was unsure how to interpret the expression but felt the intensity of Audrey's stare settle into her chest.

Audrey removed her hand and gently lowered the bottom of Cole's shirt. She looked as if she were going to say something, but instead smiled and turned to the kitchen. Cole followed her.

"How do the scars look to you?" Cole figured she might as well get a professional opinion. Cole placed her own hand over the spot where Audrey had touched her. The site of contact radiated heat from their brief connection.

"I think you are healing well," Audrey said as she placed a small pan on the range top. "You'll likely have some soreness as you begin to use the muscles in that area again, but that will eventually pass. In fact, now is probably the time to start to stretch and use those muscles so they regain their strength."

I could think of some exercises we could do together, Cole thought and then abruptly stopped her train of thought before it completely derailed. *Pull it together!*

"Make yourself comfortable," Audrey said without looking at Cole. "I'm going to make us some food."

Cole took a seat at one of the stools near the counter opening. She enjoyed watching Audrey move confidently about her small kitchen. Clearly, this was an activity she did regularly and enjoyed doing. It took all of Cole's willpower not to step close behind Audrey so that she could pull aside her long wavy hair and kiss her neck. Cole wanted to touch Audrey so badly, but she felt like Audrey was trying to keep a small amount of distance from her. Was she regretting the kisses they had shared at the club? Should Cole push her a little to find out? She was unsure how to read the situation. Cole felt out of her league with Audrey, who was so beautiful as to be intimidating and evidently a woman who liked to control the pace of things.

Audrey mixed, measured, and stirred things in the kitchen. Then the comm box near the door buzzed.

"Would you mind getting that?" She looked toward Cole. "Just hit the button and say hello."

Cole did as instructed. The voice that responded belonged to Sara. Cole buzzed Sara in, and after a few minutes, she was at the door.

"Well, hello, Cole. I didn't expect to see you here," she said with a smile as she pulled back the hood of the dark overshirt she was wearing. She tossed a slightly rumpled paper onto the counter near Cole. "What is it about a girl in a hoodie? Everyone thinks you're an anarchist, when really you're just trying to buffer yourself with a little visual privacy on the train."

"You are an anarchist," said Audrey.

"I am not!" Sara said indignantly. "Cole, don't believe a word she says."

Sara walked up behind Audrey, in the spot Cole had wanted to be just moments earlier, and inhaled deeply over her shoulder. "Yum. I can see my timing was perfect. Cole, you're in for a treat. This woman is magic in the kitchen."

"It's all about the sauces," said Audrey. She tasted her creation with a small spoon.

"Hmmm, I think this is ready. Sara, would you hand me some bowls?"

Audrey parceled the delicious smelling food while Cole leaned over to read the crumpled sheet of paper that Sara had tossed on the counter. "RETURN TO EARTH" was written in large print and underneath was a partial quote from Albert Einstein. He labeled capitalism as evil, saying the only way to fight against it was by embracing socialism.

Interesting, thought Cole.

"Let's move to the table," said Audrey. She motioned with her head as she carried two bowls toward a small table with four chairs.

As Cole moved to join them, Sara saw her reading the paper flyer. "That got shoved in my pocket on the transit. I'm sure it was the hoodie. Nothing like a dark hoodie to send the wrong signal."

After a few bites of Audrey's yummy creation, Sara then asked, "So, where's Ava?"

"She's on her way to Stockholm. She had to do a cargo flight today," said Cole.

"I found Cole alone in Avery Park and decided to bring her home and feed her," said Audrey.

"Hmmm," was Sara's only response, but she gave Audrey a knowing look, as if to say wordlessly, *Whatever you say.*

"Wow. This is really good," said Cole after she'd taken a few bites from the dish of what looked like a savory stew. Only it wasn't stew because she'd made it with elements from the synthesizer, but somehow it didn't have the usual flat taste that Cole had come to expect. "This might be the best thing I've eaten since I got here."

"I told you," said Sara. "Magic."

Audrey smiled with satisfaction.

They enjoyed the meal and talked casually and comfortably about random topics: Kate's birthday outing, the new DJ at Club Six, annoying encounters on the transit system, med lab politics. Sara smiled easily and often, and there was a friendly warmth between Audrey and Sara that Cole was happy to participate in. After a lively hour or so and second helpings from the kitchen, Sara said good-bye and headed off to meet with some other friends. She invited Cole and Audrey to join her, but Cole followed Audrey's lead and declined.

"Your loss," Sara said. As she headed toward the door, she handed a card to Cole. "The next time you're lost in the park feel free to give me a shout. Just hold this up to a public comm box and it will automatically connect."

"Thanks," Cole said. She took a moment to study the square card before shoving it into her pocket. It had a rectangular looking pattern and some numbers printed on the front, along with Sara's full name: Sara Schraff. "I'll do that."

After seeing Sara to the door, Audrey joined Cole on a small sofa with warmly patterned cushions. She sat with one leg under her so that she was facing Cole. She had picked up a handheld comm unit on the way to the sofa and began to type something.

"I'm letting Ava know that you're here." Audrey didn't look up from the small screen as she spoke. "I wouldn't want her to try to reach you and worry if you didn't answer at her place."

Cole didn't respond for a moment. She waited for Audrey to finish with the device and put it down on a nearby table.

"I told Ava that we kissed."

Audrey was visibly surprised. "Oh? What was her reaction?"

"She seemed a little upset, but I couldn't figure out exactly why."

Cole wanted to find out how Audrey felt about the kiss. She had felt intensity between them the previous night, and she could feel something between them now, but her overall lack of experience with women had caused her to doubt her judgment.

"Can I ask you a personal question, Cole?" Audrey asked.

"Of course."

"Have you been with many women?"

"How do you mean? Like, in a sexual way?"

"Yes, that's what I meant."

"No, not many. Is it that obvious?"

"I wouldn't say it's obvious," replied Audrey. "You seem very comfortable with yourself, and you have this self-assured way about you. It's quite attractive actually. I was just taking a guess."

Audrey seemed to be matching Cole's usual openness with openness. Cole appreciated the chance to just talk. And maybe talk about what was happening between them.

"I admit I'm having a hard time," said Cole. "I wasn't sure when I got here if you had regrets about what happened at the club last night."

"I have no regrets about kissing you. In fact, it's been very hard not to kiss you since the first minute I saw you today."

"I'm glad to hear you say that, because I feel the same way."

Cole shifted a little bit closer to Audrey, closing the gap between them on the small sofa. Cole's lips were only inches from Audrey's mouth. "I have wanted to kiss you again ever since I left you on the deck last night."

Audrey looked first at Cole's slightly parted lips, and then into her eyes. She felt heat rising from her center, up through her chest, and into her flushed cheeks. Audrey stood abruptly, feeling like she needed to put space between them while at the same time not wanting to. She was at odds with herself. Why was she fighting this connection with Cole? Was it about wanting to know her better before something physical happened? Or was it just fear?

Cole followed Audrey with her eyes. From her seated position, she caught Audrey's wrist to stop her escape. Audrey closed her eyes, pulling against her captured wrist, facing away from Cole for fear that her expression would give her away.

After a few seconds, Audrey turned to face Cole. In her attempt to exit, Audrey had moved away from the couch toward the bedroom door. Cole stood and slowly backed Audrey against the wall. There was no room for Audrey to move away from Cole. Audrey closed her eyes again and let out a shuddering sigh. She felt her chest rise and fall as her breathing sped up. Cole pressed tightly against her. She didn't kiss Audrey immediately. Instead she let her lips drift slowly over Audrey's neck and face with just the softest of caresses.

"I find it hard to believe that you lack experience with women," said Audrey. "You…You are…so…"

"Audrey, I have no idea what I'm doing," Cole whispered in her ear. "I just want us to be close. You drive me crazy. Everywhere you touch me I feel like I'm on fire."

Audrey looked into Cole's soft, dark eyes and surrendered to what she was feeling: the overwhelming sensation that whatever was happening between them was right and true and that it was pointless to argue against it. She pulled Cole's face toward hers and claimed her mouth with an open kiss. As the kiss deepened, Audrey began to urgently unbutton Cole's shirt. The minute she could get inside Cole's shirt to her bare chest, she began to use her mouth to touch every space of open skin between her neck and her nipples. She held Cole's narrow frame captive as she moved her mouth down her chest, her lips hot and demanding.

Audrey then spun their position around so that Cole's back was now against the wall. Consumed with want, Audrey continued her downward assault on Cole's torso. She began to work at the top of Cole's pants to unfasten them, but Cole held her hands to stop her.

"Audrey," Cole said breathlessly. "Audrey…Can we lie down?"

Audrey didn't immediately answer. She closed her eyes, breathing Cole in. *She smells so good.* With arms extended on either side of Cole so that her palms rested on the wall just above Cole's shoulders, she kissed Cole softly. A kiss meant to communicate not only desire, but affection.

"Yes, we can lie down."

Audrey pushed Cole backward through the doorway and into the bedroom. Cole sat on the edge of the bed with her shirt open and the top button of her pants still undone. She gazed up intensely as Audrey moved toward her, slowly unbuttoning her shirt. She freed each button deliberately. Her shirt fell open revealing her pink lace bra. She moved closer to Cole so that she was now standing between Cole's legs. Audrey placed her hands inside Cole's shirt at the collar and then let them slowly drift down Cole's chest. Cole's eyes were partially closed so Audrey placed a finger under Cole's chin, tilting her head up so that they could meet each other's gaze.

"Cole," Audrey said as she dropped her shirt to the floor. She wanted to put words to her feelings, but words seemed to fail her.

Audrey roughly pushed Cole's shirt from her shoulders. Cole wore nothing under her shirts so her bare chest was revealed. Audrey reached around and unfastened her bra, letting it fall to the floor. She pulled Cole's mouth to her, guiding Cole to take her breast. Audrey worked her fingers in the short hair at the back of Cole's head, giving her an indication of the pressure she needed. She leaned over and kissed Cole long and hard.

Audrey became aware of Cole's fingers at the hem of her skirt, and then the sensation of gentle caresses along the inside of her thigh, just before feeling her silk underwear being slowly lowered until she could step out of them.

At the first caress of Cole's fingers between Audrey's legs, she moaned and leaned into Cole's insistent mouth.

Somehow, Cole seemed to have taken control of her body. Exploring, stroking, teasing.

Audrey wanted to feel the weight of Cole on top of her. She wanted to feel Cole's slender hips between her legs. She unzipped her skirt so that it too fell away. She gently pushed against Cole signaling for her to lie back on the bed. Cole began to move backward up onto the bed. Now completely nude, Audrey helped Cole out of her shoes, pants, and undergarments before moving into the spot beside Cole.

There was now nothing between them. As their bodies entwined, they tenderly caressed each other. Audrey felt as if in that instant she was making some intimate discovery, previously unknown. She had the feeling that together they were bringing forth something singular, something to be cherished and not taken lightly.

Audrey moved her hands urgently over Cole's velvet ribs. She felt consumed with want and need, and then felt vulnerable and exposed by her desire. Her hips were undulating uncontrollably against Cole. Her senses were exploding.

"Audrey, this…being with you…it feels so intense that I can hardly breathe. Do you…do you feel it, too?"

Audrey began to kiss Cole's forehead, then each eyelid, then her cheeks, before placing a tender, enduring kiss on her mouth.

"Yes, I feel it, too." She was unable to not acknowledge her surrender to the wild desire that Cole had created within her.

Audrey pulled back just enough so she could see Cole's face. Audrey realized she would have never been this vulnerable had she not felt Cole's complete open acceptance of whatever she might say or do. The closeness of connection she was feeling for Cole seemed to flow around them, causing her to feel completely flushed and heated. Cole seemed to have awakened something in her. Something primal and soul-shattering.

Audrey filled her fingers with Cole's hair and pulled her hard against her mouth. They kissed with bruising ferocity. Audrey pressed herself fully and desperately against Cole, moving against her, rolling her over on her back, to press herself completely on top of Cole, straddling her so that Cole felt Audrey's hot, wet center against her midsection.

Audrey realized that it wasn't so much any single action that was different from what she'd experienced before. But rather it was the emotional intensity that traveled with each touch from Cole that seemed to pierce Audrey's chest and emanate throughout her entire being.

Audrey slowed her mouth and placed soft kisses down Cole's neck and across her collarbone. Her hair brushed across Cole's skin as she leaned over and Cole ran her fingers tenderly over Audrey's silky abdomen. Between gasps for air, Cole managed to say, "Audrey, you are so incredible."

"Hey, I don't want you to move too much," Audrey said, aware of Cole's recent injuries. "Let me do the moving, okay?"

Audrey adjusted her hips slightly on top of Cole to allow space for Cole to put her hand between them. Audrey took Cole's hand, moistening Cole's fingers inside her mouth before guiding them to where she needed them most.

Cole slid her fingers inside Audrey, gently at first. As Audrey moved against Cole's hand, Cole's thrusts became deeper. As Audrey felt herself about to peak, she whispered Cole's name in between shuddering gasps of ecstasy. She was giving herself fully to Cole as she allowed herself to be taken over the edge. Cole wrapped strong arms around Audrey and buried her face in Audrey's neck. Audrey collapsed on top of Cole, resting her head on Cole's chest. Cole stroked her hair and kissed her damp forehead. Audrey was emotionally spent in a way she'd never experienced before when making love. The realization of this as she listened to Cole's steady heartbeat beneath her ear both excited and frightened her. She felt her fear pulling her away from the moment, but Cole must have sensed it because she whispered into Audrey's hair, "Come back to me, Audrey. I'm right here. I'm with you completely."

How did she know? How could she possibly know? But somehow she did. Audrey looked up and kissed Cole tenderly as she slowly moved her fingers down the length of Cole's tall frame until they reached the space between her legs.

Audrey slid down slightly, tracing the curve of Cole's small breasts with her tongue, all the while exploring with her fingers until they found the entrance she sought. Cole reacted almost instantly, shuddering against Audrey's hand, moving her hips, thrusting slowly with Audrey's every motion until her body tensed against Audrey, trembled again, and then relaxed.

"That's it," Audrey whispered close to Cole's ear. "I've got you."

Cole felt wetness gather at the corner of her eyes. The tears surprised her. She hadn't been aware that tears were building, but as Audrey held her, a feeling of completeness washed over her, and she felt damp tendrils slowly trail down her cheeks. Audrey tenderly kissed the wet tracks, moving on top of Cole to cover her fully with her soft curves. Cole wrapped her arms around Audrey, burying her face, allowing herself to feel wholly the depth of the joining they'd just made.

❖

The late afternoon sun sent shafts of light across Audrey's bedroom. Cole was sleeping, face down, her body only partially covered by a white silk sheet. Audrey was propped up on one elbow watching Cole sleep. She gently swept her hand down Cole's back. Cole didn't stir.

Audrey realized there wasn't anything about Cole's physical technique in bed that would have told her that she had very little experience with women, but rather her emotional honesty. Cole was completely vulnerable and open with Audrey. She sensed that there were no clouds of hurt, no partial walls constructed by past encounters, rejections, or betrayals. Because of this, Cole had been fully, passionately present with Audrey. It made Audrey's chest ache for more. She knew one afternoon with Cole would not be enough.

CHAPTER FOURTEEN

The air was cold and moist as Ava stepped out of the transport and onto the platform in the cloud city of Stockholm. Jenna Bookman, senior flight officer, stepped out beside her. Jenna was probably fifteen years Ava's senior and had been a great mentor and friend. Jenna usually requested Ava as her second, especially for longer, international flights. She knew Ava needed to increase her flight time hours in order to move her ranking up.

Ava was just noticing she'd received a message on her comm unit when Jenna said, "I'm going to get some coffee and food before we prep for the return flight. Do you want to join me?"

"Yeah, that sounds good. I'm feeling kind of hungry," Ava replied without looking up from her comm unit. She was reading the text as it scrolled across the small screen. "What the hell?"

"Problem?"

"No…yes…maybe…" Ava was at a loss. "Can I just respond to this message and then I'll join you?"

"Women," Jenna mused, taking a guess at what was the issue. "Can't live with them, can't…" The comment trailed off as she walked ahead of Ava. "I'll be at the place near the central transit office. Come join me when you're finished."

"Okay, I'll be right there. Will you order something for me?"

"The usual?" asked Jenna over her shoulder as she walked away.

"Sure," Ava said. She returned to the message she'd received from Audrey. She read it again just to be sure:

"Ava, found Cole in a city park, invited her over for lunch. Didn't want you to worry."

What the hell? Just play it cool, thought Ava. She typed a response:

"Just landed and got your message. Getting food. Back in Easton in 12 hours."

❖

Audrey heard her handheld comm unit buzz from her reclined position on the bed. She leaned over, placed a soft kiss on Cole's bare shoulder as she lay sleeping, and got up to check the message. Her assumption was correct. The text was from Ava.

"When you get back we need to talk," Audrey replied and hit "Send."

"*I know about the kiss,"* Ava wrote.

"I know you know. I don't want to talk about that. I want to talk about us," wrote Audrey.

"OK," Ava responded. *"Come by my place. I'll text you when I land."*

"See you soon," Audrey replied.

Audrey closed her comm unit and placed it on the dresser. She looked back at Cole, still partially covered by the bed sheet, and draped over one side of the bed. She climbed back into bed next to Cole and began moving down her back with soft kisses while she rested her hand on Cole's pronounced hipbone.

Cole began to stir and slowly, sleepily, rolled onto her back.

Audrey moved from kissing Cole's back to kissing her stomach and then moving up to softly suck each of Cole's nipples, which grew harder and more erect with each stroke of Audrey's tongue.

"Hey," said Cole in a sleepy voice.

"Hey." Audrey paused her caresses long enough to respond. "I'm sorry. Did I wake you?"

"Hmm, somehow I don't think you're very sorry," mused Cole with a sleepy grin.

Audrey moved her hand from Cole's hip down under the sheet, between Cole's legs. "You're right. I'm not very sorry."

She began to caress Cole, who was still wet and aroused. Cole reached for Audrey's face, pulling her upward into a luxurious kiss. Audrey's touch had caused Cole's body to react as if fully awake.

"This might be the best lunch invitation I've ever had," joked Cole between kisses.

"Is that so?"

Audrey had to smile. Cole was so playful. It was refreshing to not only be incredibly turned on in bed, but to also have fun. There was no feeling that Cole was in any way distracted by external obligations, and no sense that she was in a hurry to escape from intimacy. Instead, Cole pulled Audrey on top of her so that she could hold her more closely.

Audrey could feel her body temperature rise as the feel of Cole's bare chest against hers caused her heart to race. She had never imagined anything could feel like this. And now that she'd experienced it, how could she ever exist without it?

❖

Ava pushed open the restaurant's glass doors and scanned the room for Jenna. She spotted her talking to a waitress at a corner booth. Ava slid into the booth across from Jenna.

"Everything okay?" asked Jenna.

"Not really." Ava leaned her forehead into the palm of her hand. "That was a message from Audrey."

"When are you going to quit stalling and ask that gorgeous woman out?"

"It's complicated." Ava told Jenna about all the things that had happened in the past two weeks. She trusted Jenna not to report her for spending time on the ground. After all, it wasn't as if she intentionally set down in a prohibited zone; it was due to mechanical failure and she was in her personal cruiser, not a company-issued craft. Plus, she was on her own time when it happened. Still, if the higher ups found out, it might cause problems for her commercial flight status. She'd already been written up on two occasions for dropping into the low elevation no-fly zone just for the view. If her co-pilot at the time hadn't been such a brown-nosing rule follower, no one would have even known. After two days on the ground, she now questioned the restrictions they'd been operating under. The decision to prohibit travel to the ground now seemed to have little to do with security, which was always the reason offered by the government.

"This Cole must be something spectacular," Jenna said.

"I can't explain it," said Ava. "She's just so…She's so different from anyone I've ever met. She's so real." She looked directly at Jenna. "Have you ever been on the ground? It was nothing like I expected it to be."

"No—" Her reply was interrupted by the delivery of food and drinks. As the waitress moved away from their table, Jenna continued. "I knew a guy once, an old friend from my college days. His craft went down somewhere over the central continent. He was never found."

Jenna looked up from her plate of food at Ava. "I should say, not *all* of him was found."

"Oh," said Ava. "I guess I was lucky then."

"Very lucky. Listen, Ava, you know I'm all about the ladies. The more the merrier. But you could have something real with Audrey. You two could make a life together. You can always have your little adventures on the side. Don't let this Cole steal her away from you." She winked at Ava.

Ava smiled and shook her head. She knew Jenna had quite a reputation. She used her pilot status and all its travel perks to her advantage. Jenna and her partner, Sophie, had been together for years, but it was clear they had some sort of understanding about other women. At least that's what Jenna had told Ava. And Ava was quite sure that if the beautiful Sophie didn't feel like spending an evening alone while Jenna was traveling then she didn't. On at least one occasion she'd even made a play to seduce Ava. That was a little too close for comfort for Ava. Having any sort of physical encounter with Sophie would have complicated Ava's working relationship with Jenna. While she was tempted by the offer, it didn't seem worth the risk.

"Well, Audrey wants to have a serious talk when I get back," Ava said. "So I have twelve hours to figure out what I want to say to her." Ava played with her food on her plate while she spoke. "That text I got while we were in flight was Audrey saying she'd invited Cole over to her place for lunch."

"Wow. Maybe I need to meet this Cole after all. She sure stirred up some trouble in the very short time she's been here," joked Jenna.

"It's not funny. I think something might really be going on between them." Ava pinched the bridge of her nose to ward off a rising headache. "At first I thought Audrey didn't like her at all. But now I'm not so sure that's what I was picking up on."

"Do you and Cole have any sort of agreement? I mean, does she know how you feel about Audrey?"

"How can I tell Cole how I feel about Audrey when I'm not even sure myself? We're friends. We almost made out once, due to excessive alcohol consumption. There isn't much to tell other than that."

Ava felt like she'd really screwed up. It seemed to be Ava's pattern to leave too many things unsaid and spend too much time running away because if she stood still for a moment she might actually commit to something or someone. Audrey had been in her life for several years and she'd completely taken her for granted. Did she think Audrey would just wait around forever? Could she even be the sort of person Audrey needed her to be? She quickly responded to her own internal line of questioning. No.

"You know, Audrey and I have never been intimate," Ava said. "I'm not sure if I'd ever told you that."

"No, you hadn't. I guess I just assumed you were friends with benefits," said Jenna. "What's going on with you, Ava? I mean, what's really going on?"

"I wish I knew." Ava sighed. "I feel so restless."

Jenna sat quietly eating, giving Ava room to collect her thoughts.

"I don't know what I thought. That Audrey would just be available forever. Until I was ready to settle down."

It was unusual for Ava to talk so openly with Jenna. Mostly they joked about flirtations and bantered with each other about their abilities in the cockpit.

"Even my mom is upset. She loves Audrey," Ava added. She rested her elbow on the edge of the table with her chin in her hand. "What mother wouldn't? She's perfect."

"You'll get no argument from me there," said Jenna. "If I was fifteen years younger…"

"Stop!"

"Seriously. I'd give you a run for your money." Jenna smiled and winked in Ava's direction. "That long, wavy auburn hair…Those curves…"

"Please stop," said Ava. "Don't make me hurt you."

Chapter Fifteen

Ava felt a knot building in the pit of her stomach the closer they got to Easton. Thankfully, Jenna was quiet on the flight back. Ava felt like she needed time to think. Rather than having time alone or time to think as she had planned, the past two weeks had made her life even more complex.

Post flight shutdown took a little longer than usual. The flight tower had received some bomb threats earlier in the day so the Easton defense system had logged an orange alert, requiring extra security shutdown procedures. Orange alerts had become more common in the past few weeks as the insurgents set off small explosions in various parts of the city. So far, no one had been killed and no one had been captured and held for the crimes. The residents of Easton, like other cloud cities where small acts of vandalism had happened, didn't seem to take the threats very seriously. The insurgents' message was muddy at best, a rally cry against capitalism. The ruling party had assured residents that no real harm could be organized by such a small group of malcontents. Ava's general opinion was the radicals were simply unhappy with their assigned rank in the city. Well, not everyone could be at the top. Who would be left to take the trash out? *If they really wanted to change their status they should work for it, not blow things up.*

As Ava walked toward the transit center to catch a train to her residential cube, she sent Audrey a message to say she was back. She asked Audrey for enough of a head start to take a shower and freshen up before they were to meet. After she received a reply in the affirmative, Ava realized that for the first time the power balance in their friendship had shifted. Ava had always been the one to move closer or pull away from Audrey, controlling the pace and level of intimacy between them. Ava was no longer in control of where their relationship was heading. Relinquishing control was not one of Ava's favorite positions to be in.

Ava arrived at home, dropped her flight gear by the door, and headed for a hot shower.

❖

Cole reclined at the counter near the kitchen. Audrey had stirred up another lovely smelling concoction after they'd finally gotten out of bed. Cole felt incredibly content as she sipped a warm beverage and ate the food that Audrey offered.

"I received a message from Ava saying that she's back from her Stockholm route," said Audrey. "I'm going to go over to her place for a little while."

Cole took a few bites and studied Audrey's face.

"If you don't mind, I'd like some time alone with Ava," said Audrey. "We…There are some things that she and I need to talk through."

"Of course."

"Will you be okay on your own for a little while?" asked Audrey. "You can stay here as long as you like."

"I'll be fine," Cole said, flashing Audrey a smile. "Maybe I'll finish that walk I started yesterday before I got sidetracked by your sweet lunch invitation."

Cole reached an arm around Audrey's waist and pulled her close.

Audrey leaned in and placed a soft kiss on Cole's lips. She followed that kiss with another on Cole's forehead. Audrey reached across the counter and pulled a small bag toward them. She pulled several credits out of the bag and handed them to Cole.

"Please take these with you in case you decide you need food or a drink during your walk," said Audrey. "I know you don't use credits for goods on the ground, but up here, it might come in handy to have a little cash on hand."

"Oh, thank you." Cole stashed the paper credits into her pants pocket.

They finished the last few bites of the food Audrey had prepared and then walked toward the door for one last embrace before Audrey left for Ava's place and Cole headed out for her walk. They rode the lift down in silence, leaving the same way they had arrived. As they exited the lift at the pedestrian level, Audrey paused for a moment and took Cole's hand.

"I just realized I don't know how to reach you later," said Audrey.

"It makes me very happy to think I'll see you later."

Audrey pulled a small comm unit out of her bag. "Here, take this."

Cole took the device.

"I'll call you," said Audrey.

"Okay. Just know that I miss you already."

"Be careful, Cole. The city is a big place. Pay attention."

"Are you really worried about me? I'll be careful."

"I know it's silly for me to worry. It's in my nature. I'll try and get past it."

Cole smiled. "I like that you feel protective of me, but I'll be fine."

Feeling unable to let Audrey go, Cole pulled her close and kissed her. It was as if the two of them together were able to create a space that only they inhabited, from which the world fell away, the sea of pedestrians separating to move around their embrace as if they were a craft upon the open sea. When their lips separated, Audrey reached up to wipe lipstick from Cole's mouth with her thumb.

"It seems that lately every time we're alone together you end up wearing my lipstick."

"Maybe it's a good look for me," said Cole, smiling.

"I'm a good look for you."

She stood and watched Audrey leave, until she was swallowed up by the crowd.

Cole had no plan of where to go or any particular route in mind. Each window she passed presented a glimpse into a world she had never known. And every passage, every corridor between high rises was so crowded. The pedestrian traffic was orderly, and in general, attire and demeanor seemed almost uniform, but the sea of humans seemed to extend to the horizon.

Cole had seen photos in old books of crowded sidewalks in places like New York, but that was a century ago, before the Atlantic sank the shoreline and New York's elite class rose to save themselves. Cole had never experienced such a dense population on the ground.

After a while, Cole began to feel tired and visually overstimulated so she found a spot to rest. As she sat, she realized she was missing home. Cole had only seen the smallest of manicured patches of grass within a couple of small city parks she'd passed, both yesterday and today. Cole wanted nothing more than to be sitting by the pond near her home. She closed her eyes to conjure up the smell of damp earth as it baked in the sunshine.

After walking again for quite a while, she took a seat at a small outdoor café and waited as the server brought her the hot coffee she had ordered. Cole kept her dark glasses on to avoid the unwanted attention her eye color might generate. She was grateful now that Audrey had thought to give her credits before she left.

Cole took a sip and then stared down at the inky beverage that was supposed to taste like coffee. Her mind shifted to Audrey. The past few days had been a whirlwind of new feelings and sensations for Cole.

The unexpected kiss with Audrey had happened. Audrey and the intense sexual chemistry that existed between them had completely swept Cole off her feet. Somehow, sex with Audrey felt very different from sex with Alice, the young woman she'd seen so briefly. She and Alice together had been timid and then sweet, affectionate, and at times tentative. She and Audrey together had taken Cole's breath away. With Audrey it was passionate, desperate, and intensely intimate. Was that love? The emotions that had arisen when she and Audrey were together were so strong that they'd overridden any thought of how their physical coupling would play out. If Cole was completely honest, she'd have to admit that she'd barely thought of anything the entire time she was with Audrey and certainly not while they were making love. Not the past, not the future, not the fact that she would likely be leaving soon. She'd only thought of the feel of Audrey's skin against hers and the taste of Audrey's mouth.

When would she return to the ground? It was only a matter of time, and probably not that much time, before Cole would need to return home. She couldn't just continue to float about the city. There was no place for her here. Plus, she had plans of her own back home. Cole had begun thinking of moving out and staking her own claim on a nearby spot she'd been eyeing. Her aunts supported the idea. But how would she go back to her life on the ground? The thought of not seeing Audrey again gave her a sick feeling in the pit of her stomach.

Cole was lost in thought staring into her dark beverage when she realized a shadow had been cast over her. She pulled herself out of her trance to see Sara standing with arms across her chest, studying her. Cole wasn't sure how long Sara had been standing there before she noticed her. Cole looked up at Sara.

"I didn't want to disturb you," said Sara. "But now that I have, would you mind if I joined you?"

Relieved to have the friendly distraction, Cole replied, "Sure."

Sara claimed the chair on the other side of the small table. "So, what's new with you, Cole?" Sara asked.

The smile on Sara's face gave Cole the distinct feeling Sara already knew the answer to that question.

Chapter Sixteen

Audrey rode the lift up to Ava's cube. Now that she was here, Audrey wasn't sure exactly where to begin with Ava. What did she really hope to achieve during this meeting other than some clearing of the air between them?

"Hi, Audrey," Ava said. She smiled tentatively as she opened her door. Her hair was still damp from the shower. "Can I get you a drink?"

"Sure," said Audrey. She dropped her small bag into a chair and accepted a glass from Ava. They were both quiet, waiting for the other to begin.

Audrey stood in the center of the room, feeling ill at ease in a space that had formerly been comfortable to her. Ava began to pace back and forth a few feet from Audrey as if she were trying to gather her thoughts.

Ava finally spoke. "Audrey, I'm really sorry that I left the way I did a few days ago. And then I didn't talk to you about everything when I first brought Cole back with me to the city. I know I should have. I know I hurt you by shutting you out and not telling you what was going on with me. After the friendship that we have shared, I owed you more of an explanation."

Audrey was silent, studying Ava's face. She decided that Ava did seem genuinely sorry and that helped ease what little anger Audrey was still feeling about their first encounter outside Cole's recovery room at the medical lab.

"Ava, if we're going to be completely honest, and I think at this point we owe that to each other," began Audrey, "I think whatever we shared that was beyond friendship is over."

Audrey noticed the surprised look on Ava's face. Had Ava expected something different?

"What happened between us before you so abruptly left was a symptom of something…I'm not sure what. But I'm glad we didn't take things further. I think that would have been a mistake and ultimately may have ruined our friendship," said Audrey.

Ava didn't know how to respond. She'd prepared an entirely different defense in her head for the argument that she expected Audrey to deliver. And now, Audrey was just calmly saying there wasn't ever going to be anything between them except friendship. There was never going to be a possibility for more between them. Wasn't this exactly what she'd proclaimed to her mother just a few days ago? So why was this so upsetting? For the first time, reality hit Ava that she had lost whatever chance she might have had with Audrey. She thought maybe she'd have more time to figure things out, but it was clear that she'd misread the situation. Ava decided full disclosure was her only available approach. She stepped closer to Audrey, gesturing with her hands as she spoke.

"Audrey, I have to admit, I didn't expect this to be the conversation we'd be having," said Ava. "What makes you so sure that what almost happened with us would have been such a big mistake?"

"Honestly? Cole happened."

"What do you mean by that?"

"What I mean is how I feel about Cole."

There it was. The suspicion was confirmed.

"How can you have feelings for her? You hardly know her. That's not really your style, Audrey."

"There's something intense between us that I seem too powerless to ignore. It started the day I brought her to your place after lunch, and then the other night on the dance floor things went a step further, but it has evolved even more since then."

"Evolved?" Ava felt anger and jealousy rising in her chest. "How much could things have evolved in only a few hours?"

"Enough to know that what I've been searching for might actually exist. Enough to know that I want to spend more time with Cole so I can see where this leads."

Ava was in shock. She slumped into the sofa and put her head in her hands. "Have you told Cole how you feel?" Ava purposefully didn't reveal what Cole had shared with her. For some reason, she didn't feel like making things easier for Audrey.

"Not completely," said Audrey.

"Did you sleep with her?" asked Ava.

"Yes."

Ava felt ill, but she wasn't sure exactly why. Was she sick over the fact that Audrey had sex with Cole? Would she have felt that way about anyone else or was it that deep down she knew Cole was the sort of person Audrey had been searching for, someone who could truly commit to her? She looked up at Audrey. "Audrey, I have no right to feel jealous, but I do."

"I know. And I know you care about Cole too. I watched you with her when you first brought her here from the med unit. I think we both know that there's something very special about Cole."

Ava looked at Audrey. She didn't recognize this woman. Who had she become while Ava wasn't paying attention? Wasn't this the woman she'd been friends with for years? Ava could feel the shift like a door slamming. She sighed and leaned back on the sofa.

"I can't believe you slept with Cole."

Audrey finally sat in a chair across from Ava. "I'm as surprised as you are. Believe me when I say that."

"She's going to have to leave at some point. You know that, right?" Ava said as she read the sadness on Audrey's face.

"I know." Audrey looked down, studying the drink she was still holding. "I just need a little more time."

"Where is she now?" asked Ava. She realized that she hadn't even thought to ask.

"She was going to take some time and walk around the city."

"You let her go by herself?"

"Cole will be fine," said Audrey. "I may fall apart without her, but Cole is going to be fine."

Ava knew it was out of character for Audrey to be impulsive and to take chances, and she'd just done both. What she and Audrey were experiencing was a seismic shift. And as was the reality when that sort of shift happened, things had fallen off level surfaces and shattered on the floor.

They were now sitting in silence. What Ava had expected to be a fight was in the end just the act of letting go.

Chapter Seventeen

Cole waited for Sara to take a few sips of the drink she'd ordered and then asked, "What's your story, Sara?"

"My story?" Sara repeated with amusement. "I teach math to a small group of privileged children who couldn't care less about math. And despite what Audrey might have told you, I'm not an anarchist. I'm a reactionary."

"I'm not sure I know the difference," said Cole.

"A reactionary is someone who's in favor of a return of the status quo in society, a return to the way things used to be. In my case, the way they used to be before the cities rose and we separated from the ground," Sara said. "An anarchist just wants to upend the political structure and have a free state so to speak."

Cole studied Sara quietly for a moment. "I thought people in the city wanted to be separated from the ground."

"Not all of us."

"When I asked you what your story was, I was thinking more like you'd tell me who your parents were and, well, what sort of things you liked to do for fun."

"Sorry to disappoint you. I figured after you saw that flyer at Audrey's house that she might have said something to you about my *other* life—the one where I'm not a math teacher to the rich and spoiled."

"Um, Audrey and I didn't really talk that much," said Cole.

"I can only imagine," Sara said knowingly. "Where is she now?"

"She's with Ava. I think they had some things to work out."

"That's the understatement of the year. Those two have had an unrequited crush on each other off and on for years. I think they're the only two people in the city who weren't aware of it."

"Really?" Ava's remote response to the news that Cole and Audrey had kissed began to make sense. "Why do you suppose they never acted on it?"

"Because they know each other well enough to know they can never meet each other's needs. Audrey wants forever. Ava wants right now. Had they ever attempted to date, they would have ruined a friendship and ended up with nothing to show for it."

Cole contemplatively sipped her coffee.

"You really like Audrey, don't you?"

"I'd say *like* isn't really a strong enough word for what I've been feeling."

"Audrey is amazing. I hope you know that."

"Yeah, you'll get no argument from me there."

Sara returned to sipping her drink before leaning back in her chair to observe Cole. "Cole, I think you should come with me to a meeting. I was heading there when I saw you, but we won't be that late if we go now."

"What sort of meeting?"

"A meeting with people that would be very interested to know you. You may not realize this, but you're sort of amazing also." Sara stood and dropped credits on the table. "Come on. You need to see this."

Sara led Cole down the pedestrian corridor and across a raised walkway between two tall buildings, then down a set of stairs past the transit platform. She opened an unmarked steel door just under the platform and turned left once inside. They were met with more stairs leading downward, followed by another landing, and then more stairs past massive pipes and encased cable networks. Cole was fascinated that so much space and infrastructure existed below street level. And that at the lower levels you could hear the steady hum of the huge turbine engines that held the city's altitude at a consistent level.

"Are you sure you know where you're going?" Cole finally asked.

"We're here," said Sara. She pushed open a door as she smiled back at Cole.

They entered a room crowded with people, mostly young, some middle-aged, mostly women, but there were also some young men standing about. There was a raised landing at the front of the industrial looking space and an intense looking woman who was shouting to the crowd that gathered. Sara paused for a minute to hear the woman speak as the crowd cheered in response.

"Apathy *is* death! We must fight back against the corrosive power of the mega banks and food corporations that have created this enormous economic divide! The cocoon of wealth and privilege permits the rich to turn those around them into compliant workers, hangers-on, servants, flatterers, and sycophants. Wealth breeds a class of people for whom human beings are disposable commodities."

The woman paused to allow the crowd to respond. There were booming yells and applause in support of her statements.

"Colleagues, associates, employees, kitchen staff, servants, tutors, personal trainers, even friends and family, bend to the whims of the wealthy or disappear," she shouted as she continued to pace back and forth across the platform as she spoke. "Once oligarchs achieve unchecked economic and political power, as they have in the cloud cities, the citizens, too, become disposable. We must rise up against the system that seeks to destroy us! Even in a system designed to favor the elite, only a rare few truly benefit. In the end, we will be no better off than those left behind on the ground."

The crowd was charged with emotion.

"Return to Earth! Return to Earth! Return to Earth!" the crowd chanted. The woman speaking had to wait for the chants to die down before she could speak again.

"The philosophers warned us that oligarchs are schooled in the mechanisms of manipulation. They use subtle and overt repression and exploitation to protect their wealth and power at our expense. How do they manipulate the masses, you ask? Foremost among their mechanisms is the control of ideas. Yes, ideas are very dangerous things."

As the woman continued speaking, Sara took Cole's arm and began pulling her through the tightly packed crowd to the front of the room.

"Ruling elites ensure that the established leadership is subservient to an ideology. In this case, the separation from the ground and the empty worship of commerce," the woman said loudly as she began to notice Sara approaching the stage with Cole.

"The blanket dissemination of an ideology through the media and the purging, especially in academia, of critical voices have permitted our oligarchs to orchestrate the largest income inequality gap in the history of the world!" She paused for dramatic effect. "Meanwhile, without the slightest tug on their conscience, the oligarchs have convinced us to abandon the majority of the Earth's population on the ground—never to benefit from the wealth that we, the few, the city dwellers, benefit from on a daily basis up in the clouds. But to what end? We have forsaken our ancestors. We have forsaken our earthly birthright. We have abandoned the *REAL* for the *SYNTHETIC*."

The woman stopped speaking when Sara pulled Cole to the edge of the raised platform. Cole, still unsure of what she had gotten herself into and only vaguely understanding what this woman had been shouting about, stood calmly as Sara reached up and removed the dark eye shades she'd been wearing. As the woman on stage saw what Sara was revealing, she stopped in her tracks. She stared at Cole for a long moment before she stepped off the platform, walked up to Cole, and took Cole's face in her hands. The woman was taller than Cole. She had long, thick, wavy, silver hair that framed her green eyes like a wild mane. She wore metallic clothing, a sterling overcoat, and heavy black boots. Cole noticed as the woman grasped her face that, despite her strong persona, the woman's hands were soft and warm. The crowd mumbled in hushed tones as they watched the scene unfold. Those nearest to the stage relayed to those in the back what was transpiring.

"Brown eyes!" the woman finally spoke. "You are a groundling."

Cole had never heard that word, but she figured that described the fact that she lived on the ground.

"Yes," Cole responded simply.

Those individuals standing closest to Cole began to reach out and touch her. They brushed their fingers along her arms, her shoulders, and her hair. They were responding to her as if she were some foreign, yet sacred object in their midst.

The mass of people began to move like a wave to the front of the room to see and touch Cole. Sara and the woman who had been speaking quickly became aware that the crowd was closing in. Before things could get completely out of hand, the woman pulled Cole protectively into her silver coat, and with Sara in tow, led them both out a door at the far corner of the platform. The crowd continued to push forward, but no one followed as the door closed behind them.

Cole realized they were now in a small corridor and the tall, silver-haired woman motioned for them to follow her through another nearby steel door. Once inside the room, Cole saw that it had a couple of desks, chairs scattered about, beverage containers, and the walls were covered with what looked like maps of the city.

"Please, sit," said the woman as she motioned for Cole to take a seat near one of the desks. Then the woman took a seat facing Cole; Sara stood off to the side.

"May I touch your hands?" the woman asked.

Cole extended her hands, and the woman took them in hers. She felt the palms of Cole's hands, pausing to rub her fingers over a few calluses. "A worker's hands," she said.

"I suppose so," said Cole, still unsure what to make of this woman who was now intently studying her face.

"What did you think of what I said out there?" the woman asked.

"I didn't understand all of it. Who are you?"

"Of course, forgive me. I am simply known as Meredith," the woman said. "And you?"

"Ruth Coleman George. Everyone calls me Cole."

"It's a pleasant surprise to meet you, Cole," said Meredith as she leaned back in her chair and crossed her arms in front of her chest. "When Sara told me she had met you, I admit I doubted her. My apologies, Sara."

"No need to apologize," said Sara.

Meredith turned her attention back to Cole. "We are in the middle of a revolution here, Cole. We're fighting the ruling elite for your inclusion in the city states."

"Why?"

"Why? Because those of you left behind on the ground have suffered long enough at the hands of the rich. You have been denied basic health care, career advancement, an upper tier existence."

"We don't really need anything on the ground," said Cole. "Each person benefits from their own labor. No one takes anything from us. Life is actually pretty good on the ground."

Meredith sat back in her chair and regarded Cole with some astonishment before she continued. "You only say that because you don't know the difference."

"Well, your medical care is definitely better in the sky cities. I'll give you that."

"And I'm sure there are other deficiencies of life on the ground which you should not have to suffer."

Cole was starting to take offense at this woman who seemed to be fighting for needs she assigned to Cole and her fellow groundlings whether they wanted them or not.

"Have you been on the ground?" asked Cole.

"No. Not personally," Meredith replied. "But some have returned to tell of the conditions there."

"I'm feeling like you should check your sources," said Cole. "Life is mostly good there. We have everything we need and in fact, we never really think about the cities."

Meredith seemed completely puzzled. She looked over at Sara and then back at Cole. You could see by the look on her face that she was thinking of her next move. After a few contemplative moments, she spoke. "I understand that you are proud and that it might be hard for you to accept our help in making your life better."

Cole furrowed her brow and listened.

Meredith continued. "We do this in your honor—for the betterment of all your people on the ground."

"I don't want my silence to give you the idea that I agree with what you're saying, because I don't," said Cole.

Cole could tell by the woman's face that she was not used to having anyone question her or disagree with her.

Sara chimed in. "Meredith just wants to help the working class on the ground, Cole."

"Whether they want it or not, I imagine," replied Cole.

"I can see you aren't capable of following the complex ideas I put forth a few minutes ago when I was speaking in the larger room," said Meredith in a full-blown condescending tone. "Better that you let those who are wiser in the ways of the elite do these works on your behalf."

"Wow." Cole shook her head. "You obviously have your own ideas about life on the ground despite being confronted with facts that contradict those ideas."

"Cole, maybe we should go," Sara said.

Meredith raised a hand in Sara's direction. "No. You stay. I'll get Cole an escort to the surface."

Meredith punched a button on a small comm box on one of the desks. In response, two very intimidating women stepped into the room. Meredith spoke to them in a hushed tone. "See that she gets to the surface—in such a way that she can't lead anyone back to this location."

As if, thought Cole. But she was happy about being shown the door. One of the two female escorts gruffly reached for Cole's arm, and she pulled away. The second escort pulled a dark sack from a drawer as the first woman again grasped Cole's arm. It was obvious to Cole that the woman meant to place the dark cover over Cole's head.

"I don't think that will be necessary," Sara said.

Meredith shot her a look for contradicting her.

"It's okay, Sara," said Cole without trepidation. She decided not to fight the situation for Sara's sake. Cole gave Meredith one last intense glare before the dark bag was placed over her head.

Cole tried not to trip as she was shoved up yet another flight of metal stairs. The bag over her head was stifling and was causing a sense of claustrophobia. She tried to calm down. Surely they were almost at street level by now and she would soon be released by this ridiculous duo. She was hoping that Sara was okay. Cole would have preferred for Sara to leave with her.

She heard the hinges of a door opening and felt fresh air hit her arms and hands. One of the women shoved her forward and then removed the hood. Cole blinked and rubbed her eyes with her hands. She turned just in time to see the door close as the two women retreated back below street level.

Great. Where the hell am I now? She looked around for anything familiar that she might be able to use to gather her bearings. She could see a transit station a block or so away and headed in that direction thinking that there might be a map of routes that would be helpful.

Chapter Eighteen

Ava's comm unit buzzed, signaling that someone was downstairs. She and Audrey both assumed it was Cole but were surprised to see a breathless and frightened Sara appear at the door to Ava's apartment.

"Is Cole here?" Sara blurted out before even saying hello.

"No, she was out for a walk when I saw her last," replied Audrey. "Sara, what's wrong? You look like something is wrong."

"It's all my fault," she said. "I saw Cole at a café and I invited her to one of my meetings. And then it didn't go so well. She challenged the woman who leads the group, and the woman had two of her butch goons escort Cole out with a bag over her head!" Sara was breathless.

"Slow down, Sara!" said Ava as she took Sara's arms in each of her hands, forcing Sara to face her. "You took Cole to one of your damn meetings? And you left her alone?"

"Meredith, the woman in charge, she wouldn't let me leave. I was scared. I didn't know what to do."

"I'm sure they didn't hurt Cole. Why would they?" asked Audrey.

"I don't think they would. They just put a hood over her head so she wouldn't know the location of the meetings at sublevel, but I have no idea where they took her," said Sara. "The minute I could leave I got to the street level as fast as could, but I couldn't find her."

Ava shook Sara. "I can't believe you, Sara. You and your stupid resistance movement."

"It gets worse," said Sara.

Audrey stepped closer to Ava and Sara. "What do you mean it gets worse?"

"What did Meredith say? Something like *events are already in motion*." Sara paced back and forth in front of them. "There were schematic drawings on her desk. I'd never seen those before. And along one wall was a large map that looked like a topographic map of the western half of the North American continent. I have no idea what that has to do with anything."

"Sara, you aren't making sense. What schematic drawings?" Ava asked.

"Of Easton. Schedules and times written on each of the drawings in locations all around the city." Sara buried her face in her hands as she continued to pace.

"You must have been mistaken." Audrey reached for Sara's arm. "Sara, look at me."

"I got involved with the resistance only because of assurances that the movement would remain non-violent. But in recent weeks, things have slowly been shifting. I never imagined that Meredith endorsed the violent behavior or that the small acts of aggression were leading to something more sinister."

They were distracted by a flash of light as an explosion ignited in the distance. They all ran to the window.

"That was an explosion!" exclaimed Audrey.

"There will be more," said Sara breathlessly. "There were plans on the desk…on the desk where Meredith's inner circle meets. Detonation times were listed for locations in all four quadrants of the city."

"What!" said Ava.

"I think Meredith is planning to set off a chain reaction that would destroy the entire power grid. I think she wants to bring the whole city down to prove a political point."

"Bring it down where? Into the ocean?" exclaimed Audrey. "And Cole is out there somewhere in the middle of all of this!"

"Sara, we've got to let the authorities know," said Ava, snapping into action. "If there needs to be a mass-scale evacuation of the city then they need to start that now."

"Maybe I'm wrong. Maybe I read the diagrams incorrectly," said Sara. "Could she really bring the whole city down? Is that even possible?"

"Yes, it's possible. Given the right engineering schematics and advanced understanding of the floatation mechanisms," answered Ava. "If she takes out enough of the city's flight turbines she can definitely take it down. Even if she only took out enough engines to cause the whole city platform to list to one side, that would still be enough to make it lose altitude drastically."

Just then, there was another flash of light, this time closer, and it was followed by a slight shock of sound waves on the window of Ava's apartment.

"Oh, no! This can't be happening!" Sara slumped into a chair near the window, tears streaming down her cheeks.

"Ava, I just remembered that I gave Cole my handheld comm unit. See if you can reach her and find out where she is," Audrey said, ignoring Sara's meltdown.

Ava grabbed her unit and punched in Audrey's number.

❖

Cole had been thrown to the ground by the second blast. The detonation had been close enough to break windows nearby and shower shattered glass on the street and passersby. Screams and cries of fear sounded all around her. Cole was sitting on the ground, shaking broken glass out of the folds in her shirt as people ran past her. Then she felt a buzzing vibration in her pocket. *The comm unit.* She'd forgotten that she had it.

"Hello?" she said then pressed the button on the device again. "Hello?"

"Cole!" said Ava. "Can you hear me?"

"Barely!" Cole yelled back. She scrambled out of the way as people ran in all directions to get away from the blasts.

"Cole, before we lose the connection, tell me where you are. We're coming to get you."

"Uh, I see a building number—3467 South Cross Street." Just as she was about to say something else, another blast went off. Cole's ears began to ring and smoke drifted all around her. The comm link went dead.

❖

Ava looked at the comm unit in stunned silence. "I think another blast went off very close to her."

Audrey went to the window. "I see three distant flames with smoke. We need to hurry."

Ava grabbed her flight bag and they headed toward the lift. At street level, Sara started out with them in the direction of the aircraft hangar.

"No, Sara, you have to get to your own evac unit," Ava pushed her in the opposite direction. "Cole isn't a citizen so she doesn't have an assigned unit. We'll have to get her out in my cruiser. It won't carry four!"

"I'm so sorry!" said Sara. "I'm so sorry."

As they separated Audrey asked, "Will the cruiser carry three?"

"It'll have to. If Cole is hurt she's going to need you," said Ava. "Come on, hurry!" They ran toward the hanger on the flight deck six blocks away.

Other pilots were scrambling to ready their cruisers for departure when Ava and Audrey arrived. Ava tossed her bag in the cockpit and hurriedly ran through preflight.

"Get in," she said.

Ava climbed in the pilot's seat and charged the cylinders. The craft began to rise as the hydrogen boosters kicked in. Ava checked to make sure the solar grid was coming online. She closed the hatch as the cruiser began to slowly rise. Ava then eased the accelerator forward to clear the hangar deck.

"Don't strap in yet," Ava said. "If I can't set the cruiser down you may need to pull Cole in."

Ava maneuvered the craft just above street level as two more blasts sounded on the other side of the city.

"Sara was right. That crazy woman is trying to set off a chain reaction," said Audrey. "I was hoping that Sara had overreacted."

"We're close to Cross Street. Help me look for Cole," said Ava as she began to circle the area. There was a lot of smoke and a lot of movement on the ground as people rushed to evac units. The citywide emergency alarms had begun to sound, signaling that a believed threat of structural collapse was imminent.

"There's too much smoke. I can't see anything on the street!" said Audrey.

❖

Cole thought she glimpsed Ava's cruiser for a moment through the shifting smoke. She was looking up rather than at the chaos around her, fleeing pedestrians collided with her, sending all of them to the ground.

"Damn!" Cole said.

She got to her feet just as the city's foundation seemed to slant to one side. Everyone nearby stumbled; several people fell down completely, including Cole. Another blast sounded, and Cole threw her arms over her head as small pieces of mortar cascaded around her onto the paved surface.

❖

Audrey was desperately searching as Ava brought the craft around again for another pass.

"There!" Audrey exclaimed and pointed. "Over there! I see Cole."

Ava saw an open space nearby that was large enough to get her cruiser on the ground. She released the hatch so Audrey could climb out and get Cole who still hadn't spotted them.

"Hurry!" Ava yelled after Audrey. She kept the cylinders charged for immediate liftoff the minute Audrey returned with Cole.

Audrey was running toward Cole, yelling, "Cole! Over here!"

Cole spotted Audrey through the smoke and headed in her direction. Audrey took a few seconds to give Cole a brief embrace as they collided.

"Cole, I'm so happy we found you! Hurry, we need to get out of here!"

Audrey and Cole were only a few feet from the cruiser when a blast struck nearby. They were knocked to the ground as debris rained down on them. Cole's right temple was bloody from impact with a flying object. She scrambled to her feet and reached for Audrey.

She pulled them both into the cruiser, and Ava hit the boosters to lift the cruiser off the street before the hatch had completely closed. As they were beginning to rise, a secondary blast erupted, sending small shrapnel ricocheting through the cockpit and igniting sparks. Cole and Audrey were sharing the second seat so Cole instinctively reached around Audrey to protect her.

Ava felt a sharp pain in her side, but ignored it. She felt the piercing sting again as she made a move to seal the hatch.

"Cole, can you get the hatch?"

Cole reached up and locked the seal. Ava banked the cruiser to rise above the blast area. As they gained altitude, they could see smoke streaming in every part of the city. They were almost at the edge of the cloud city boundary when a huge detonation occurred close to their flight path hurling the cruiser sideways. Ava fought to regain control, and felt the sharp ache again in her side. She put a hand over the spot. When she pulled it way, her hand was covered in blood. *Keep it together. You've gotta get this bird on the ground. Just stay alert.*

As they left Easton, they looked back to see the two forward quadrant platforms of the city begin to tilt and lose altitude. Evac units were jettisoning off in every direction as the city went down. The emergency pods were programmed to automatically travel to one of the three cloud cities closest to the evacuation site.

Ava set the GPS coordinates for Cole's farm into the nav computer. Her hand was shaking, but she managed to hide the fact from Cole and Audrey.

Cole leaned her head back into the second seat.

"Thank you, Ava, for coming to get me," said Cole. "You are one of the bravest women I know."

"You would have done the same for me if you knew how to fly this thing," Ava joked. "Won't Ida and Vivian be surprised to see us for dinner?"

Cole smiled back in response.

Audrey, seated in Cole's lap, leaned her head on Cole's shoulder. She pressed her lips into Cole's neck, feeling incredibly grateful to have found her safe and now be sitting enfolded in her arms. She couldn't bring herself to contemplate what an alternative outcome might have been had they not been able to find her. Audrey hoped that Sara made it safely out of the city before it was too late.

They were thirty minutes into the flight when Audrey noticed Ava's head droop forward.

"Ava? Are you okay?" Audrey noticed for the first time that Ava's face was damp and her color wasn't good. *How did I miss this?* So much was going on that these details had escaped her. "Ava?"

Cole could hear the alarm in Audrey's voice and glanced over at Ava. Ava seemed to be struggling to stay awake. They were beginning to lose altitude over the treetops. Cole could now see that they were fast approaching the large hay field near her home on the ground. Cole reached over to steady Ava's hand on the nav stick.

"Something's wrong," said Audrey.

"Ava!" yelled Cole. "Talk to me. How do I set this thing down?"

"What?" Ava said. "Oh…cut the thrusters." She pointed toward a readout on the control panel. "Try and keep it level. Level it out, Cole. …I'm sorry…" Ava said before slumping forward in her seat.

Cole struggled to pull the nav stick back so they wouldn't nosedive into the ground. The cruiser bounced once, and then twice, and then it slowed, cutting a path through the tall dry hay before coming to a complete stop.

"Quick, Cole, pop the hatch so I can get to her," said Audrey.

Cole reached up and punched the release. The hatch slowly rose, and Cole climbed across the central console and positioned herself in front of Ava. She propped Ava back into the seat and saw a dark red stain spread across the side of Ava's shirt. Cole leaned in to examine the open wound. She felt the spot and realized there was a narrow piece of metal shrapnel protruding from it.

"She must have been hit when that last explosion sent pieces of debris inside the cockpit. There's a piece of it sticking out of her side."

"We need to get her out of here and get the bleeding to stop," Audrey said, looking at Cole.

Cole and Audrey lifted Ava out of her seat and placed her gently onto the ground next to the cruiser.

"Cole, grab that white box. It's a med kit." Audrey ripped Ava's shirt open so that she could better examine the wound. She then took gauze from the kit and wiped away some of the excess blood.

Audrey was in complete medical trauma mode. She worked quickly to get a compress over the wound to slow the bleeding.

"We can't stay here. We need to get her to medical care. She needs more than I have here in this first aid kit. Or at the very least we need to move her somewhere more stable so I can remove this object from her wound and close the hole."

"We're close to my house," said Cole. "You wait here. I'll get help."

Cole placed a kiss on Audrey's forehead before she ran in a full sprint in the direction of her cabin.

Audrey watched Cole disappear across the field and then turned her attention back to Ava.

"Ava, can you hear me? We're on the ground. Cole is getting help," Audrey said to Ava while still keeping pressure on the wound. Ava didn't stir.

Audrey remembered the radio in the cruiser. She thought maybe she'd reach someone and be able to get an evac team for Ava, even though they were on the ground. She quickly climbed into the pilot's seat, noticing for the first time, how much blood Ava lost. There was blood all over the seat. She reached for the transmitter.

"This is J5468. Our pilot has been injured and we require medical assistance."

No response.

Audrey assumed that Easton's tower was down. She switched channels and tried to reach Boston Cloud City tower.

"This is J5468, requesting emergency assistance."

"J5468, this is Boston Cloud City tower. All emergency personnel have been dispatched in response to the Easton Cloud City Collapse. We are unable to dispatch assistance at this time."

She had expected as much. Audrey climbed back down onto the ground near Ava. She checked her pulse. She felt cold. Audrey removed the light sweater she'd been wearing and covered Ava, and then for the first time, looked up to survey where they'd landed. She was hyper aware that she was alone, on the ground, and the sun was going down. The wind rustled the tall grass slightly, and the late afternoon sun created a golden glow across the field.

This is what Ava had meant when she said things on the ground were not what they'd been told. It was beautiful. And it was clear that Ava had been touched by this place; it had shifted something inside her.

Audrey turned in the direction that Cole had run. *Hurry, Cole!* She bent down again to check Ava.

Audrey had hoped to visit where Cole was from at some point, but not this way.

❖

Cole was out of breath by the time she reached the cabin. Vivian was working in the yard with a harness attached to a plow. When she saw Cole she dropped what she was doing and ran to embrace her.

"Cole! What happened?" Vivian held her at arm's length.

"Vivian, I'm so glad to see you. I'm fine, but we have to hurry. Ava is hurt." Cole tried to calm her breathing. "We need to get her to the house. I left her in the lower hay field behind the old schoolhouse ruins."

"I'll hitch the horse up to the buckboard," said Vivian.

"Is that Ginger?" asked Cole, looking at the horse near their barn.

"Yes, Marc traded her to me for rights to cut some timber on the lower acres."

"I'm going to grab a blanket." Cole passed Ida as she ran through the house.

"Cole! I didn't know you were back. What's going on?" Ida said.

"Ava is hurt. Vivian and I are going to get her in the wagon," said Cole as she retrieved a blanket. "We'll bring her to the house. I'll explain everything when I get back."

Once outside, Cole helped Vivian finish the rigging of the horse.

CHAPTER NINETEEN

Audrey worried it was taking too long for Cole to get back with help. Time was of the essence. If she was feeling chilly as the sun dropped below the horizon, then she knew Ava was also. If she hadn't been so concerned for Ava she might have been able to relax a little and enjoy her first sunset from the ground, but Audrey was tense as the moments continued to slip by.

After what seemed like forever, Audrey saw something dark on the horizon approaching. She could hear and feel the pounding of the large animal pulling a wooden transport of some kind. *Is that a wagon?* Metal clanged against the wooden rods on either side of the horse as the antique carriage drew closer. She panicked for a moment and then recognized Cole with another dark-haired woman on the buckboard seat beside her. As they got closer, Cole jumped off while the wagon was still rolling and rushed to Ava's side.

"How is she?" asked Cole.

"I don't know. I need to get a better look at the wound, and I need something to clean the injury to guard against infection."

Audrey knew Cole would be able to see the stain of tears on her cheeks. She closed her eyes as Cole brushed the dampness from her cheek with her thumb.

"Ava is going to be okay," Cole said.

The woman Cole was with joined them, carrying the blanket.

"Audrey, this is my aunt Vivian. She's going to help us get Ava back to the house."

Vivian quickly nodded hello. They spread the blanket out and gently moved Ava on top of it. Holding it tightly, they used the blanket as a makeshift stretcher to lift Ava into the back of the buckboard.

"Wait." Audrey jumped down and ran back to the cruiser. She grabbed Ava's flight bag, Cole's bag, and the med kit. Then she used a remote device to close the hatch and climbed back into the wagon.

Audrey and Cole sat on either side of Ava to try to keep her still during the bumpy ride to the cabin. Audrey had to hold on to Ava's hand to keep her from touching the gash. Ava moaned and her eyes batted with pain. She was definitely hurting, and the jarring ride was not helping.

When they arrived at the house, another woman was on the porch to greet them. "Audrey, this is my aunt Ida," Cole said as Ida stepped down off the porch to help carry Ava inside.

"Hello, Audrey," Ida said. "I cleaned off the kitchen table, as I thought that's where we'd have the best light to work."

Audrey gave Ida a grateful look as they carried Ava in and placed her on the wooden plank table. Ava tried to lift her head.

"Ah, this hurts," were the first words Ava had spoken since they got her out of the cruiser and onto the ground.

Audrey placed a hand on Ava's shoulder. "Please don't move, Ava." She brought her face closer to Ava's. "Can you hear me? There's shrapnel in your side. I'm going to have to remove it. Do you understand what I'm saying?"

Ava moaned and turned her head toward Audrey, but she didn't seem to completely understand. Her hair clung to her forehead, and Audrey brushed loose strands aside with a gentle caress.

"Cole, we need some boiled water and some clean rags," said Audrey, springing into action. "I'm going to need something to stop the bleeding and then something to stitch the wound. We'll need to sterilize the needle."

Cole took Audrey's face in her hands. "We're going to help you do this." She brushed a loose lock of hair behind Audrey's ear.

Looking at Cole closely for the first time, Audrey noticed the dried blood at Cole's right temple. She turned Cole's head to see the cut more closely.

"You're hurt."

"It's just a scratch. It can wait."

Audrey returned her attention to Ava. She pulled her blood-soaked shirt up and away from the laceration. She then gingerly removed the white gauze, now also soaked red, so that she could get a closer look at the site of entry.

Vivian placed a lantern at the edge of the table. She brought another and placed it at a slightly more elevated position on the counter near the stove where Ida had set water to boil. Ida brought a bowl of the piping hot water and some clean pieces of cloth to Audrey.

While Audrey was wiping away excess blood from around the protruding metal shrapnel, Cole slipped into the pantry and returned with a bottle that she placed on the table near the bowl of hot water. "Here, for sterilizing things. It's alcohol."

"I need to remove this piece of metal, otherwise I'm not going to be able to stop the bleeding completely," Audrey said, looking up at Cole. "Can you hold her down? You have to keep her still while I remove this. Vivian, it might be good if you helped as well. We need to keep her as still as possible."

Cole and Vivian nodded. Cole braced herself against Ava's shoulders and upper body. Vivian leaned across Ava's legs.

"Ava, if you can hear me, this is going to hurt, but I have to do it," said Audrey softly.

Ava's eyes flitted in response. Audrey turned and nodded to Cole. First, she poured some of the alcohol across the wound, which caused Ava to try to break free from their hold as she reacted to the burning sensation. Audrey gripped the sliver of metal with a fresh cloth. The blood was making it too slick for Audrey to grab the metal with her fingertips. Audrey took a deep breath and pulled with a quick, sharp movement. Ava cried out.

Cole tried to keep Ava from moving. "Ava, it'll be okay."

When Audrey looked back at Ava's face she realized that she had passed out. She quickly poured more alcohol over the wound causing a combination of the clear liquid and blood to wash across Ava's torso. She placed a clean cloth over the wound and pressed firmly. At that point, Ida was at her side with a jar of white powder.

"This is yarrow. If you pour it over the wound it will stop the bleeding," Ida said. "After the incident recently with Cole, I thought we should have some on hand for emergencies. Trust me, army medics used to use this in the field to dress wounds as far back as the American Civil War."

Audrey took the jar with her free hand. She was in a foreign place. She had no choice but to trust Cole's aunt. "Thank you." She pulled the compress cloth back, doused the hole with yarrow, then replaced the compress.

"Do you have anything I could use to close the wound?" Audrey asked, looking at Ida. "Something like a needle and some thread of some kind. The thread would need to be very strong. And we would need to sterilize both."

"The best thing would be horse hair," said Vivian. "I've seen Maddie use it before to stitch up knife cuts."

"Maddie is the local healer," said Cole. "But she's a long ride from here."

"I'll fetch a needle," said Ida. "We can sterilize it all with the alcohol."

Vivian and Ida were back quickly, and after pouring alcohol over the horsehair, Audrey threaded the needle and got ready to do the stitching.

"Can you hold her again? I don't want her to wake up in the middle of these stitches."

Vivian and Cole nodded and resumed their positions. Audrey took a deep breath and braced herself for the task at hand. As she began the first stitch, both Cole and Vivian looked away.

The yarrow helped slow the bleeding. It took a few minutes for Audrey to complete the neat line of stitches. Then she clipped the horsehair, tied it off, poured alcohol on another clean cloth, and wiped any remaining blood from the stitched area. Audrey then took gauze from the med kit she'd brought from the cruiser and taped it over the wound.

Audrey had done everything she could do with limited resources and equipment. Now they just needed to let Ava rest and keep her warm. Cole brought more blankets from the spare room and placed a small pillow under Ava's head. She took one of the remaining clean cloths, dampened it with warm water, and wiped Ava's forehead.

Audrey moved to stand beside Cole. Taking the same cloth, Audrey wet the other side of it, then took Cole's face in her hand and wiped away the dried blood from Cole's temple. With the cloth still in her hand, she slumped against Cole, and Cole held her close.

"You did good, Audrey," Cole said close to Audrey's ear.

Cole felt Audrey shake in her arms and knew that she was crying. Cole kissed the top of her head and looked over in the direction of her aunts, who were also holding each other in a comforting embrace.

Ava seemed to be resting peacefully under the pile of blankets. After several minutes, Audrey pulled away from Cole and wiped her own face with a clean spot on the cloth she still had in her hand.

"I'm sorry. I don't usually get so emotional providing medical care," Audrey said as she smiled and looked at Vivian and Ida.

"Don't give it one more thought," said Ida. "If I'd had to do what you just did I'd be passed out on the floor, a complete mess."

"I second that," said Vivian.

Audrey smiled at them. "I hope it's okay to use your table like this. I don't think we should move her right away. I'd like to keep her as quiet as possible for a little while. I don't want her to move and open up that wound again."

"Of course," said Ida. "I think that's a wise thing to do."

"I'm sorry to just show up in such a way," said Cole. "I'm sure we gave you two a fright. Everything just happened so fast."

"I want to hear the entire story," said Ida. "But it can wait until I get the two of you something to eat and drink. Cole, you look thin."

Ida cradled Cole's face in her hands and placed an affectionate kiss on her cheek. "I have biscuits and cider. And some leftover fried potatoes. We can take them in the sitting room by the fire so as not to disturb Ava. And then you girls can tell us all what's happened since we last saw you, Cole."

"Thank you, Ida," said Audrey. "I'm suddenly feeling very tired and hungry."

They removed the lantern, leaving Ava in the dimly lit room. They moved with heaping plates of food to chairs near the stone fireplace in the sitting room. It was warm out, so no fire was lit, but the room held the comforting, rustic aroma of a previous wood fire.

Between mouthfuls, Cole relayed the story of the past several days to her aunts, concentrating on the actions that led up to the collapse of the cloud city of Easton, but not touching what had been developing with Audrey. She didn't know how to begin to tell that part of the story.

The food did much to revive them. Audrey found Cole's aunts both comforting and amusing at the same time. She reclined back in her chair and for the first time felt herself relax a little. Audrey hadn't had any time to soak in her surroundings, or to even connect with Cole, since she'd left her on the street in front of her place in the city. She hadn't even stopped to absorb the fact that the life she had on Easton was now likely destroyed or had changed dramatically. She closed her eyes and leaned her head back against the chair.

Cole reached over and put her hand on Audrey's shoulder. "You should lie down. You've had a very stressful day."

Cole stood and took both of their plates with her. "My aunts and I can sit up with Ava while you rest a little."

"I think that's a very good idea," said Ida, standing and taking the plates from Cole. "You go get Audrey settled and we'll sit in the kitchen with Ava. If you need anything, Audrey, don't hesitate to ask."

As Cole walked her toward her room, Audrey realized she was emotionally exhausted. Cole guided her into the room with a gentle hand on her elbow and helped her sit on the edge of the bed. Looking down, Audrey realized that she had spots of blood all over the front of her shirt. She was shocked that she hadn't noticed this earlier. She began to wonder what else she hadn't noticed as Cole closed the door and pulled a clean cotton shirt from her dresser.

Cole kneeled on the floor in front of Audrey, handed her the shirt, and began removing Audrey's shoes for her.

"You can put on one of my shirts, and I'll put your shirt in some water to soak," said Cole.

"Your aunts must think I'm insane," said Audrey. "I'm wearing a blood-soaked shirt. I'm a mess."

Cole muffled a laugh. "Well, what did they expect? You just performed surgery in their kitchen."

Audrey ran her fingers through Cole's rumpled hair. "You are so handsome. Do you know how handsome you are?"

"I'm not nearly as handsome as you are beautiful. I know that much."

Cole helped Audrey out of her blood-soiled clothing and into the fresh shirt she'd pulled from the dresser. Audrey stood and slipped out of her pants. Cole pulled the covers back for Audrey to climb into bed. Cole leaned over and kissed Audrey's lips for a sustained moment.

"Can you stay with me for just a little while?" said Audrey. "I feel…I feel very unsettled."

Cole stretched out on top of the covers alongside Audrey. She pulled Audrey into her arms and Audrey sunk her face into Cole's shoulder.

"This is the only place I want to be," Audrey said.

"You were amazing today, Audrey." Cole's lips brushed Audrey's hair. "I've never been so proud of anyone in my whole life. You and Ava are both brave women. I don't know what would have happened to me if you and Ava hadn't come to find me in the cruiser."

Audrey shivered to think of what might have happened, of what could have happened.

"Ava insisted we come find you," said Audrey. "After I told her everything that had happened between us, you were her first concern."

"I'm very grateful for that. She's saved me twice now."

Audrey smiled and snuggled into Cole's warmth.

CHAPTER TWENTY

Cole jerked and opened her eyes. She must have dozed off holding Audrey. Cole gently moved her arm, placed Audrey's head on the pillow, and then kissed her forehead. She slipped off the bed and went back to the kitchen. Her aunts were seated, talking quietly. The light in the room was low and Cole wasn't sure how late it was.

"I'm sorry," Cole said as she came back into the room. "I think I must have fallen asleep for a few minutes. What time is it?"

"It's very late," said Ida. "It's good you fell asleep because now you can spell us for a little while."

Cole moved to stand beside Ava, looking down at her intently. "How is she?"

"Mostly sleeping, but a couple of times she woke up and we had to talk to her to quiet her down," said Vivian. "Will you be okay by yourself for a little while?"

"Yeah. I'll be fine. You should get some rest." And then she added jokingly, "I'm younger and I need less sleep."

Vivian smiled at her.

Ida embraced Cole. "I'm glad you're back, sweet Cole."

Ida and Vivian quietly moved to their bedroom to get some sleep. Cole pulled a chair beside Ava and took one of her hands between hers.

"Oh, Ava," Cole whispered. She brushed her lips across the back of Ava's hand. How strange that their friendship had started in much the same way, only with the roles reversed.

The house was very quiet as it slipped into the latest part of the night. Cole was swimming in her own thoughts about the last several days, contemplating all the emotions that had run through her during the time she'd spent with both Ava and Audrey. As recently as a month ago, she'd had no plan for the future other than to move out and create her own home on Black Mountain. There had been no glimmer of romance on the horizon for Cole. And now, only a few months after the celebration of her twenty-second year, she had made love to a remarkable woman. Could she really hope for a future with Audrey? What did she have to offer Audrey here on the ground? Would Audrey offer her a life in the city? Was that even an option? As far as she knew the urban centers were a closed system. Would she even want to live in the city if she could? Could she even be happy there?

Cole wasn't sure how long she'd been sitting in the dark. This was the first time in days that she'd had time alone to think through all her recent experiences. She was lost in contemplation when she felt soft hands on her shoulders. Audrey had walked up behind her and she hadn't even heard her approach. Cole looked up.

"Hi." She smiled at Audrey. "Did you get some sleep?"

"I did, thank you," said Audrey. The faintest pink hue was beginning to appear through one of the kitchen windows. The sun was not up, but the horizon line was beginning to show the slightest notion that the sun was on its way.

Audrey moved past Cole and placed her hand on Ava's forehead. Ava felt slightly warm, but it could have just been all the blankets she was under. Audrey pulled the top blanket back and placed it on a nearby chair. Then she pulled the lower blanket back so that she could see how the bandage over the wound looked. There was some blood showing through the gauze, but the bleeding had stopped. She decided not to pull the bandage up to replace it with a fresh covering just yet.

"Has she woken up at all?" Audrey asked.

"No. Aunt Ida said she woke up a couple of times with them, but she hasn't so much as stirred since I've been sitting here."

"Cole, you look really tired. Why don't you get some rest? I'm awake. I can stay up with Ava."

"Okay. I guess I am really tired," said Cole. "There's water in that pitcher if you want any, and there are biscuits in that skillet if you're hungry. I'm sure my aunts will be up before me, but they would want you to get whatever you need from the kitchen, okay?"

Audrey nodded. "Get some rest, Cole. Ava will hopefully be awake soon and she'll be able to tell us how she's feeling."

"Okay."

Cole was tired, and was asleep moments after she lay down on the bed. She didn't even remove her clothes.

❖

Audrey had only been alone with Ava for about an hour when Ida and Vivian joined her.

"Around here you have to get up with the chickens," said Vivian. She grabbed a basket and headed out of the house toward the barn.

"How is our patient?" asked Ida.

"I think she's doing well," said Audrey. "She felt a little warm earlier, but now that seems to have passed. I'd like to move her to a bed if you have one to spare."

"Oh yes, we have a spare room. We can move her in there," said Ida. "Should we carry her or should we wait until she wakes up?"

"I feel like she's going to wake up soon, and it would be good to get her to walk a little, even if it's only across the room," said Audrey. "At the hospital, we get patients up to walk within twelve hours of surgery."

"This young woman was very lucky to have brought a surgeon down to the ground with her."

"Oh, I'm not a surgeon. I'm just a general practice doctor. I make rounds sometimes on the surgical recovery floor."

There was silence between them for several minutes.

"I've never been on the ground before," said Audrey.

"Well, I've never been up in one of the cloud cities before, so I guess that makes us even."

"I suppose it does."

Ava's eyes began to flutter, and she ran her tongue over her dry lips. "Ava, would you like some water?" Audrey asked.

"Yes," rasped Ava. "Please."

Audrey placed a hand behind Ava's head to help her rise enough to sip from the cup she offered. After a couple of small sips, Ava wanted to lay her head back down on the pillow.

"Ida?" Ava said, somewhat confused.

"I'm here, dear. You're at our house in the mountains. Do you remember?" Ida placed a comforting stroke across Ava's forehead.

"Is Cole here, too?" Ava asked, still trying to get her bearings.

"Yes, she's resting," Audrey said. "She sat up with you all night. She'll be very sorry that she wasn't here to see you wake up."

Ava blinked and swallowed. "Can I have a little more water?"

Audrey assisted her with a few more sips.

"Ava, take a little bit longer to wake up, then I think we should move you to a more comfortable place," said Audrey, holding Ava's hand as she spoke. "I know it won't feel very good, but I think it would be best if we helped you get up and walk to the next room. Do you think you feel up to that?"

"I think so. I sort of feel like I've been hit by a cruiser rather than just having flown one."

Audrey smiled. It was good to see that Ava was coming out of the fog a little.

It wasn't long before Audrey and Ida were able to get Ava up and moved to the spare bedroom. They helped her roll over and slide off the table slowly so that Ava wouldn't put too much pressure on her stomach muscles to lift herself up. They helped her to the bathroom first and then Ida and Audrey stabilized her as she tentatively walked between them to the spare room.

After swallowing a few bites of food and some hot tea, Ava drifted back to sleep. The tea contained Echinacea. Ida also mixed a small amount of goldenseal in water to ward off infection. Audrey was learning that Ida had quite a working knowledge of medicinal herbs. Audrey had only ever seen mention of such herbs in books. She had never actually seen them used in practice.

❖

It was early afternoon before Cole was up and about. She got some lunch and then offered to show Audrey around the farm.

Audrey had hardly been outside the house since they had arrived and was extremely curious to see more of her new environment. They didn't stray too far from the house in case Ava needed them. Cole walked Audrey around the outbuildings, past the chickens, and up the ridge a little way so that she could get a better view of the entire place. Audrey remembered what Ava had told her about how good everything smelled. She was right. Her senses were on overload. And not just from her surroundings.

Audrey felt her body react every time there was even the slightest physical contact with Cole. A simple brush of their hands, a touch on the arm or shoulder, would cause heat to rise in her center. Audrey was sure that Cole's aunts noticed her attraction to Cole. She felt it was impossible to hide her feelings. And truthfully, she didn't really want to.

During the course of the afternoon, Ava got up once more with help from Audrey and Cole. She made two circles around the kitchen and sitting room before collapsing back in bed.

Ida made food for everyone, and then before they knew it, the house was dark and it was time to retire for the night. Everyone was tired and eager to get a full night of rest. With Ava recuperating in the guest room, that meant that Audrey and Cole were sharing Cole's room.

Cole handed Audrey another clean shirt from one of the dresser drawers. "Hopefully, this will fit. It might be a little snug since you're more…um…" Cole's face reddened as she spoke, but it was hardly noticeable in the low light from the lantern.

"Since my breasts are larger?" said Audrey. She smiled knowing she was making Cole pleasantly uncomfortable.

Audrey began to unbutton her shirt and Cole quickly turned away to offer Audrey some privacy. Cole was still holding the clean shirt out for Audrey to take.

"Am I embarrassing you?"

"No. Truthfully, just looking at you might be more than I can handle at the moment," said Cole.

Audrey moved up behind Cole, wrapped her arms around Cole's waist, pressed against her, and kissed the back of her neck. Cole shut her eyes, leaning into the embrace.

"That's not really helping," said Cole. "Just the heat of you against me makes me feel excited."

"That's the best compliment I've had in a long time," said Audrey. "Okay, you can turn around. I'm dressed."

But Audrey wasn't completely dressed, she had donned the borrowed shirt, but left it unbuttoned and was wearing nothing else.

"I can't believe that people aren't paying you compliments all the time, Audrey." Cole's eyes widened at the sight of Audrey, barely covered, and warmly lit by candlelight from the bedside table.

"I don't get many compliments that have such sincerity." Audrey caressed Cole's face and kissed her. "Aren't you going to get undressed for bed?"

"Um…"

Audrey began unbuttoning Cole's shirt. She'd allowed Cole to be bashful, but now she had the powerful desire to feel Cole's skin under her hands. The house was quiet; she reasoned they were the only ones left awake, so she kept her voice to a whisper. Audrey needed to feel close to Cole, after everything that had happened in the last several hours: the blast, Ava's injury, the unscheduled landing on the ground. She wanted some validation that everything that had happened in the last twenty-four hours could end in a good place.

"Cole, it's been very hard to be so close to you all day and not be with you like this." Audrey slipped her hands inside Cole's shirt and stroked her chest. Cole inhaled sharply, responding to Audrey's teasing fingertips.

Audrey whispered against Cole's cheek. "I need to feel the weight of you on top of me. I want to feel you between my legs. Can you do that for me?"

Cole nodded as Audrey loosened the buttons at the front of her trousers and pushed them down over her hips. Audrey pulled the covers back, climbed in bed, and pulled Cole on top of her, spreading her legs and then wrapping them tightly around Cole's midsection.

Cole pulled the light summer quilt over them, then settled on top of Audrey.

"Cole, I'm so turned on, all you have to do is move on top of me." She put her hands on Cole's firm ass and began to slowly grind against her. Cole feathered kisses all across Audrey's collarbone and neck. Audrey swept her hand up under the back of Cole's shirt, dragging her nails lightly down toward the small of her back. Audrey was so close. Cole's slow erotic rhythmic movements were bringing her swiftly to the edge. As she felt the intense release of all that she'd held so tightly all day, she buried her face in Cole's neck so as not to scream and wake the entire household.

After the tremors of her climax passed, Audrey moved a thigh between Cole's legs and allowed her fingers to travel down between them. She knew Cole was close.

"Come for me, baby," Audrey whispered.

Cole's eyes were moist as they met her gaze. Audrey had never experienced such a strong joining with anyone. This connection only added to the heat that erupted between them every time they touched.

Cole moved against Audrey's hand, and it was only a matter of minutes before her body became taut and then she settled against Audrey.

"I think I'm afraid," said Audrey. She kissed Cole's forehead as she ran her fingers through Cole's hair.

"What are you afraid of?"

"I don't know."

But the truth was Audrey did know. She was afraid that she had finally found what she'd been searching for. Her fear was now that she'd found it she wouldn't have the courage to claim it. That she wouldn't have the courage to make Cole hers. Cole was everything she'd been looking for in a lover and partner, but to make this real would mean everything in her life would have to change. Change of that magnitude frightened Audrey.

Audrey realized that while she'd been staring at the ceiling lost in thought, Cole had been looking up at her.

"Audrey, I'm here with you. Don't be afraid. Whatever you're afraid of, we can figure it out."

Audrey didn't respond, she merely pulled Cole up into a tender kiss.

CHAPTER TWENTY-ONE

The next morning as Ida was making quiet rumbles in the kitchen, Cole exited her room, rubbing the sleep from her eyes. She yawned as she stumbled into the kitchen. In the low morning light, Ida had set a lantern near the stove. She motioned for Cole to come closer.

"I need to have a look at you," she said, studying her features. "Don't think I didn't notice that you didn't use the bedroll in the living room last night."

"Hmm?" said Cole.

"It's clear to me that you have feelings for the young doctor."

"Aunt Ida." Cole blushed as she tried to step away from her aunt's grasp.

"Now don't pull away. I'm not finished yet." Ida tilted Cole's head to see the cut on her right temple and lifted her shirt slightly to see the two scars at the side of her lower torso from her previous injury. She pulled Cole into a maternal embrace. Cole relaxed into her arms.

"I'm glad you're home safe, sweet Cole," said Ida.

Audrey exited the bedroom a few moments behind Cole. Cole pulled back from Ida's hug, only to have Ida embrace her again and whisper into her ear, "We'll revisit this topic later."

"You're too thin! I'm going to fix you a big breakfast," said Ida.

"I wasn't doing much in the city to work up an appetite. And… well, sometimes the food didn't agree with me," she said, beaming in

Audrey's direction, as Audrey joined them in the kitchen. "Except for the two meals I had at Audrey's place. She's a very good cook. You two could share some secrets for sure."

After eating everything Ida put on their plates, Cole carried a dish into Ava's room. Audrey followed.

"Ava, are you awake?" Cole whispered.

Ava stirred and opened her eyes as Cole set the dish on the bedside table.

"We thought you might be hungry," said Cole.

Audrey moved to sit at the edge of the bed, and Cole shifted so that she was standing near the footboard. Ava adjusted herself slightly so that she was facing Cole. Her eyes were sleepy, but she seemed much better than the previous day.

"I was lying here thinking that I can't believe the complete circle of events that have befallen us," said Ava, wincing slightly as she adjusted herself a bit more to take a sip of the coffee that Audrey had handed her. "Not too long ago our positions were completely reversed."

"I know. I promise not to say it was 'meant to be,' but you've got to admit that there seems to be some larger force at work here," Cole said as she leaned on the bedpost at the corner of the footboard.

"Yeah, definitely a larger force—a sociopath with a knife and a load of C-4," said Ava.

"C-4?" asked Cole.

"Plastic explosives," said Ava.

"Oh, well, I'm at least glad things worked out so that I could help you for a change."

"For a change?" Ava asked. "You rescued me first. Then I punched you in the nose. Then I rescued you after the one-sided knife fight. Then you saved me from—"

"Audrey is really the one who saved you," interrupted Cole.

Ava reached out and placed a hand over Audrey's hand. "Thank you."

Audrey held the plate for Ava to take a few bites. Cole shifted, stowing her hands in her pockets.

"Well, Aunt Ida needs me to cut some wood for the stove. I guess I'll go do that and let the doctor have a look at you." Cole squeezed

Ava's foot under the blanket. "You look much better today, Ava," Cole added, grinning at Ava as she left the room.

There was an awkward moment of silence before Ava spoke.

"Thank you for what you did, Audrey. I would have been in real trouble if you hadn't been with us."

"You're going to be fine, Ava. You just need a couple more days of rest and then you'll be able to fly yourself out of here."

"Am I the only one who'll be flying back then?"

"I didn't mean it that way. I assume I'll be leaving with you."

"Oh." Ava tried to read Audrey's expression. "I guess I thought you might stay with Cole."

"That would be a pretty big move wouldn't it? I have my work in the city, which I assume is piling up in the wake of the explosions. And besides, Cole hasn't extended the invitation to stay."

Audrey stood up, all of a sudden feeling unsettled. She didn't really want to talk with Ava about what she was feeling, and she was afraid the look on her face revealed her conflicted emotions.

"Where did you and Cole sleep last night?" asked Ava.

That's all you really care about isn't it? Whether we had sex or not. When in fact, whatever is going on with Cole and me is about so much more than just sex. Although, the sex is amazing.

"I slept in Cole's room and she slept with me," Audrey answered flatly.

They were quiet for a moment while Ava ate a few more bites of food. Then she spoke. "I think you should use the radio in the cruiser to contact Jenna and let her know where we are. I'm sure Easton needs every available pilot at the moment, and I feel bad that I'm stuck here and Jenna has no idea where I am."

"I'll see if Cole can walk me over to the cruiser. I'm not sure if I could find it on my own." Audrey was happy to have a task and happy to have a reason to leave the room. "It would be good for me to check in with my medical team, too. I'm sure the med lab is swamped."

Audrey turned to leave. As she shut the door she said to Ava, "Get some rest."

Ava sunk back into the pillows and closed her eyes. How had she managed to lose both Audrey and Cole? She felt like she'd practically set them up with each other. She delivered Cole right to Audrey's doorstep. *Maybe this was meant to be.*

Ava laughed at herself for even thinking the words that Cole was so fond of using. She knew she should be happy for Audrey for finding someone that truly cared about her. But instead she felt a little angry and a little lonely and maybe a little jealous.

❖

Audrey found herself alone in the main living space of the cabin. She walked to the fireplace and leaned her forehead against the smooth cool surface of the hardwood mantel. She exhaled and traced the edge of the stonework with her fingers, feeling the rough texture and uneven surface of the rocks within her reach. She dragged her hand across each surface nearby as she made a slow circle about the room—the upholstered chair, the woven blanket thrown over the back of the slightly threadbare loveseat, the roughhewn boards of the rectangular kitchen table, to the black iron of the wood cooking stove, still warm to the touch.

How was it possible that she could feel so at ease in a place so foreign? Could a person feel kinship to a place they've never been before? It was as if she carried some memory at a cellular level of ancestors who lived in such a place long ago. If she allowed herself to be honest, it felt right to be here. The familiarity of the formerly unknown place gave her a strange sense of déjà vu.

Audrey heard a sound she didn't recognize and walked out onto the porch to find Cole. She spotted her near the barn, cutting wood with an axe.

Audrey watched Cole swing the axe with broad, sure strokes, splintering chunks of wood with a single strike. Her shirtsleeves were rolled up to her elbows, her chest glistening at the opening of the partially unbuttoned shirt, and her dark cropped hair fell across her forehead with each downward drive. She was placing another chunk of wood on the stump to splinter it into smaller wedges with the axe when she noticed Audrey watching her. Cole regarded Audrey with an unexpectedly intense and direct gaze, which caused Audrey to catch her breath.

This is Cole in her natural habitat. Lean, rugged, skilled at making a life in this rustic world. At that moment, Audrey found Cole to be a gorgeous mix of feminine and masculine energy, and Cole was looking at Audrey with the same raw desire that Audrey had experienced at the club that first night they had kissed.

Cole hesitated for a moment, still breathing hard from the physical exertion of chopping wood. Audrey watched intently as Cole made a short stroke, wedging the axe into the stump so that it would stay in place. Cole's hand lingered on the axe handle as she moved her hand lightly up and down, stroking the wooden shaft. The suggestive gesture surprised Audrey; she inhaled sharply and looked from where Cole's hand rested on the axe handle up to meet her dark eyes.

Cole took a few steps toward Audrey, captured her hand, and pulled her past the woodpile to the back of the barn, and into the shadows of a small thicket of trees. Cole pulled Audrey roughly against her into a deep kiss. After a moment, they pulled apart. Audrey felt flushed, breathless.

"I'm sorry if I was being too rough. You just looked so…" Cole said.

"It's okay to be rough sometimes," said Audrey, her lips almost touching Cole's. She ran her fingers down Cole's slender, muscular forearms, and then entwined her fingers with Cole's. "I've never seen anyone do what you were doing. That was hot."

"Chopping firewood?" asked Cole. "Really?"

"Yes. Really." Audrey leaned in for another long kiss. When she pulled away she asked, "Where's Vivian?"

"Down in the lower field I suppose."

"Will anyone see us here?"

"No, why?"

Audrey gave Cole a firm, deep kiss, and pushed her back against a large nearby tree. She began to move her fingers inside Cole's shirt, feeling how slightly damp she was from her exertion with the axe. Audrey moved her hands down Cole's chest to unfasten the buttons at the waist of Cole's pants and slipped her hand inside. She held Cole's mouth captive with a passionate series of deep, open-mouthed kisses.

Cole shuddered at the touch of Audrey's fingers across her stomach as they dropped inside her trousers. Audrey slipped her other hand inside the back of Cole's pants, grabbing her firmly, and pulling her against her probing fingers. Cole had her hands at the back of Audrey's neck, fists full of hair, pulling her into a fierce kiss. Audrey felt Cole's insides tighten around her fingers as she came. She held Cole tightly as she shuddered in response to the unexpected orgasm that coursed through her body.

"Audrey," Cole breathed out her name.

"I can't get enough of you, Cole," Audrey whispered as she pulled back so that she could look into Cole's eyes. She removed her hand, which caused Cole to inhale sharply. Then Audrey rested her body against Cole.

Audrey felt Cole's hands drift down her body, moving slowly downward until they came to rest at her hips.

"Stay with me, Audrey."

"I'm here, baby. I've got you."

"I mean…stay with me," said Cole. "Don't leave."

"Oh, Cole…" Audrey closed her eyes tightly and pressed her cheek into Cole's shirt. "You know I want to…" But she didn't finish the thought.

Audrey smiled uncertainly at Cole and placed a tender kiss on her lips before pulling away to walk back toward the house. She didn't want Cole to see the tears well up and run down her cheeks. *How will I leave, Cole? How can I bear it?*

❖

After Audrey walked away, Cole sank to a seated position at the base of the tree. She sat there for a little while, head in her hands. Cole felt like her insides were in knots. She wanted to say more to Audrey. She wanted to say what she suspected, that she was falling desperately in love with Audrey. But she was afraid to say the words out loud and have them rejected.

Cole knew that Audrey had strong feelings for her. Every time they were alone it seemed obvious that this intense connection she felt was mutual. And what if it was? What if Audrey was falling in love with her also, then what? Could she really expect Audrey to leave Easton permanently and live on the ground with her? While that was exactly what Cole hoped for, she knew how unrealistic that notion was.

Cole gave herself a little longer to calm down and get herself together before she walked back to stack the wood she'd just split.

CHAPTER TWENTY-TWO

Cole decided it would be quicker if they rode Ginger down to the cruiser so that Audrey could use the radio. Audrey stood on the raised porch as Cole pulled up on the friendly mare.

"Have you ever ridden a horse?" asked Cole.

The answer from Audrey was *no*. Audrey was more than a little nervous about climbing up on the large animal. Cole's self-confidence in the saddle atop Ginger assuaged her nerves only slightly.

"Put your foot just so in the stirrup and I'll pull you up," said Cole as she reached a hand down to Audrey.

Audrey took Cole's hand and partially launched herself and was partially pulled up into the space behind Cole. She was glad she'd been able to fit into trousers she'd borrowed from Ida, which made climbing onto the horse much easier than trying to attempt it in her usual city attire. She wrapped her arms around Cole's waist and snuggled up close behind her, resting her cheek on Cole's back.

"Not too bad, huh?" said Cole over her shoulder.

"So far."

Cole led Ginger at a slow pace down the ridge, past the remnants of the old stone building, and across the grassy field to where the cruiser rested. Once they reached their destination, Cole helped Audrey climb down, and then dismounted, letting the reins drop loosely to the ground.

Cole stood far enough away from the cruiser so that she couldn't hear what was being said. But she could tell that Audrey had made contact with someone. After a few minutes, Audrey joined Cole.

"So, did that go okay?" asked Cole.

"Yes. I was able to reach Jenna, Ava's senior flight officer. She was relieved to hear that we're all okay. Unfortunately, she doesn't know Sara so I wasn't able to get an update on her status. I suppose I'll find out when we get back."

She said it again. She's definitely leaving. Cole pushed the thought down inside her chest.

"I thought we might head over to my friend Marc's farm and say hello," said Cole. "This is his field. He may not have seen the cruiser yet since he's probably busy with the baby coming. But it would be neighborly to check on him."

"Okay."

"Besides, he's one of my closest friends. I'd like for you to meet him," added Cole.

❖

Audrey realized she hadn't really met any of Cole's friends. She didn't even know anything about them. Their first forty-eight hours on the ground had been consumed with getting Ava stabilized and on the mend.

They walked along beside the horse, in the opposite direction from where they'd come. Cole seemed quiet. Audrey suspected it was her imminent departure that was to blame. She took Cole's hand as they walked, intertwining their fingers. The sky was bright blue and cloudless. Autumn colors had begun to appear on the trees surrounding the hay field. Eventually, they came to a dirt path at the edge of the pasture and began following it toward a farmhouse that Audrey saw in the distance. *Everyone has so much space here.*

In another fifteen minutes, they were walking up the steps onto the porch of a wood-sided white house. There were chairs on the porch and planters with ferns. Cole stepped up to the door and knocked.

"Coming!" they heard a male voice yell from somewhere in the house. In a moment, Marc was at the door. He smiled warmly at Cole.

"Boy, are you a sight for sore eyes. Look at you, Cole," he said. He grabbed Cole and pulled her roughly into a friendly hug. "I haven't seen you in weeks!"

"Hey, Marc, this is Audrey," said Cole.

"Hi, Marc," Audrey said, smiling and extending her hand, which he ignored and instead pulled her into a hug.

Marc was a bit taller and more stout than Cole, but with the same easygoing nature. Audrey thought maybe he was a bit more gregarious than Cole, but then again, she hadn't gotten to spend that much time with Cole she realized. Marc stepped to the side and motioned for them to enter the house.

"Come in, come in. Hannah is going to want to see you for sure," said Marc.

Audrey was curious about the interior of the house. It had a similar feel to Cole's place, but the furniture seemed to be of a different era, maybe slightly more modern. Marc motioned for them to follow him into a sitting room where a very pregnant Hannah sat lounging on a sofa.

"Look who just stopped by," said Marc. "And she brought one of her city friends, Audrey. Ida had stopped by to bring a pie to Hannah, knowing she was in the last days of her pregnancy and likely needing to be off her feet. She told us all about Ava's crash landing and the knife attack."

"Crazy stuff, huh?" said Cole.

"I just feel kinda bad that I've been so distracted with the coming of this baby and shouldering all the farm chores that I haven't been much of a friend the past few weeks," said Marc.

"Please don't worry about it, okay?" Cole patted Marc's shoulder and gave him a genuine broad smile.

"Audrey, the color of your eyes is really something. Even in the low light they practically sparkle," said Hannah. She tried to sit up as they entered the room, but Cole quickly moved to her side.

"Please don't get up. We can come to you," said Cole. She reached down and hugged Hannah warmly. "You're glowing, Hannah."

"I might be glowing, but I feel like I'm about to bust. If this baby doesn't come soon I don't know what I'll do." Hannah looked in Marc's direction. "Poor Marc, he's had a lot to contend with during this pregnancy."

"Oh, sweetheart, it's been a cake walk," Marc said, grinning.

"Yeah, right," Hannah said with a smirk in his direction.

"Hannah, it's very nice to meet you," said Audrey as she stood a few feet from the sofa where Hannah was reclining.

"Oh! The baby is kicking up a storm. Do you want to feel it?" said Hannah.

"Uh, yeah. You don't mind?" asked Cole. She was seated at the edge of the sofa next to Hannah.

Hannah took Cole's hand and placed it in on her belly. Cole had a look of wonder on her face. She looked up at Marc. "Wow, you can really feel it."

"Would you like to feel it?" Hannah said, directing the question to Audrey.

"Are you sure?" asked Audrey.

Cole moved so that Audrey could take her seat. "Sit here, Audrey," said Cole. "Audrey is a doctor in the city. She works in one of the hospitals."

"Really?" asked Marc.

"Yes, but I've only ever seen one baby delivered," said Audrey as she settled in next to Hannah. "It was like witnessing a miracle."

Audrey allowed Hannah to take her hand and place it on her stomach. Audrey smiled when she felt the baby move.

"Amazing," Audrey said.

Hannah kept her hand over Audrey's as they shared the intimate gesture. "How far along are you?"

"It should be any day now," said Hannah. "And it can't happen soon enough. I'm so big now I can hardly move. Poor Marc has to do all the chores by himself. I can barely manage to get any food on the table at the end of the day."

It was obvious by the huge grin on Marc's face that he couldn't care less. He beamed with pride and love for Hannah. Cole reached an arm over his shoulder.

"You're gonna be a dad, Marc! Can you even believe it?" asked Cole.

"Hardly," he said humbly.

It was decided that they'd have tea on the porch so Audrey and Cole assisted Hannah to a chair while Marc got the tea and glasses. Cole sat on the top step of the porch leading down to the yard, Marc leaned on the porch railing, and Audrey and Hannah occupied the two chairs.

"Have you been to the far side of your hay field lately?" Cole asked Marc. "There's a cruiser parked in the tall grass."

"Seriously?" asked Marc.

"Yeah, the other woman who came with Audrey and me is a pilot. That's Ava, who Ida told you about. Only, she was injured in this big explosion as we left the city, so she's resting up until she's well enough to fly," said Cole. "I figured you wouldn't mind it if we parked the cruiser there for a little while. I just didn't want you to be surprised if you happened upon it."

"A big explosion?" asked Hannah.

"It's a long story," said Cole.

"Well, sometime I'd like to hear it," said Hannah.

"Wow. What's it like to fly?" asked Marc.

"It's pretty astounding. You can see so far," Cole said, looking off as if picturing it in her head. "It actually makes you feel very small."

Audrey watched Cole. She'd never thought of the experience of flying in that way. She looked around the small farmhouse and yard and toward the open landscape in front of them. The expanse of the sky, the openness of this place, made her feel exposed. In the city, everything was compact, orderly, for maximum use of space.

As Cole and Marc began to talk about something else, Audrey allowed herself to study them, not really listening to what they were saying. Cole lounged on the top step, leaning back against one of the support posts of the porch. She was handsomely fit and comfortable in her own skin, her dark hair perfectly tousled at the front. Just beyond her, Ginger slowly meandered about the yard, eating dry autumn grass.

Marc was enjoying whatever they were talking about. He smiled warmly and often. His brown eyes sparkled in the midday sunlight. Hannah was smiling and watching the banter between Cole and Marc. She is glowing, thought Audrey. Everyone seemed happy and the fondness between the three friends was easy to see.

Audrey was pulled from her thoughts when she spotted someone approaching the house from the dirt path. It was a young woman wearing a collared white shirt and rust colored pants that were rolled up just slightly over the top of ankle-high shoes. Her hair was light brown and straight, with blond highlights from the sun, and it was cut in a straight line just below her jaw, not quite touching her shoulders. She smiled as she approached the house, waving with one hand, carrying a basket in the other.

Cole stood as the young woman approached. "Jess, nice to see you."

Jess held her hand up to shield her eyes from the sun and smiled up at Cole, cocking her head slightly to one side, as she was not quite as tall as Cole.

"Hi, Cole. I didn't expect to see you here."

Audrey could now see that despite the work clothing she was wearing that she had a thin, girlish figure. She's pretty, thought Audrey. She noticed the way Jess regarded Cole and felt a jolt of jealousy in the pit of her stomach. *And she's attracted to Cole.*

Cole turned in Audrey's direction. "Audrey, this is Jess."

"Hi," said Audrey.

"Hi," said Jess.

"What's in the basket?" asked Cole. She playfully made a move to peek at the contents.

"Some fabric for a new dress," said Jess and looked over at Hannah. "For the wedding."

Hannah smiled and began to explain to Audrey. "As soon as I recover from having this baby, Marc and I are getting married." Marc looked lovingly at her. "There will be drinking, music, and dancing… lots of dancing."

"It'll be a great party," said Jess. She moved to take a small jar from the basket and handed it to Marc. "I traded eggs and some muscadine wine for the fabric and for this—it's sourwood honey for you." Jess extended the jar in Hannah's direction.

"Oh, I do love fresh honey," breathed Hannah.

"I know you do." Jess smiled. She hesitated before making her exit. "Well, I best be headed home. Good to see you all. It was nice to meet you, Audrey."

Jess's over-the-shoulder glance at Cole didn't go unnoticed by Audrey.

"So, Audrey, do you have family in the city?" asked Hannah.

"Uh, no, actually I don't. My parents died when I was young. I grew up in a boarding school in the cloud city of London. A boarding school is a kind of like an orphanage, but with a study program. And students live there year round."

As Audrey watched Cole listening intently she realized they'd never talked about their parents. They had been too focused on the intense feelings of the present.

"I'm sorry. That must have been difficult for you," said Hannah.

"I miss them of course," said Audrey. "But sometimes you don't get to choose the path your life takes, do you?"

"That is a true statement," said Marc.

"And do you find being a doctor fulfilling work?" asked Hannah.

"I do," said Audrey. "I get joy from helping people."

Audrey noticed Cole still watching her so she looked in Cole's direction and smiled. The direct gaze made heat rise to her cheeks. Audrey felt her face flush slightly.

"Say, Cole," said Marc, "I wonder if you'd help me with something while you're here. I need a second set of hands out in the barn to reset the plow."

"Sure," said Cole.

"We'll just be a minute, ladies," said Marc as he and Cole walked toward the barn.

Audrey turned in Hannah's direction. Hannah was studying her. Audrey smiled and blushed shyly, realizing that Hannah probably could tell by the way she watched Cole walk away that she had feelings for her.

"Have you known Cole for long?" asked Audrey.

"Not as long as Marc. They've been best friends forever. I only got to know Cole better once Marc and I got together. That's been several years now."

"I…I have…" Audrey wasn't sure what to say. She looked down at her hands holding the glass of tea.

"I can tell you have feelings for her," Hannah said. "More than a few young women in this area have tried to get Cole's attention and without success. You must be quite something."

Audrey laughed lightly. "I think Cole is quite something."

"That is for sure. Cole is extremely honest, loyal, and I dare say if she fell in love with someone her heart would be completely unguarded."

Audrey looked up to meet Hannah's gaze. "I understand."

"You seem to be a genuinely nice person, in addition to being stunningly beautiful. But Cole doesn't have a lot of experience with love. I would hate to see her get hurt. What are your intentions toward her?"

"I don't know," answered Audrey truthfully. She was a little taken aback by Hannah's candor, but at the same time, found it refreshing. "Our situation is…complicated."

"Try your best not to hurt her, okay?"

"That's the last thing I want to do," said Audrey, looking directly at Hannah. "Believe me when I say that."

"I do. But we don't always get what we want do we?"

Before they could talk further, Cole and Marc returned. Cole suggested that they should probably head back to her house and leave Hannah to rest. There were hugs all around before they climbed back on top of Ginger and rode up the dirt path and out across the hay field. Marc waved after them as they rode away up the rutted path.

"Your friends are nice," said Audrey.

"I thought you'd like them," said Cole, "Audrey, I'm sorry I never asked you about your family."

"That's okay. We haven't spent much time talking have we?" Audrey smiled, leaning against Cole's shoulders.

"No complaints from me about that. I hope we have lots of time together. I want to know everything about you."

Audrey squeezed Cole just a little tighter, while Cole placed her hand over Audrey's arms at her waist.

❖

As they rode up to Cole's house, they saw Ava reclining against a post on the porch. She waved in their direction as they rode up. Cole helped Audrey dismount and then she rode over to the barn to stow the saddle and get Ginger feed and water. Audrey stepped up on the porch near Ava.

"You look much better, Ava." Audrey placed her hand on Ava's forehead. "And your temperature seems good. How do you feel?"

"Restless," replied Ava.

"I'm sure."

"Did you reach Jenna?" asked Ava.

"I did. I told her after another day or so you'd probably feel well enough to fly us back to the city."

"And how are things there?" asked Ava.

"Two of the city quadrants are currently floating on the ocean. Their propulsion systems collapsed completely. The other two are still in the air but at a much lower altitude to better help with the repairs."

"I suppose it could have been much worse."

"Jenna thinks it'll be another three weeks before all repairs are complete. She said she's been flying in supplies and engineers from all over."

"You two were gone for quite a while," Ava said, looking at Cole who was now walking toward them. "Where did you go?"

"We rode over to see my friend, Marc," answered Cole.

"How long have you been up, Ava?" asked Audrey. "Should you lie down for a while?"

"Maybe so." Ava smiled weakly. "The house was so quiet. I just thought I'd get some fresh air. Ida and Vivian will be back shortly. They said they were going to the 'lower field,' whatever that means."

"It means they are likely digging potatoes," said Cole. "I should probably go help them. Are you two okay here for a little while?"

"We'll be right here when you get back," said Audrey. She smiled at Cole and they held each other for a bit with their eyes. Audrey then offered a hand to Ava and helped her into one of the chairs on the porch. They watched Cole walk away, and then Ava turned to Audrey.

"There's such a strong attraction between the two of you that I could cut it with a knife," said Ava. "I must have been blind to not notice it sooner."

"I know."

"It doesn't matter," said Audrey. "I can't stay here. And she can't live with me in the city."

"Just like that?" asked Ava. "You won't even try?"

"It could never work." Audrey was starting to have doubts that this was the case. *Maybe it could work and I'm too scared to even try. I feel if I really give myself to Cole I could completely lose myself in her.* That thought was what scared Audrey more than living on the ground. Audrey knew that when they were intimate, Cole held nothing back. But the same wasn't true for Audrey. Fear or something else kept small barriers in place between them.

Those same barriers had never been an issue with other lovers before, but Audrey could tell that a love affair with Cole set a different expectation for emotional intimacy. Audrey wanted this, she had sought it out, and yet it scared her more than she wanted to admit.

CHAPTER TWENTY-THREE

The day turned to evening, and evening turned to night. Everyone had retired to their separate quarters, however, Cole wasn't sleeping. Audrey was snuggled into her shoulder as Cole lightly caressed her hair. Cole lay awake reflecting on the day. A loud knocking at the door echoed through the darkened house. Cole jumped up and headed toward the door only to find Marc, out of breath, with a panicked look on his face.

"Marc!" Cole said with surprise.

Vivian and Ida came from their room also to see who had come so late to knock at the door.

"What's wrong?" asked Ida.

"It's Hannah," Marc gasped, breathing hard. "The baby is coming and something isn't right!"

Just as he said that, Audrey appeared at Cole's side. "Marc?"

"Audrey, I need your help," Marc pleaded. "It's Hannah. Something is very wrong." He looked as if he were about to start crying.

"Marc, of course I'll help if I can," Audrey said. She put her hand on his arm. Then she turned a questioning look toward Cole. "Cole?"

"We'll hitch the wagon. That will be fastest," said Cole. "Marc, you ride back to Hannah. We're minutes behind you."

"I'm going with you," said Ida, joining the huddle.

"We're all going!" said Vivian. "Cole, help me with the wagon."

Marc climbed back on top of his horse and headed off into the night at a fast clip. Moments later everyone but Ava was in the wagon headed out behind him. Ava stood in the doorway, wrapped in a blanket, and watched them leave. Audrey feared the ride in the wagon would be too rough for Ava so she asked her to remain behind.

Vivian pushed Ginger into a full gallop. The minutes seemed to drag by. They all clung to the wagon to stabilize themselves during the frenzied ride.

As they pulled up in front of Marc and Hannah's house, they heard a scream from inside. Audrey was swiftly out of the wagon and through the front door with Ida right on her heels. Marc appeared at the door to their bedroom, his face sweaty and blood-streaked.

"I don't know what to do to help!" Marc was near panic. "She's in so much pain. It's been going on for hours!"

"Marc, I think you should wait outside and let Audrey take over," said Ida. She placed her hands on his arms and pushed him out of the room. "Everything is going to be okay," she added as she closed the door in front of him.

Marc stood stunned in the center of the room. Cole moved to him and threw her arms around his shoulders. He clung to Cole and let the tears come. Vivian placed a comforting hand on his back while Cole consoled him.

After a short while, Ida appeared at the door. "We need clean cloths and hot water."

Cole and Vivian launched into action. Cole delivered the cloths and the water to the door, briefly getting a glimpse of the scene inside. She could see Audrey bending over Hannah who was moaning and writhing in pain.

Ida pushed Cole away from the door. "Go be with Marc, Cole. He needs you now." She closed the door as Hannah screamed.

Inside the room, Audrey had assessed the situation.

"Hannah, I'm going to help you okay?" Audrey leaned over so that Hannah could see her face and stroked Hannah's sodden forehead. "I need to turn the baby. The baby's shoulder is stuck."

Hannah nodded but didn't respond.

"This is probably going to hurt, but I need to get the baby moving through the birth canal..." *so that the baby can breathe.* Audrey didn't finish the thought so as not to frighten Hannah.

Audrey then looked at Ida. "Are you ready for this?"

"I'm ready."

❖

Hannah's screams ripped through the room like a lightning strike. Marc paced the floor while driving his fist into his abdomen; tears stained his cheeks. Cole felt helpless. She decided to match his pacing, from time to time, taking his arm and telling him everything would be okay, and that Audrey wouldn't let anything happen to Hannah or the baby.

After what felt like an eternity, Hannah's cries subsided and there was nothing but quiet from the bedroom. The silence was broken by the unmistakable wail of an infant. Marc stared at the door of the room where Hannah lay.

A brief second later, Audrey appeared at the door, holding the baby, still red and fresh from the womb, wrapped in a small blanket. Her arms and sleeves were covered in blood. Despite that, she smiled, and spoke to Marc. "You have a daughter."

Marc moved to stand beside her. "Hannah?"

"She's doing fine," said Audrey. "Let's take the baby to her."

Audrey handed the tenderly wrapped infant to Marc. He carried the little one back to Hannah's bedside. Ida was seated on the bed next to Hannah, holding her hand and wiping her face with a cool cloth.

"She's beautiful," said Marc with wonder in his voice. He looked down at Hannah who smiled weakly.

Cole and Vivian had gathered in the doorway. Audrey wiped her arms and hands with a clean, damp cloth. Cole took Audrey's hand. She was so grateful that Audrey had helped her friends.

"Audrey, how can we repay you?" Marc asked. "I feel certain that our daughter would not be here on this Earth if it wasn't for you."

Audrey had been happy to help. Being able to witness and help bring the gift of life was a gift in and of itself.

Hannah turned her head so that she could meet Audrey's gaze. "What's your middle name, Audrey?"

"Emma."

Obviously sensing what Hannah was suggesting, Marc smiled and kissed his new baby girl. "Hello, Emma. Welcome to the world."

Hannah reached up to touch Marc's arm. He lowered himself to sit beside her on the bed.

"Is that okay with you, Audrey?" Hannah asked.

"Yes." Audrey's voice broke as she felt a knot of emotion rise in her throat. "I'm incredibly touched."

Cole stepped closer to Audrey and put a protective arm around her shoulders.

In a flash, Ida took charge of the situation. "Now, Marc, you leave the baby with me, as we need to let our new mother get some rest." Ida reached for baby Emma and motioned for everyone except Hannah to leave the room. "Cole, you three go on back home to Ava. I'm going to stay here tonight with Hannah."

"Thank you," whispered Hannah.

Exhausted but incredibly happy, they climbed into the wagon and headed out into the darkness toward home. Vivian was in the front seat, guiding Ginger, while Cole and Audrey sat in the bed of the wagon with their backs against each side of the bed, facing each other. Cole watched Audrey's face in the moonlight. She seemed deep in thought. Cole decided to let her be.

Eventually, Audrey looked up and met Cole's unwavering gaze. Cole smiled. Audrey moved to the other side of the wagon and buried her face in Cole's chest.

Cole held her close. "Audrey, you did real good. You are an incredible gift." *I love you.* Cole didn't say the last part aloud. She felt that she finally knew what being in love meant. She kissed the top of Audrey's head.

Audrey wrapped her arms around Cole's waist. They held each other the rest of the way home.

By the time they reached the house, it had gotten quite chilly. Vivian even remarked as they unhitched the wagon that they might see frost in the morning. They watched their cold breaths as they walked to the porch.

Audrey and Cole were wide-awake from the night's events so Cole decided to build a fire. *Hot tea and the warmth of a fire would be just the thing to take the edge off the day.*

As Cole carried the hot tea from the kitchen, Audrey stood near the fireplace, clasping her arms about her chest and staring into the flames. She had never experienced an open fire and was mesmerized by its soothing warmth.

"I've never sat by a fire before." Audrey reached for the mug of tea that Cole offered. "And now I think I might never leave this spot."

"There isn't much that's more of a purveyor of the comforts of home than a stone fireplace and a wood fire," mused Cole. She sat in a nearby chair and sipped her tea.

The room was dark, only lit by the soft, warm glow of the fire. As its flames stretched, the fire crackled and popped a hot cinder onto the hearth. Cole stretched out her boot and kicked the red ember back to where it belonged.

"Everything matters down here," she finally said, almost more to herself than to Cole. She was staring into the fire as she spoke.

"What do you mean?"

"I'm not used to being the sole physician on hand, like this evening with Hannah. What if I had misread the situation or used the wrong technique?" Audrey turned to look at Cole. "There was no backup. No surgical team. No other doctors to call in. Just me. What if I hadn't been enough?"

"But you were enough."

"But what if I hadn't been? Everything I did tonight saved Hannah and the baby, but if I had done something wrong, one or both of them might not…might not have lived." Her voice broke as she thought about what might have been. "That's what I mean by everything matters. Everything is so visceral, so close to the surface, so immediate."

"You do what you can do," said Cole. "You do the best you can and everything else is in God's hands."

Audrey studied Cole's face and thought about what she said. "What does that even mean?" Audrey had never heard someone speak in those terms.

"It means you, we, don't control everything. Some things are out of our hands and are in the hands of God, a higher power. A power greater than ourselves."

"I'm not used to thinking about things in that way," said Audrey. "As a doctor, you feel responsible for the person you're attending."

Cole stood and put her arms around Audrey, pulling her close. "And tonight, the doctor was miraculous."

Cole kissed Audrey lightly on the lips. Audrey then leaned into Cole's shoulder.

"Thank you."

"If this had happened in Easton, the care they would have received would have been based on their level of income." Audrey considered her words. "Here on the ground, care is given if care is available, with no regard for monetary payment." Audrey watched the flames intently. "Marc and Hannah wanted to give me something in return so they named their baby after me. What could carry more value than that?"

"It's important for people to give in kind for works they receive," said Cole. "But sometimes just the gift of being able to help is all the return you need. I would say this was one of those times."

CHAPTER TWENTY-FOUR

The next morning, after coffee and breakfast, Vivian and Audrey rode over to check on Hannah and the baby and to take Ida a fresh change of clothes. Cole stayed behind with Ava. Cole sat on the top step leading from the porch down to the yard and was enjoying her cup of coffee. She seemed deep in thought to Ava, who decided to join her.

"How are you doing, Cole?"

Cole looked up at Ava. "I'm fine. Why do you ask?"

Ava took a seat beside her on the top step. "I feel like I'm responsible for turning your life upside down. If I hadn't crashed nearby that first evening then you wouldn't have met me, you wouldn't have spent time in Easton, and you wouldn't have met Audrey."

"You know, I never told you this," Cole said without turning to look at Ava. "But the night I released the hatch on your cruiser I knew my life was about to change. I had this flash forward moment, and I just knew that after releasing that hatch, things would never be the same. I knew that everything that followed would be a result of that one act."

They were silent for a bit before Ava spoke.

"I think we'll probably leave tomorrow."

"I figured," said Cole.

Ava wanted to say something about Audrey leaving, but she didn't know what to say. She knew that Audrey was conflicted about her feelings for Cole, and even Ava wasn't sure exactly what that meant, so how could she offer any comfort to Cole? From Ava's perspective, the past few days on the ground had not been as pleasant as her previous visit. She knew it wasn't anyone's intention to make her feel like the odd woman out, but that's how she felt. It was clear that Cole and Audrey had intense feelings for each other, whereas she and Cole had simply shared an affectionate friendship. Ava was also restless and ready to get back to her work, even though she didn't know exactly what to expect when they returned to the city.

"Do you think you'll ever come back here?" Cole asked.

"I don't know. Would you like it if I did?"

"Of course I would. I care about you, Ava. I had hoped that we were friends."

Ava smiled. "We are friends, Cole."

"And I don't want to be the person who hurts your friendship with Audrey."

"Audrey and I will always be friends. We're just going through some sort of transition," Ava said, hoping she was right. She knew that she and Audrey shared too much history to not at least be friends, but emotions were swirling inside Ava that she hadn't quite figured out. A mixture of jealousy, anger, and just plain regret intermittently surfaced, and she seemed to have no control over any of these emotions whenever she was alone with Audrey. The *might have beens* now haunted her thoughts.

"Audrey is definitely going back with you, isn't she?" asked Cole.

"I think so."

Ava had questioned Audrey for not staying with Cole. But if she were in Audrey's place, would she make a different choice? To stay would mean giving up her entire life for a relationship that was in its infancy. Ava guessed she would choose to go back to the city, too. She'd be too afraid to take such a risk, despite her feelings.

"If you don't mind, I'm going to go for a walk," said Cole. She set her coffee cup on the porch railing. She then walked back into the house for a jacket before heading out toward the tree line. Ava suspected this might be one of those times when Cole needed some time alone to think on her special granite overlook.

Ava was actually fine with a little alone time. She smiled at Cole as she struck out on her walk. In a couple of hours, Audrey and

Vivian would be back, and she and Audrey could begin to plan their departure.

❖

The trip to see Marc, Hannah, and little Emma had been quite pleasant. Vivian hadn't pressed Audrey to talk on the way over, and seeing the baby doing so well cheered Audrey considerably.

After returning to Cole's house, the rest of the day was spent doing the usual chores, with spells of rest on the porch soaking in the sun. The morning had been chilly, but the temperature had climbed to a nice early autumn level by late afternoon. As the sun began to dip, the chill began its return to the air.

Cole and Audrey had cooked dinner together, much to the entertainment of Ava, who watched from the kitchen table. Audrey realized that cooking non-synthetic food presented a whole new learning curve for her.

That evening, Ava turned in early and Cole asked Audrey to go for a walk. Audrey sensed that there was something Cole wanted her to see. Cole picked up a small lantern as they left the house, telling Vivian they would return in a little while.

❖

The evening was cool and clear. The shadows were growing long and dark as they walked the mile between Cole's place and Black Mountain. They had been holding hands during their stroll through the woods. Audrey was highly sensitive to the pulsing sounds of the cicadas around her.

"So, where is this you're taking me?" Audrey finally asked after about twenty-five minutes of walking, the last bit of which was quite steep.

"You'll see," said Cole, now walking ahead of Audrey as the path became narrower. "It's one of my favorite places."

The trail crested at the ridge and emptied them into an opening upon which resided an old tower structure. It looked to be about twenty-five feet off the ground, set atop heavy beams. The structure at the top was square with a wraparound deck and a tin roof that slanted gradually up on all four sides to a peak in the center. The moon was nearly full so visibility was fairly good as they climbed the stairs to the landing.

"It's an old government fire tower," said Cole. "I've always loved this place. I'd like to turn it into a house that I could live in one day."

Cole stepped into the interior and looked back at Audrey. "Just be careful not to lean on the railing. Some of it is rotted and needs to be replaced. Too many years exposed to the elements I suppose. But the interior is solid."

There was a combination wood-cook stove in the center of the main room. Cole began to start a fire with the small logs and kindling she kept stashed to warm the room.

Audrey walked around the inside of the space, taking note that there were candles and some heavy blankets rolled up in one corner.

"I keep a few things here so that I can spend the night sometimes," said Cole. "I'll spread out the bearskin and we can sit by the fire."

Cole spread the large, thick black fur in front of the stove as Audrey enjoyed the view from the windows that were set on all sides of the abandoned lookout. The moon cast a bluish light on the trees and ridges that surrounded them, creating a magical setting.

Audrey felt her heart rate increase as she realized they might do more than just sit by the fire. They were truly alone together for the first time since they'd made love in her residential pod in the city. She looked across the room toward Cole. Audrey noticed, even in the low candlelight, that Cole watched her with penetrating intensity. It was a look that shot straight through her chest. Her heart skipped. The room began to feel warmer from the fire Cole had lit, or was it just the flushed heat rising in Audrey's cheeks? She wasn't sure. She found the whole scene incredibly romantic. She moved to stand closer to Cole.

Cole ran her hands slowly up and down Audrey's arms. Audrey wanted to feel Cole's hands on her bare skin so she began to unbutton her shirt. As the last clasp fell away, Cole placed her hands at the base of Audrey's neck and pulled her into a tender kiss. Then Cole moved her hands inside Audrey's shirt, pushing it down off her shoulders and onto the floor. Cole began kissing Audrey's neck, then her shoulders, before pulling her bra strap aside to kiss the mark where the strap had lain.

Audrey began to moan quietly as Cole ran her fingertips across Audrey's breasts.

Cole had decided that if Audrey was going to leave, she was going to give her one last night to remember. Maybe it would be enough to convince her to someday return. At any rate, Cole was going to take her time with Audrey tonight. She felt like they deserved this time together after everything that had happened, and she wasn't going to be rushed.

As Audrey reached to unfasten her bra, Cole unbuttoned her own shirt. She pulled Audrey to her so that Audrey's bare breasts brushed hers inside the opening of her shirt.

"Oh, Cole," whispered Audrey. "I want you so badly."

Cole responded with a deep, open-mouthed kiss, pulling Audrey down onto the bearskin rug in front of the glowing stove. Cole braced her body on one elbow as she ran her other hand over Audrey's breasts and torso. Every spot that Cole touched seem to shudder from the heat of her stroke.

Cole was having a hard time going slow. While she was enjoying the luxury of this pace, she felt like she was on fire and needed to possess Audrey, to take her, now. She pulled Audrey into a searing kiss.

Pulling away from Audrey's mouth only momentarily, Cole began to unfasten Audrey's pants and slip them down over her sensuous hips, and off. Then Cole dropped her own shirt to the floor and did the same with her trousers, then lay back down beside Audrey.

"Are you cold?" Cole asked. "Do you want a blanket?"

"Maybe."

Cole pulled a blanket over their mostly naked bodies. She removed Audrey's underwear and moved on top of her, placing her hips between Audrey's thighs. Bracing herself on her elbows above Audrey, Cole began to explore Audrey's breasts with her mouth. Audrey roughly fisted Cole's hair as a signal for her to take more of each breast into her mouth, which Cole was happy to oblige.

Audrey began to grind slowly against Cole. She reached down to push Cole's loosely tied briefs past her pronounced hipbones. Audrey needed to feel Cole's exposed center on hers.

"Please, Cole," breathed Audrey. "I need to feel you inside me."

Cole raised her head so that her face was very close to Audrey's. She wanted to look at Audrey as she came. Cole moved her hand down between Audrey's legs, caressing the wet folds, before answering Audrey's request.

"Look at me, Audrey. I want you to look at me while I'm inside you."

Their lovemaking was so intensely intimate that Audrey was having a hard time breathing. But she opened her eyes and looked into Cole's gaze as she felt Cole enter her. Audrey's hips thrust slowly at first, and then harder and with more ferocity, grinding relentlessly against Cole's strong hand, pulling her deeper. She felt the orgasm rise with such force that she felt like she would explode from pleasure. Audrey's mouth opened and her eyes began to flutter and close.

"Stay with me, Audrey. Look at me," said Cole. She closely studied Audrey's face as she climaxed.

Audrey tried to do as Cole asked, but as waves of ecstasy coursed through her body, she had to grasp Cole's shoulders and bury her face in Cole's neck to stabilize herself. She was shaking as tears began to brim and spill slowly down each of her cheeks. Audrey had never felt an orgasm with such force. Her loss of emotional control scared her.

"I've got you, Audrey. You're safe."

"Cole, I've never felt anything so intense." She clung to Cole's neck, whispering the words.

Cole took one of Audrey's hands and pushed it down so that Audrey could feel how wet she was. She pushed her fingers inside and Cole began to move rhythmically on top of her. Cole moved slightly so that she now straddled one of Audrey's thighs and could press her thigh against Audrey's still wet center. Audrey kept her fingers inside Cole as Cole moved against her hand, first slowly, then rapidly with more pressure.

Audrey realized that Cole was bringing them both to climax at the same time. Audrey dug the nails of her free hand into Cole's shoulder as she felt the orgasm take her over. Cole dropped from bracing herself above Audrey so that her full weight was on top of Audrey. She captured Audrey's mouth and kissed her long and hard. Audrey had never had anyone make love to her with such emotional force. She felt every nerve in her body twitch with arousal. But if Cole kept this up she was going to pass out. She pulled Cole's head down to rest on her chest and began to stroke her head and then her back. Audrey closed her eyes, savoring the weight and warmth of Cole's body over hers.

"I want to make you come again," said Cole.

Audrey moved to roll Cole on her back. She sat straddling Cole's hips so that they touched and could feel each other's wet arousal. Audrey began to kiss Cole's neck, then moved down to her firm nipples, all the while allowing her long hair to fall across Cole's torso. Cole relaxed into Audrey's tender caresses. After exploring Cole's subtly muscled torso with her mouth, Audrey sat up, flipping her hair back over her shoulder.

Cole raised up, placing her arms around Audrey's waist, she pulled her close so that she could put her mouth on Audrey's breasts again.

Audrey allowed Cole to pleasure her and then she pushed Cole back down until she was once again lying on the thick fur rug. She moved her hands from Cole's shoulders down across her small, aroused breasts, and across her long, lean torso. Audrey moved down so that she was now lying between Cole's legs and she began to kiss the inside of Cole's thighs, moving within inches of where she knew Cole wanted her but stopping before giving Cole release.

Cole was moaning and raising her hips toward Audrey's mouth. Finally, Audrey relented and put her mouth on Cole, pushing her tongue inside. Cole had her hand in Audrey's hair, at the back of her head, pushing her mouth harder against her. Cole was writhing from the stimulation, but Audrey refused to release her. Audrey wrapped her arms around Cole's hips and pressed even harder, feeling Cole climax under her touch. As she felt Cole gyrate, she lifted her mouth and pushed inside Cole to feel the muscles tighten around her fingers.

Cole was breathing hard and begged Audrey to stop for just a minute, but Audrey refused to move her hand. She pressed her body on top of Cole to ground her, while keeping her fingers in place.

"Cole, it's okay. I've got you this time." Audrey kissed Cole's neck.

After a few minutes, the shuddering subsided, Audrey withdrew her hand, and they lay holding each other in the moonlit room. Audrey rested her head on Cole's shoulder, rubbing her fingers lightly across Cole's chest. Cole turned her face slightly to place a long kiss on the top of Audrey's head.

"Audrey, what's going to happen to us?" Cole asked quietly.

"Oh, Cole. I don't know." Audrey rolled away from Cole so that her back was against Cole's bare chest. "I wish I knew the right thing to do."

"I don't know how I'm going to survive without you."

"I've never felt this way with anyone," Audrey replied, watching the embers dance inside the old stove. *And the way I feel about you scares me to death.*

Cole pressed against Audrey's back so that Audrey could feel Cole's small, erect nipples against her shoulders. She moved Audrey's hair so she could place a kiss on the back of her neck, then she moved down to Audrey's shoulders.

Audrey was becoming aroused again as she felt Cole's strong hand caress her lower back and then her hips before she moved to slip her hand between Audrey's legs from behind. Audrey exhaled sharply at the feeling of Cole moving to roll her over so that she could take her from behind.

Cole moved down so that she could place kisses at the small of Audrey's back, then trailed kisses up her spine to the base of her neck, all without removing her slowly stroking hand from between Audrey's legs. Audrey lay on her stomach. She moved so that Cole could press her thigh between Audrey's legs pushing them further apart. Cole held a handful of her hair and Cole's mouth was pressed to the base of Audrey's neck as she pushed her fingers inside her from behind.

"I want you to come again for me, Audrey."

Audrey didn't know if it was the fact that Cole had her pinned so that she couldn't help but let Cole gain entry to her hot, wet center, or if it was Cole's lips brushing her ear, or a combination of everything, but Audrey began to move underneath Cole, pressing into Cole's hand as she pushed deeper and deeper.

"Oh, Cole. I can't, please…"

Cole pumped harder and faster, filling Audrey more completely with each thrust. Audrey muffled a scream into the blanket as the orgasm claimed her entire body. She tried to roll over to face Cole, but Cole refused her. After letting Audrey rest for a moment, Cole began to move slowly again inside her, building steadily upward with gentle thrusts to make Audrey climax again. Audrey came fast, her body began to shudder with rippling aftershocks. Only then did Cole release her and allow her to roll over. She pulled Audrey into a tight embrace, kissed her forehead, and then her quivering lips.

Audrey was breathing hard and her face felt hot against Cole's chest. "You are an amazing lover," she breathed. She brushed her lips across Cole's chest.

"So are you, Audrey."

Audrey found her mouth searching out Cole's nipple, which she began to tease with her tongue, as she moved her hand down between Cole's legs. Audrey pushed her fingers inside and began to move slowly against Cole again.

Cole was so close already that she came fast and hard against Audrey's palm. Audrey held Cole tightly until she felt Cole relax against her. Then Audrey pulled the blanket up around them and snuggled into Cole's shoulder. *How am I going to leave you?*

Floating through the open door of the tower came the sounds of the tree frogs and crickets singing their late night rhythmic chorus, like some nocturnal heartbeat. Lulled by the soothing woodland sounds and completely spent, Audrey, holding Cole in her arms, drifted off to sleep in the soft light of the moon.

Chapter Twenty-five

Two months had passed since Audrey left with Ava back to the cloud city of Easton. Two months had passed without a word from Audrey about whether she'd ever return to Cole. Their final kiss good-bye had been heart wrenching for Cole. There was one desperate, hopeful moment when Audrey hesitated to board the cruiser. It led Cole to think she might stay on the ground with her. But then Audrey whispered, "*I'm sorry,*" against Cole's neck, climbed into the cruiser, and soared up.

Cole had waited for several minutes after the cruiser disappeared over the horizon, not yet able to accept that Audrey had left. As the realization of her loss sank in, a fog of profound sadness took her over. There seemed to be no words of comfort that her aunts could offer that would lift her spirits. The only person who could console her was Audrey. It was as if Audrey took a part of Cole with her when she left that day.

For weeks, Cole clung to the idea that Audrey had felt the same intense bond that she had felt and that this would be what brought Audrey back to her. But with each passing day, Cole had to fight the doubts that began to arise. To try to shake her heartache, Cole poured all her energy into the renovation project she'd begun on the old fire tower on Black Mountain. The busier she was, the less she could contemplate what might have been with Audrey, or so she hoped. At least the sheer exhaustion from the physical labor made it possible for her to sleep some at night. But the aching space she felt deep in her chest never left.

Cole wanted to create a living space in the tower now more than ever because it was where she and Audrey had spent their last night together. If nothing else, she wanted to be in the space that now felt almost sacred to her. When Cole dawdled in the rays of the setting sun, she could almost feel Audrey beside her. She savored these moments before stowing her tools and walking the mile back down the ridge to her aunt's cabin.

❖

Audrey felt like she'd been sleepwalking through her life since she returned from the ground. When she closed her eyes to sleep at night she couldn't escape the sensory memories of Cole inside her, on top of her, beneath her. She would awake aroused in the middle of the night unable to shake the intense feelings she had experienced the last time they made love. Like a ritual, Audrey would then pour herself a drink and stand at the window of her apartment to look out toward the horizon and wonder what Cole was doing at that moment. As she sipped the golden brown elixir, she would hold the shell between her fingers rubbing its even, raised ridges. Cole had pressed the shell into her palm as they said good-bye. What had Cole said about the bleached, weather-beaten seashell? That it was an object that reminded her of epic forces at work. *Forces greater than ourselves.*

Despite her sleeplessness, Audrey regularly put in requests for double shifts at the med lab. Keeping busy with others that needed her attention kept her from dwelling on what she'd found and then chose to leave behind.

Easton was still in the early stages of recovery from its near collapse. Certain transit lines weren't quite operational, and some citizens hadn't been able to return to their residential units because construction repairs hadn't been completed.

One morning, a teenage boy was brought into the med lab with a broken arm from a bad fall near one of the construction sites. He was tall, lean, and with his short dark hair, he could pass for a younger version of Cole. Audrey was so caught off guard by the resemblance and the rush of emotion that followed that she had to request one of the other doctors attend to the young man. Audrey blamed a weak stomach before excusing herself and running to the nearest restroom where she collapsed against the door and sobbed.

Audrey's colleagues could see that something was troubling her, but when asked, Audrey would only say that she was tired. The explosions had traumatized large numbers of people, so most assumed that Audrey had suffered some hardship related to these events and didn't press for details.

Audrey had also avoided contact with Ava since they returned to Easton. This wasn't too hard to achieve since Ava's flight schedule was so hectic. The day after they returned, Ava was assigned to several intensive routes with Jenna. They had been handling shuttle flights for medical supplies and emergency personnel around the clock.

It took two months for the flight engineers to get the cloud city back to its former elevation, and still not all turbines were operating at full capacity. Authorities held several individuals from the underground movement in custody, but the woman in charge, Meredith, had so far managed to elude them. Audrey had spoken with Sara briefly a couple of times. Sara had distanced herself from the movement since the day of the explosions and was still trying to come to terms with what role she'd played in the injuries and damages that had followed. The two of them had not talked about Cole or about the days that Audrey and Ava had spent on the ground. Sara tried to ask once, but Audrey told her she couldn't talk about it just yet. Sara must have sensed how fragile Audrey was feeling, and let her be.

Despite Audrey's heavy heart, the days after she returned to Easton passed quickly. Before she knew it, those days turned into weeks, and then those weeks turned into months, and Audrey was no closer to forgetting Cole than if she had left the ground yesterday.

CHAPTER TWENTY-SIX

On the ground, the first days of winter had come and gone. Despite the frigid cold snap, everyone had turned out to support Marc and Hannah on their wedding day.

As Marc's best friend, Cole stood with him at the church altar. Marc fidgeted with his pressed shirt, waiting for his bride to appear at the rear of the sanctuary.

"She'll be here. Why are you so nervous?" Cole leaned close to Marc so no one could hear her.

"You tell me when you're in the same position. I'm just nervous is all," said Marc. He straightened his collar for the hundredth time. "Getting married is a big deal."

"You're already a father. I would think being a husband would be easy at this point," said Cole. She shoved him playfully with her elbow. Ida shot them both a look that read, *Behave*.

Ida was holding baby Emma as she sat in the first row with Vivian. The church was packed with friends and neighbors who came to show support for this union.

The piano began to play the "Wedding March." Cole and Marc stood taller and turned to look toward the back entrance of the church. Jess Walker appeared first, as Hannah's maid of honor. She walked down the aisle before Hannah, carrying an arrangement of colorful ribbons, as flowers were out of season. Jess smiled at Marc and Cole as she walked carefully yet joyfully to join them.

Cole was struck by how pretty Jess looked in her new dress. Jess had made it especially for this day, cut from floral fabrics to complement what Hannah was wearing. The style of the dress highlighted the svelte curves of her slim frame. Jess's light brown hair was pulled back and pinned to show off her oval face and hazel eyes. Cole watched her walk to the front and stand across from them, leaving an open spot for Hannah to stand next to Marc. The minister joined them in preparation for the bride's arrival.

As Hannah entered the sanctuary from the back, all those who were seated stood and turned to admire her. Hannah practically glowed as she walked down the aisle

Marc smiled broadly and even blushed as Hannah reached the front and stepped to stand beside him. They faced the minister as he began his eulogy on commitment and the responsibilities of each to the other in this union.

Cole chanced a glance in Jess's direction. Jess caught Cole's eyes and smiled shyly. Marc and Hannah exchanged their vows, exuding love that seemed to envelop everyone.

After the ceremony, the wedding party reconvened in the fellowship hall for dancing, food, and general merriment over the event of the day. Two fiddle players, a guitar player, and someone on a standing bass joined the piano already in play to conjure up a rousing dance number. The floor became overrun with couples, old and young, enjoying the festive music. Dances didn't happen very often in the community, so on the rare occasions when they did, everyone turned out to participate.

Cole was slowly sipping a drink, lost in her solitude as she stood idly at the edge of the dance floor. Vivian spotted Cole and headed her way.

"Nice crowd for the wedding don't you think?" said Vivian as she stood beside Cole.

"Yeah, it was a nice service, too. I've never seen Marc so happy."

"I could stand to see you a little happier," Vivian said.

Cole smiled weakly. "Sorry."

"I think you should ask Jess to dance."

"What?" Cole turned to look at Vivian.

Vivian motioned in the direction where Jess was talking with a couple of other women. "She keeps looking over here at you. You haven't noticed?"

"No," replied Cole. But actually, she had noticed once or twice. Cole had been mostly keeping her gaze to herself because Margaret was also standing in that general direction and she didn't want to send any wrong signals her way.

"Go ask her to dance. She's a sweet girl and she's all dressed up for the occasion," said Vivian. "I feel certain she'll accept your invitation." Vivian gave Cole a nudge in Jess's direction. "Go. Be young. Dance."

Cole walked up to Jess, feeling shy and not very confident about her abilities as a dancer. "Would you…would you like to dance, Jess?"

Jess blushed at the question. "Yes, I would like that."

Cole extended her hand and Jess accepted. As they moved toward the dance floor, she noticed Margaret, who was standing several feet away, glaring at the two of them.

"I'm not sure I'm a very good dancer," said Cole as she led them onto the dance floor.

"Me either," replied Jessica with a sweet grin.

After a few minutes, the rapid rhythm of the tune slowed and took a more romantic, slow pace. Cole hesitated, not sure whether they should continue to dance or leave the floor. To her surprise, Jess took the slow tune as an opportunity to step closer to Cole, placing an arm around Cole's neck and leaning her head against Cole's shoulder. Cole was unnerved at first and responded rigidly. But then she gave in to Jess's generous gesture and held her close.

❖

Having danced through several songs, Cole asked Jess if she'd like to walk outside for some fresh evening air. They held hands as they left the large, crowded room. The sky was clear and the January air was quite chilly. Cole and Jess walked out under an oak tree, near a patch of moonlit open grass. Cole leaned up against the tree, enjoying her view of the quarter moon. She pulled her jacket tighter to ward off the chill. While Cole was looking up at the moon, Jess leaned in and placed a tentative kiss on her cheek. This took Cole by surprise. She smiled at Jess, who was standing very close to her.

"What was that for?" asked Cole.

"You just seem so sad. Like maybe you just need someone to be sweet to you." She caressed Cole's arm with her small, delicate hand.

"I'll be okay. But thank you."

"You miss her, don't you?"

"So much so that it makes my chest ache." Cole felt a knot in her throat. She fought back the sadness rising in her chest. She didn't want to cry in front of Jess. It was supposed to be a jubilant night. She didn't want to bring her melancholy to those who were actually able to enjoy themselves.

Jess continued to stroke Cole's arm. "It's okay if you want to cry. There's no shame in showing your feelings, Cole. There's no one here but us."

And that was all it took—that sweet gesture from Jess gave Cole permission to allow her grief to rise to the surface. Cole buried her face in her hands and let the tears come. Jess put her arms around Cole. "Everything is going to be okay. Just let it out. You can't keep holding all of this sadness in."

After a few minutes, the sobs subsided. Jess brushed a remaining tear away from Cole's cheek with her thumb.

"Feel better?"

"Yeah, I guess I do," said Cole. She sniffed and wiped her cheek with the back of her hand. "Thank you, Jess."

"Oh, Cole, I wish I could make it better for you." Jess squeezed Cole one more time.

Cole put her arms around Jess and allowed herself to be comforted by the sincere embrace. After a lasting moment, they separated.

"Do you feel like dancing a little more?" asked Jess.

"Yeah, that'd be nice," replied Cole.

Jess hooked her arm through Cole's and they walked back toward the sound of a cheerful melody.

The feeling of Jess's embrace surprised Cole. It hadn't had the overwhelming fire that she'd felt with Audrey, but it had warmth and tenderness, and it cast a warm glow in the center of her chest. Just acknowledging her sadness and letting go of some of it with Jess had lightened Cole's mood just a little.

Jess and Cole kept close to each other the rest of the night, laughing, talking, and dancing. And for a little while, Cole forgot to be sad.

CHAPTER TWENTY-SEVEN

Audrey spotted Ava, Kate, and Sara at a corner table. They waved and she moved through the café to join them. It had been four months since the explosions that had rocked the city, and life was only now beginning to get back to normal in certain sections of the commercial district. Sara looked tired and a bit crestfallen. The death of idealism had claimed a harsh toll.

When Kate messaged Audrey to invite her out for lunch, Audrey thought maybe enough time had passed since the destruction of her city and her leaving Cole, and that it would be nice to see her friends again, including Ava.

"Hi, friends," said Audrey, as she took an empty chair at the table. "Have you already ordered?"

"Yeah, but just now," said Ava and gave their waitress a wave.

"Audrey, I've hardly seen you. Where have you been hiding?" asked Kate, taking a sip of her beverage. "And have you lost weight?"

"Oh, you know, I've just been putting in some extra hours at the med lab. They needed the help and, well…" her voice trailed off.

"She needed the distraction," finished Ava.

Audrey shot Ava an annoyed look.

"Distraction from what?" asked Sara. "Oh, sorry."

"Not from what, but from whom? Right, Audrey?" said Ava.

Audrey shot Ava another look. Was she intentionally trying to be a jerk? Or was she just that insensitive?

"I feel like I'm missing part of the story here," said Kate.

"You remember Cole," said Ava. "She was at your birthday party at Club Six."

"Oh yeah, she was really cute. Kinda quiet if I remember correctly," replied Kate.

"She and Audrey had a thing," said Ava.

Ava knew she was making Audrey angry by being so obnoxious about what had happened between Audrey and Cole, but she couldn't stop herself. Somewhere, deep inside, she was still angry about it all and she wasn't even sure why. It could have been the loss of her, it could have been because of the loss of some potential relationship with Audrey, or it could have been that she knew that she'd lost Audrey to Cole and she wasn't used to losing. Losing made her want to lash out at Audrey for the hurt she was feeling.

"I'm sure Cole is in good hands down on the ground," said Ava. "Did you ever get to meet Margaret? I'll bet she rushed in to comfort Cole the minute the cruiser lifted off."

Ava continued, ignoring the hurt look on Audrey's face. "Margaret has it bad for Cole. I saw it firsthand. I wouldn't be surprised if Cole finally gave in to her. She's pretty. As a matter of fact, she looks a lot like you, Audrey." Ava regretted the hurtful words the minute she said them, but it was too late to take them back.

"Please stop! Please stop talking about this," Audrey said. "I know you're hurt, Ava. But there's no need to be so cruel. I don't know who Margaret is, but thinking of Cole with her is the last thing I need to hear about right now."

For some reason, the tone of Audrey's voice caused Ava's temper to flare. Having Audrey point out that she was acting badly in front of her friends just made her even more furious.

"You know, suddenly, this table is feeling very crowded. I have to get back to work anyway. Enjoy your lunch." Ava stood and glared back at Audrey.

Ava dropped her cloth napkin on the table and turned to leave, almost running into the waitress returning with their food. "Sorry," Ava muttered as she continued her exit.

Everyone sat in shocked silence for a few minutes while the young woman set several plates of food on the table. Kate was the first to speak.

"What was that all about?"

Audrey covered her face with her hands and exhaled. Sara reached over and covered Audrey's hand with hers.

"Are you all right?"

"Okay, stop. Will someone please tell me what is going on?" said Kate.

"Audrey, sweetie, do you feel like talking about this?" asked Sara.

Audrey sighed and leaned back in her chair. "I fell in love."

"With Cole?" asked Kate. "But I thought she…"

"Are you going to see her again?" asked Sara.

"How? How can I see her? One of us would have to be willing to give up our entire life to be with the other. It's just not realistic."

"Since when does love listen to reason?" said Sara.

"Never," quipped Kate. "Absolutely never."

Audrey gave them a painful smile before she buried her face in her hands.

"I admit, I don't know what to do. I thought I'd be miserable if I stayed with Cole, but the truth is I feel twice as miserable here. I think about her all the time. I think about her every minute."

Audrey looked up at Sara. "Did I make the wrong decision?"

"I don't know if I can answer that. Tell me how you feel about Cole. I mean, you guys definitely have chemistry. Even I picked up on that. But talk to me. How do you feel about her for real?"

Audrey was quiet for some time, rolling a fork over and over on her napkin, watching her reflection repeat on its shiny silver surface. Sara and Kate ate quietly while they waited for her to speak.

"Truthfully? I don't know if I can live without her. She's like no one I've ever met. When I'm with her, she is completely there. When I think about what it was like to be held by her…" Audrey's voice trailed off. "I felt contentment. I felt loved, completely, without reservation."

"Wow," said Kate. "Audrey, I've never heard you talk this way about anyone."

"I know." Audrey felt tears rise in her throat. "I feel like I made a huge mistake and now so much time has gone by. I haven't even spoken to Cole. How would she ever trust me again? I'm sure she thinks I've forgotten her. We haven't spoken since I left four months ago. I thought I was doing the right thing for both of us. But the truth is I didn't really give Cole a choice. I just left."

"This isn't all on you, Audrey," said Sara. "I mean, did Cole even ask you to stay with her?"

Audrey didn't answer.

"Oh, I'm so sorry, Audrey." Sara moved to sit closer to her and put her arm around her. "I had no idea all this was going on with you. I'm so sorry."

Audrey dabbed at her eyes with her napkin. "Did I tell you that I delivered a baby while I was down there?" She sniffed and smiled at the memory. "Cole's best friend, Marc, and his girlfriend, Hannah—I suppose his wife now—they were planning to have their wedding this month. Anyway, I delivered their baby. That was only the second time I've ever gotten to be present when a child was born. They were so grateful that they actually named the baby after me."

"Wow, that's incredibly touching. What a sweet gesture," said Sara, with her hand still resting on Audrey's shoulder.

"What am I going to do?" Audrey asked as she gave them a pleading look. She knew there was no easy response.

CHAPTER TWENTY-EIGHT

Cole had actually gotten some decent sleep after dancing with Jess for a few hours at the wedding party. She sleepily walked toward the smell of coffee brewing and found Vivian was dressed and ready to go. Not only that, but a crossbow was laid out on the kitchen table.

"Good morning," said Cole. "You're up early."

"I thought we should go look for a deer," said Vivian. She was wearing a thick wool jacket with large buttons and she had a knitted cap on her head pulled down to her ears. "It's going to be cold for a few days so it's a good time to cure the venison."

"Okay," said Cole with a yawn. "Just let me get dressed."

When Cole returned a few minutes later, Vivian reached for the crossbow and a sheath of arrows, which she handed to Cole, "We'll be back in a few hours if all goes well." She leaned over to give Ida a quick kiss.

"You two be careful out there," said Ida. "Just remember you aren't the only ones hunting today."

Cole stopped to kiss Ida on the cheek before following Vivian out into the still dark morning. "We're always careful," she called back over her shoulder.

❖

The air was biting cold and dry in Cole's lungs as she and Vivian struck out and up the ridge behind their house and down the other side. They picked up a deer trail and walked for another long stretch, up another ridge, and down a gradual descent to the edge of an oak flat. It was the time of year when bucks were getting antsy as their testosterone levels rose, and the amount of available daylight began to shrink. Mature deer tended to move out of their usual thicket hideouts so they could nose around for does. The goal for Cole and Vivian was to find a place with thick cover but also with food value, like greenbrier. They found a spot and took up positions several feet apart making sure to be camouflaged by the greenery. They then waited in a kneeling position.

The pink of the sun had begun to appear as they'd come down the last ridge, but it had not warmed things up yet. The air was still chilly enough that they could see their breath as they sat silently, waiting. Cole shifted and rubbed her hands together for warmth as her body temperature dropped from sitting in the frigid air motionless.

Quietly, almost in a whisper, Vivian began to speak. "Did I ever tell you that I fell in love before I met your aunt Ida?"

"No," replied Cole. Not only had Vivian never mentioned this, but Vivian rarely talked when they were in the woods together hunting.

"I was young, and I got my heart broken pretty badly. As a matter of fact, I thought I would never be in love again. I thought I'd never be able to trust anyone enough to truly love."

Vivian had a wistful look on her face as she recounted the events from her past. "I thought I'd had my one chance at true love and that I would have to be alone forever since it hadn't worked out," said Vivian. "And then I met Ida and realized I had been terribly wrong."

Cole was quiet for a few minutes, reflecting on her aunt's words.

"You think that's what is going on with me, don't you?" asked Cole.

"I can't know what's really going on with you, Cole. I just want you to keep yourself open. Don't let sadness close off your heart."

Cole assumed that Vivian was talking about Jess. They had enjoyed each other's company at the dance following the wedding, but Cole was feeling too raw to think of Jess in any way except as a friend.

"I just need some time," said Cole. "I promise not to be sad forever."

"You can be sad as long as you need to be." Vivian put her hand on Cole's shoulder. "Just be mindful of others and the happiness they might have to offer. You never know what life has in store for you; that's all I'm saying."

Cole gave her a weak smile and nodded. After that, they sat in silence. Cole was unsure how long they'd been crouched there when she caught Vivian stirring quietly. She trained her eyes in the direction Vivian was looking. There was a rustling sound but no sight of what was causing the noise yet. Then she saw it. A young buck had moved into their field of vision in the midst of the stand of oaks.

For Cole, there was something elemental about hunting, something deep-seated and hard-wired that linked her to the land. Cole never took life ungratefully, unnecessarily, or without honoring the sacrifice of the animal.

Cole waited for Vivian to take the shot. She was likely to be more accurate with the crossbow, and since she'd spotted it first, Vivian should get the prize. But Cole sensed something wasn't right with Vivian. As Cole waited, Vivian continued to hesitate. She looked over at Vivian, who slowly lowered her weapon and nodded to Cole, a clear indication that she wanted Cole to take the shot.

Cole quickly brought the bow to full tension in front of her, raising herself slightly on her knees in order to get a clear shot but also to remain hidden from view. Few skills relied so heavily on the connection between body and mind as shooting a bow. From the soles of your feet to the position of your head, it all had to come together for the true shot. As Cole's forward arm pulled taut against her back arm, she exhaled and released the arrow. In a split second, the buck was down. Her shot had hit its mark. A chest shot just behind the shoulder blade, through its lung and heart. The animal was dead by the time they reached its side.

Cole kneeled next to the magnificent animal, placing her hand on its neck to feel the warmth and the life force escape its body. She could see the transition by watching the animal's eyes. After a respectful pause, Cole looked up at Vivian. "Are you okay, Aunt Vivian?"

"Yeah, I'm fine. Thank you for stepping in. That was a great shot."

Vivian then knelt so that she was eye level with Cole.

"This is the first time I've used the bow since, well, since the day you were hurt." She swallowed, searching for words. "I saw the woman's face when I raised the bow."

"Oh," responded Cole. She hadn't really thought of how the tragic event might have affected her aunt. She didn't know how to respond to this revelation.

"I used to be tougher. Maybe I'm getting old," Vivian said. "I think I'm still just a little shaken up. I'll get past it." She smiled tentatively at Cole. "Let's get the deer back to the house."

"If you start, I'll find a small tree we can use as a brace to carry him."

Before she moved away, Cole put her arms around her aunt and held her for a minute. Cole was grateful for many things, not the least of which was the bravery and love that Vivian had always shared with her. Vivian returned the embrace.

"You're a good kid, Cole," Vivian said as she pulled away and roughed up Cole's hair. "Now let's get to work."

CHAPTER TWENTY-NINE

The renovation of the tower was coming along nicely. There were still some boards along the railing that needed to be replaced, but Cole had decided to finish the interior space first. She could always continue to work on the exterior details after she moved in. It would be much easier to do the finishing work if she was living in the space and not spending so much time walking back and forth from the farm. A mile wasn't so far, but it made for a long walk. And at this time of year, when the days were shorter, the time it took to walk seriously cut into the daylight hours for working on the structure. Vivian and even Marc had helped out on occasion, but they both had their own tasks to complete on their homesteads. Vivian was managing most of the daily chores on the farm to give Cole a chance to work on the tower.

The renovation project had been well timed. Cole had wanted to turn the old fire tower on Black Mountain into a permanent house since she was a young kid. The repair work on the structure had sometimes been quite hard, but it provided a much needed focus and distraction for Cole. She welcomed any project that could occupy her mind and move her thoughts away from Audrey and the ache that Audrey's departure had left behind.

Cole was hammering some short boards into a corner so she didn't hear Margaret until she was already inside. As Cole reached for another nail, she jumped at the sight of Margaret before her. Margaret was holding out the small bucket of nails in Cole's direction.

"Margaret?" was all Cole could muster. She stood up to face Margaret, who set the pail of nails on a nearby table.

"Hey, Cole." Margaret attempted a sweet smile. "I just thought I'd come see how your place was coming along. Marc told me it was looking really fine, so I just wanted to see it for myself."

Cole doubted very seriously that Marc had said much, if anything, to Margaret, but she wasn't going to argue. There was no snow on the ground, but the weather in February was cold enough to warrant a fire in the old tower's wood stove to warm the interior space. Margaret unfastened her coat and dropped it onto a nearby, straight-backed wooden chair.

"I can't believe you'd walk all the way up here just to say hello," said Cole. "This is quite a hike from your place."

"Well, I had to drop some things off with Jess, so I was sort of in the neighborhood." Margaret fingered some of the tools scattered about. "Besides, you never did take me up on my offer, so I thought I'd just bring myself by in person. You know, as a reminder of what you're missing out on."

Margaret leered slyly in Cole's direction, slightly tilting her head as she spoke.

A knot began to form in the pit of Cole's stomach. She didn't want to be alone with Margaret. And the tone in Margaret's voice made her uncomfortable. She cleared her throat and moved so that the table offered a physical separation between them. But Margaret was quick to maneuver and was now standing on the same side of the roughhewn wooden table.

Margaret was dressed in her usual revealing style. Her dress was unbuttoned enough to show cleavage, with a light sweater to ward off the chilly air. If Cole didn't know Margaret, she might even find her attractive. Her buxom curves were definitely easy to find attractive, but it was her motives that always stopped Cole from accepting Margaret's advances. There was something about Margaret that set Cole on edge. She didn't feel safe around her.

"I know all about your little fling with the doctor," said Margaret. "I know you must be feeling very used and abandoned. It's just not right."

Margaret continued to inch closer to Cole. She reached over to run a finger across Cole's forearm, which made Cole pull away reflexively.

"I'm okay, Margaret. Besides, I can't just suddenly turn off feelings and feel something for someone else," said Cole nervously.

"I'm not so sure. I saw you with Jess after the wedding." Margaret gave Cole a seductive look. "It seemed like you were having a good time to me. That's all I'm talking about, having a good time."

Cole had run out of space to back away from Margaret any further. She was now pressed against a built-in cabinet along the far wall. Margaret moved into Cole's space, placing one leg between Cole's thighs.

"We could have a really good time together, Cole," said Margaret. She ran a finger along the inside of Cole's shirt collar before letting it meander down her collarbone. "You're building the perfect hideout up here. Surely you aren't planning to stay up here all by yourself."

"Margaret, I'm flattered that you would want to spend time with me." Cole thought the best offense might be a flattering defense. "I'm, well, I'm just not ready to be involved with anyone right now..." Margaret hands continued their downward motion. Her palms were now resting on Cole's chest.

They were standing very close, and Cole had no way out. Margaret pressed her breasts against Cole's chest. Cole turned her head so that her mouth would be a bit more out of reach, but Margaret pressed her lips close to Cole's ear instead.

"You might not be ready to be involved, but your body is telling me something different," said Margaret as she ran her hands across Cole's erect nipples. The shirt fabric was thick, but not so thick that Margaret could miss this detail. Margaret took one hand and firmly grabbed Cole's crotch. She began to move her hand back and forth slowly over the fabric of her trousers between her legs.

Cole didn't want to respond to Margaret's physical proximity, but she was becoming aroused in spite of herself. She turned to face Margaret, feeling flushed, and knowing that her speeding heart rate was giving her away.

"Touch me," Margaret whispered close to Cole's mouth before grabbing Cole's hand and pressing it against her breast. As Cole's hand remained pinned under Margaret's, images, scents, thoughts of Audrey came flooding to her. *Audrey, I miss you so badly. And now you seem even farther away.* Cole fiercely pulled her hand away and pushed Margaret roughly back enough so that she could slip away.

"I can't…I can't do this." Cole gasped as she tried to put distance between herself and Margaret.

"Are you serious?" Margaret said. "You can't put your hands on me like that and then just leave me hanging. You know you want this as much as I do. I can feel it."

Margaret raced to intercept Cole who was now trying to escape through the open door to the outside deck. Margaret reached again for Cole's arm. This time, Cole reacted to Margaret's clutch and jerked her arm away with such force that it caused Cole to stumble backward. As Cole attempted to regain her balance from deflecting Margaret's advances, a small stack of boards just outside the doorway caught the back of her foot, causing Cole to stumble into the railing at the edge of the tower's deck. Before Margaret could reach for Cole, the railing gave way with a loud crack, causing Cole to tumble to the ground below. Time seemed suspended as she felt herself topple through the railing. She swung her arms to right herself, but failing to do that, in the last second tried to protect her head with her arm as she struck the ground. Her last instant of awareness was darkness.

❖

Audrey was near the intake desk at the med lab when she felt a strong internal jolt. She reached out to grab the edge of the counter to steady herself. She felt lightheaded and sick. She swallowed hard and brushed her forehead with her hand.

"Audrey? Are you okay? You look like you're going to pass out. Let's find you a place to sit down," Audrey's colleague, James, said, guiding her by her elbow to an unused examining room on the floor.

"I'm…I'm okay," Audrey said. "That was the strangest feeling."

"Are you sure you don't want to sit down?" James hadn't yet released his gentle grip of her elbow.

Audrey placed her touchscreen pad on the counter and steadied herself.

"I'm almost done with my shift. Would you mind covering for me?"

"Sure, Audrey, whatever you need," said James. "But are you sure you're okay to leave?"

"I have to leave," she said over her shoulder. "Thank you. I owe you one."

Audrey broke through the med lab doors into the crisp, cold air. She couldn't explain it, but she knew that what she felt had something to do with Cole. Something was wrong. She'd felt a wave of pain pass through her as if she'd been hit by something hard—some immovable force. She cued her handheld comm device to call Ava and raced to the transit center while she waited for Ava to answer.

"Hello?"

"Ava, this is Audrey."

"Audrey?"

"Where are you? I need to talk to you…now." Audrey had been prepared to ask Jenna to take her to Cole but she felt she owed it to Ava to ask her first.

"I'm at my place."

"I'm on my way over."

About ten minutes after placing the call, Audrey was standing at Ava's door.

"Audrey, I was surprised to hear from you. What's up?" Ava stepped aside to allow a slightly breathless Audrey to enter her apartment.

"I came to ask you to fly me down to the ground to be with Cole." Audrey had decided that the most direct approach would get the quickest results. Whether Ava's response was yes or no.

"Just like that?" asked Ava. Her posture read as defensive, but her voice carried a slight tone of hurt.

"Yeah, just like that." Audrey pulled her into an embrace, despite Ava's defensive pose. "I never should have left her in the first place. I think even you knew that." She released Ava so that she could see her face. There were tears on Ava's cheeks. Audrey realized she'd never seen Ava cry before.

"I'm sorry I've been so awful to you lately, Audrey. You didn't deserve it. I'm not even sure I understand why I've been acting this way."

"I'd like to think it's just growing pains."

Ava laughed and wiped away tears with the palm of her hand. "You think?"

"Our relationship needed to change and grow, Ava. But I've never stopped loving you, my friend."

"I love you too, Audrey."

They hugged for several moments. Audrey relished the closeness she'd been missing from their friendship.

"Now, will you take me to Cole? Please."

❖

Forty-five minutes later, Audrey was throwing clothes into a travel bag when she heard the buzzer announce Sara's arrival at her apartment. She let Sara in, leaving the front door ajar so she could return to her flurry of packing.

"You're going back, aren't you?" said Sara.

"Yes." Audrey stopped and looked at Sara. "I have to. Something is terribly wrong with Cole. I can feel it as sure as I can feel my own heart beat."

Audrey pushed the last garment into her overstuffed bag and yanked the zipper. "I called Ava. I'm meeting her in a few minutes."

Audrey shouldered her bulging bag and gave Sara a wistful smile.

"Listen, everything is going to be okay. You'll see Cole and everything will be okay," said Sara.

"I hope you're right." Tears began to brim at the edge of Audrey's lashes. "Sara, I'll miss you terribly. You have always been an amazing friend to me." Audrey wiped a tear with the back of her hand. "I hate feeling like I've had to make a choice between my lover and my friends."

"Even though that's kind of what you're doing?" said Sara with a teasing smile.

"Yeah," responded Audrey, sniffling and wiping another tear. She pulled Sara into an embrace. "I love you, my friend. Be well."

They held each other close and then Audrey pulled away. "I've got to go. Ava is meeting me at the hangar deck in like ten minutes."

Audrey reached for the two bags she'd packed. "I'm leaving the keys for you. Someone might as well stay here and eat all the food I've left."

"And sleep in your cozy bed. No roommates. Ah, this will be heaven." Sara watched Audrey prepare her exit. "Seriously, be happy, Audrey. You owe that to all of us."

And with one last look over her shoulder, Audrey was out the door and down the hallway toward the lift.

Ava was prepping her two-seated cruiser as Audrey walked up with her two bags. Ava looked up and could tell Audrey had been crying.

"Hey, my flying isn't that scary…okay, well maybe it is," she joked as she took one of the bags from Audrey and stowed it in a compartment under the booster.

"Thank you," said Audrey. "I don't know what I would have done if you had said no."

"Despite my bad behavior lately, I do want you to be happy. I'm your friend and I love you."

Ava stowed Audrey's bag and helped her into the passenger seat. Ava pulled the lever to lower the hatch as the cruiser lifted and rotated in the direction of the launch tube. Audrey leaned back against the seat and closed her eyes. Soon she would be with Cole. She had no idea what to expect when she got there. Would Cole be happy to see her? Or would she just be angry? Would she even be okay? Worry over Cole's safety overtook Audrey's mind. She braced for launch as Ava notified the flight tower of their takeoff.

Audrey watched as the lights in the launch tube began to flicker at ever more rapid intervals in front of the sleek craft indicating that a launch sequence was in progress. In a matter of seconds, the small cruiser would be sent swiftly down the metallic tunnel and out into the cloudless sky and she would be closer to Cole than she'd been in weeks.

CHAPTER THIRTY

Audrey stood in the doorway of Cole's room, taking in the scene. The group of women who had gathered around Cole's bed turned as she stepped into the room. Ida rushed to embrace her.

"Audrey! Thank the Lord you are here!" Ida said. She pulled Audrey into a hug. "I've never been happier to see anyone my entire life."

Audrey smiled weakly and looked in Cole's direction. "Somehow I knew she needed me. I don't know how. I just knew I had to come."

Audrey hurried to Cole's bedside and began to run her fingers over Cole, asking what had happened. Jess moved quietly aside to make room for Audrey.

"She took a bad fall from the deck of the tower," said Vivian.

"The fire tower?" asked Audrey. Thoughts of the night they had shared in that space came flooding back.

"Cole's been renovating it, and it's about a twenty-five-foot drop from the deck," Vivian said. "Margaret was there when it happened." Vivian motioned in Margaret's direction.

"It was an accident!" said Margaret. "I swear, we were just talking and she fell through the railing."

"Uh huh," responded Vivian with a doubtful look on her face. "If I find out different when Cole wakes up I'm going to…" Ida put a calming hand on Vivian's arm before she could finish her threat.

Audrey gave Margaret an intense onceover. *I'll deal with you later. Right now, I need to focus on Cole.*

"Margaret was there when it happened. She ran to Jess's house. Then Jess and her brother Matthew got Cole here as quick as they could in the wagon. Is it bad that she hasn't woken up yet?" asked Ida. "I'm also worried that her arm is broken." Ida pointed toward a swollen, bruised area on Cole's forearm.

Audrey ran her fingers gently over the injured area. "It might just be a bad bruise or it could be a fracture. Do we have anything we can use for a splint, just to be safe?" She looked over at Vivian and Jess. "I'll need something to wrap it with and to hold the splint in place."

"I'll get something," said Vivian. As she moved to exit the room, she nearly bumped into Ava, who'd been standing back while Audrey rushed to Cole's side.

"Ava!" Vivian pulled her into an embrace.

Ava moved inside the room. She stood close enough to Audrey to be of help, but just far enough to be out of the way.

"Ava, love, so good to see you," said Ida, looking up from the bedside.

Audrey continued to examine Cole. Her pupils seemed even, her heart rate was good; aside from the small swelling on her arm, and at the back of her head she seemed okay. There might be some bruising on her ribs, but there seemed to be no other fractures.

Cole moaned slightly. Audrey leaned close to her face and placed a gentle kiss on her cheek.

"Cole, I'm here. Wake up, Cole," said Audrey as she brushed her hand along Cole's brow. She leaned in again and spoke near Cole's ear. "I came back. I'm here, baby. Please wake up for me. I'm sorry it took me so long to get here. I've done nothing but miss you since I left. I've been so stupid. I should have stayed with you…"

As Audrey said the last words, Cole began to open her eyes. "Audrey?" She blinked repeatedly as she fought to come out of the fog. "Am I dreaming? Are you really here?"

"I'm really here."

Cole moved to put her arm around Audrey and then let out a groan.

"Don't move your arm, Cole. You've got a bad bruise and maybe a fracture," said Audrey as she lovingly squeezed Cole's hand.

"I'm sorry you had to come back for this. I'm a mess," said Cole.

"You're not a mess." Audrey leaned over and kissed her lips. "You're perfect."

"Ava?" Cole glimpsed her standing behind Audrey.

"Hi, Cole."

"I think you saved me again." Cole's comment was meant for Ava, but her eyes were on Audrey.

After the painful process of tightly wrapping Cole's arm between two slender splints made from stripped birch branches, Audrey left Cole to rest, although leaving her for even a few minutes was almost more than Audrey could stand. Ava had stayed around to make sure everything was okay before she left Audrey and headed back to Easton. Her flight schedule was still tight from the reconstruction effort, so her time to linger was limited.

"Audrey, you're going to be okay, right?"

"I'm really okay. Actually, I'm better than okay. I feel like I'm home. As crazy as that sounds, that's what it feels like to me." Audrey put her hand on Ava's arm. "Thank you so much, Ava. You are a true friend. You have given me a great gift. A second chance."

"I don't know about that. But I'm glad I could do something to make this right. You and Cole are good together." Ava looked back toward the women and Matt who were sitting and standing near the front of the house. "They all love you. It shows. And as a doctor, you could do a lot of good down here on the ground."

"It does feel great to be needed," admitted Audrey. "And to be wanted. I hope the same for you someday."

"Well, I'm leaving you, but I want you to keep this communication beacon. I'm leaving a solar charger with it. If you ever need me…or anything, just press this button, and the beacon will transmit your location." Ava handed the small device to Audrey.

Audrey kissed Ava on the cheek. "Thank you."

Ida and Vivian walked over to say good-bye.

"Please take care of my friend," Ava said.

Vivian put an arm around Audrey's shoulder. "You have our word on that," Vivian said with a smile.

Ava and Audrey walked away to where she'd left the cruiser. They embraced once more with a promise that Audrey would contact Ava if she needed anything. Then Audrey watched her leave. The cruiser rose slowly, rotated, and accelerated over the trees toward the eastern horizon.

Audrey was alone with her thoughts as she watched the cruiser disappear. She took a deep breath and exhaled. The cold, crisp air held the scent of pine and rich earth. Audrey felt a calm peace descend into her chest as she turned to walk back to the house. She had brought two suitcases with her and had left all her other belongings behind. She felt like she'd left everything and found everything at the same time. A feeling of serenity washed through her as she stepped up onto the porch.

CHAPTER THIRTY-ONE

The first night after the fall from the tower, Cole and Audrey stayed with Cole's aunts. But tonight, they desired time alone, and so had decided to spend the evening in the newly renovated tower.

Since Cole hadn't officially moved in, Marc and Vivian had transported a bed and other small items of furniture so that they could spend their first night in the tower with some level of comfort. Audrey and Cole walked the mile between the house and the tower at a leisurely pace. Audrey wanted to enjoy the fall of night and the woodland serenade that the darkness brought forth from the small but vocal creatures that seemed to surround them as they walked.

As Audrey climbed the steps to the tower landing and stepped through the front door, sensations came back to her in a rush of the night she'd spent with Cole so many months ago. The bearskin rug was still in front of the small wood stove in the center of the space, but now she noticed that a high, four-poster bed rested along the back wall. She turned and smiled at Cole, who had just finished lighting a candle set under a glass globe. The glass covering was designed to block the breeze from open doors and windows, but its surface also seemed to amplify the dancing flame cast around the walls of the room.

"It's magical."

Audrey moved close to Cole, with one hand at Cole's waist, she allowed her other hand to stroke Cole's arms where the splint had been tightly bound.

"How does your arm feel?" Audrey traced the bruise with her fingertip.

"My arm is fine. But there are other places on my person that need your immediate attention." Cole smiled down at Audrey.

"I know the feeling."

Audrey closed her eyes as she felt Cole's fingers at the back of her neck under her thick hair. Audrey kept her eyes closed to relish the feel of Cole's touch, the press of Cole's lips to hers. Audrey found the buttons of Cole's shirt and began to release each one from its tether so that she could push inside the shirt's opening to Cole's bare chest. Her fingertips registered the shiver Cole's body surrendered under her touch.

"Audrey, I missed you so much." Cole brushed hair away from Audrey's face. "When I would lie down at night, I felt like a lead weight was sitting on my chest. I was so low that even the air felt heavy."

"I labored under the same heaviness without you." Audrey caressed Cole's face. Candlelight flickered in Cole's eyes. "Right now I don't want to think about that. I want to focus on the lightness I feel when I'm with you. Kiss me, Cole."

Cole obliged. She delivered a long, deep, unhurried, luxurious kiss. Audrey thought the kisses they'd shared previously were breathtaking, but this kiss seemed to pierce her soul. She swore she felt the earth move, or maybe it was just weakness building in her knees. In either case, she wanted to lie down. Audrey pulled Cole toward the bed where they watched each other undress, dropping clothing on the floor in unconcerned patterns.

After climbing into bed, Cole leaned up, bracing on one elbow. The blanket fell to Cole's waist, revealing her naked shoulders and back. She looked over, noticing the way Audrey's long, lush auburn hair fanned across her pillow like a feather pressed between the pages of a book. A shimmering mixture of moonlight and candlelight cast soft shadows across her lovely features. The crest of one pastel shoulder was visible at the edge of the blanket.

Cole settled back down on the bed and propped herself up on the pillow. She reached out with her other hand to tenderly caress the shape of Audrey's exposed milky shoulder with her fingertips.

Cole marveled at how they fit together like puzzle pieces when they made love, physical opposites creating a whole. Even the thought of Audrey's soft curves pressed against her caused a stirring at her center that urged her to take Audrey in a heated rush. But she tamped down the fire at her core just enough so that she could savor this moment of closeness.

"What are you thinking?" said Audrey.

"That you are beautiful." Cole leaned into Audrey, kissing her neck tenderly. She slid down slowly, covering Audrey's breasts with feathery kisses. "You are beautiful and I feel like I'm on fire when I'm close to you like this."

Audrey swept her hands through Cole's hair, pulling Cole's mouth firmly against her breasts. "Cole, four months of wanting you…of needing you…I don't think I can take this slow."

"Okay," was all that Cole uttered before she moved on top of Audrey and settled her hips between Audrey's legs and slowly moved against Audrey's wet center. The temperature in the room seemed to spike. Cole kicked the blanket off of them, moved her hand between them, and after a few teasing strokes, pushed inside. Audrey gasped for air as Cole brought her to orgasm, pressing her open mouth against Cole's neck and raking her nails down Cole's back.

Audrey fisted the hair at the back of Cole's neck, pulling her down into a deep, slow kiss. Feeling the weight of Cole on top of her and the now relaxed, firm hand cupping the tender spot between her legs, Audrey felt at peace, knowing this was exactly where she should be. She shifted so that her thigh was between Cole's legs and then moved her hand down so that she could touch Cole.

"Cole, look at me." Audrey wanted to read the intense connection on Cole's face.

Cole managed to maintain eye contact until Audrey's strokes brought forth a shuddering climax. Audrey pulled Cole's head to her chest, caressing her hair and then her shoulders with a gentle motion. She placed a lingering kiss into Cole's hair. "Ruth Coleman George, I will never get enough of you."

Audrey felt complete and content. She knew the source of her serenity was Cole, who made her feel safe and cherished. Cole relaxed into the lush softness of Audrey's breasts.

They drifted off to sleep encircled within the shelter of each other's arms.

❖

Morning light streamed in through the open doorway of the tower. Audrey stretched sleepily and reached over to find that Cole was already up. She rolled on her side, pulling Cole's pillow close to her chest, registering the white seashell resting on a small square table near the bed where Audrey had placed it the night before. The shell represented for her the epic forces that brought them together and had been a sentimental talisman while they were apart, reminding her of her time with Cole on the ground.

She pulled a sweater around her shoulders and walked out to where Cole stood leaning on the now sturdy railing that Vivian had repaired while Cole was recuperating. Cole was sipping a steaming cup of coffee, and surveying the view of the valley and rolling hills before them. Morning fog still nestled between the Blue Mountain ridges. The air was cold and fresh, and somewhere nearby, an owl spoke with a haunting call. Cole had brought a knitted throw out with her, and it draped across her broad-shouldered, lean frame as she enjoyed the view.

"Good morning," said Audrey as she walked up and snuggled into Cole, who opened the small throw so that Audrey could share in its warmth against the morning chill.

"Morning," said Cole smiling, punctuating the greeting with a kiss on the top of Audrey's head.

"Mmm, you smell good." Audrey nuzzled her nose into the spot just under Cole's ear.

"You feel good," said Cole, pulling Audrey closer.

"I need to thank Vivian for replacing that railing." Cole looked at the spot where she'd fallen through. "So, what do you think now that it's daylight?"

"Cole, the tower is really beautiful. And the view is amazing."

"It was the highest spot I could find. It was the closest I could get to you."

Audrey was struck by Cole's words. "That's really what you thought?"

"Yes."

"Cole…"

"Audrey, I hope you know that I was fixing up this place for you…for us." Cole paused. "It was always for us."

Audrey looked up at Cole. "There's something I want to ask you."

"Ask me anything," said Cole.

"During that time when we didn't talk, when we were apart… how…how did you know that I would come back? I mean, not that I won't be forever grateful for your faith in me, but how did you know that we would be together? You said you did all this for us. How did you know?"

Cole smiled at Audrey. "You know that book I keep with me? The small black one with the frayed leather cover?"

"Yes."

"There's a passage in that book that I kept repeating to myself after you left." Cole had a distant look in her eye as she called up the text from memory. "It says, 'We fix our eyes not on what is seen, but on what is unseen, since what is seen is temporary, but what is unseen is eternal.'"

"Unseen? What is unseen?"

"Love." Cole looked at Audrey with glistening eyes. "Love is the greatest unseen force in the universe. I had faith that love would bring you back to me."

Audrey felt an intense warmth flood through her body as she let Cole's words sink in. It was true. Love had brought her back to Cole.

"I love you, Cole." Audrey knew she could finally say those words to Cole, without reservation.

"I love you, Audrey. I think I have since the first moment I held your hand in mine."

Audrey buried her face into Cole's neck and kissed her. Audrey felt content, loving Cole and being loved completely.

About the Author

Missouri Vaun grew up in rural southern Mississippi, where she spent lazy summers conjuring characters and imagining the worlds they might inhabit. It might be a little-known fact that Mississippi breeds eccentrics, and eccentrics make for good storytelling. Missouri spent twelve years finding her voice as a working journalist in places as disparate as Chicago and Jackson, Mississippi, all along filing away characters and concepts until they seemed to rise up, fully formed. Her stories are heartfelt, earthy, and speak of loyalty and our responsibility to others. She and her wife currently live in northern California. Missouri can be reached via email at: Missouri.Vaun@gmail.com.

Or on the Web at: MissouriVaun.com.

Books Available from Bold Strokes Books

The 45th Parallel by Lisa Girolami. Burying her mother isn't the worst thing that can happen to Val Montague when she returns to the woodsy but peculiar town of Hemlock, Oregon. (978-1-62639-342-4)

A Royal Romance by Jenny Frame. In a country where class still divides, can love topple the last social taboo and allow Queen Georgina and Beatrice Elliot, a working class girl, their happy ever after? (978-1-62639-360-8)

Bouncing by Jaime Maddox. Basketball Coach Alex Dalton has been bouncing from woman to woman, because no one ever held her interest, until she meets her new assistant, Britain Dodge. (978-1-62639-344-8)

Same Time Next Week by Emily Smith. A chance encounter between Alex Harris and the beautiful Michelle Masters leads to a whirlwind friendship, and causes Alex to question everything she's ever known—including her own marriage. (978-1-62639-345-5)

All Things Rise by Missouri Vaun. Cole rescues a striking pilot who crash-lands near her family's farm, setting in motion a chain of events that will forever alter the course of her life. (978-1-62639-346-2)

Riding Passion by D. Jackson Leigh. Mount up for the ride through a sizzling anthology of chance encounters, buried desires, romantic surprises, and blazing passion. (978-1-62639-349-3)

Love's Bounty by Yolanda Wallace. Lobster boat captain Jake Myers stopped living the day she cheated death, but meeting greenhorn Shy Silva stirs her back to life. (978-1-62639334-9)

Just Three Words by Melissa Brayden. Sometimes the one you want is the one you least suspect. Accountant Samantha Ennis has her ordered life disrupted when heartbreaker Hunter Blair moves into her trendy Soho loft. (978-1-62639-335-6)

Lay Down the Law by Carsen Taite. Attorney Peyton Davis returns to her Texas roots to take on big oil and the Mexican Mafia, but will her investigation thwart her chance at true love? (978-1-62639-336-3)

Playing in Shadow by Lesley Davis. Survivor's guilt threatens to keep Bryce trapped in her nightmare world unless Scarlet's love can pull her out of the darkness back into the light. (978-1-62639-337-0)

Soul Selecta by Gill McKnight. Soul mates are hell to work with. (978-1-62639-338-7)

The Revelation of Beatrice Darby by Jean Copeland. Adolescence is complicated, but Beatrice Darby is about to discover how impossible it can seem to a lesbian coming of age in conservative 1950s New England. (978-1-62639-339-4)

Twice Lucky by Mardi Alexander. For firefighter Mackenzie James and Dr. Sarah Macarthur, there's suddenly a whole lot more in life to understand, to consider, to risk…someone will need to fight for her life. (978-1-62639-325-7)

Shadow Hunt by L.L. Raand. With young to raise and her Pack under attack, Sylvan, Alpha of the wolf Weres, takes on her greatest challenge when she determines to uncover the faceless enemies known as the Shadow Lords. A Midnight Hunters novel. (978-1-62639-326-4)

Heart of the Game by Rachel Spangler. A baseball writer falls for a single mom, but can she ever love anything as much as she loves the game? (978-1-62639-327-1)

Getting Lost by Michelle Grubb. Twenty-eight days, thirteen European countries, a tour manager fighting attraction, and an accused murderer: Stella and Phoebe's journey of a lifetime begins here. (978-1-62639-328-8)

Prayer of the Handmaiden by Merry Shannon. Celibate priestess Kadrian must defend the kingdom of Ithyria from a dangerous enemy and ultimately choose between her duty to the Goddess and the love of her childhood sweetheart, Erinda. (978-1-62639-329-5)

The Witch of Stalingrad by Justine Saracen. A Soviet "night witch" pilot and American journalist meet on the Eastern Front in WW II and struggle through carnage, conflicting politics, and the deadly Russian winter. (978-1-62639-330-1)

Pedal to the Metal by Jesse J. Thoma. When unreformed thief Dubs Williams is released from prison to help Max Winters bust a car theft ring, Max learns that to catch a thief, get in bed with one. (978-1-62639-239-7)

Dragon Horse War by D. Jackson Leigh. A priestess of peace and a fiery warrior must defeat a vicious uprising that entwines their destinies and ultimately their hearts. (978-1-62639-240-3)

For the Love of Cake by Erin Dutton. When everything is on the line, and one taste can break a heart, will pastry chefs Maya and Shannon take a chance on reality? (978-1-62639-241-0)

Betting on Love by Alyssa Linn Palmer. A quiet country-girl-at-heart and a live-life-to-the-fullest biker take a risk at offering each other their hearts. (978-1-62639-242-7)

The Deadening by Yvonne Heidt. The lines between good and evil, right and wrong, have always been blurry for Shade. When Raven's actions force her to choose, which side will she come out on? (978-1-62639-243-4)

Ordinary Mayhem by Victoria A. Brownworth. Faye Blakemore has been taking photographs since she was ten, but those same photographs threaten to destroy everything she knows and everything she loves. (978-1-62639-315-8)

One Last Thing by Kim Baldwin & Xenia Alexiou. Blood is thicker than pride. The final book in the Elite Operative Series brings together foes, family, and friends to start a new order. (978-1-62639-230-4)

Songs Unfinished by Holly Stratimore. Two aspiring rock stars learn that falling in love while pursuing their dreams can be harmonious—if they can only keep their pasts from throwing them out of tune. (978-1-62639-231-1)

Beyond the Ridge by L.T. Marie. Will a contractor and a horse rancher overcome their family differences and find common ground to build a life together? (978-1-62639-232-8)

Swordfish by Andrea Bramhall. Four women battle the demons from their pasts. Will they learn to let go, or will happiness be forever beyond their grasp? (978-1-62639-233-5)

The Fiend Queen by Barbara Ann Wright. Princess Katya and her consort Starbride must turn evil against evil in order to banish Fiendish power from their kingdom, and only love will pull them back from the brink. (978-1-62639-234-2)

Up the Ante by PJ Trebelhorn. When Jordan Stryker and Ashley Noble meet again fifteen years after a short-lived affair, are either of them prepared to gamble on a chance at love? (978-1-62639-237-3)

Speakeasy by MJ Williamz. When mob leader Helen Byrne sets her sights on the girlfriend of Al Capone's right-hand man, passion and tempers flare on the streets of Chicago. (978-1-62639-238-0)

Venus in Love by Tina Michele. Morgan Blake can't afford any distractions and Ainsley Dencourt can't afford to lose control—but the beauty of life and art usually lies in the unpredictable strokes of the artist's brush. (978-1-62639-220-5)

Rules of Revenge by AJ Quinn. When a lethal operative on a collision course with her past agrees to help a CIA analyst on a critical assignment, the encounter proves explosive in ways neither woman anticipated. (978-1-62639-221-2)

The Romance Vote by Ali Vali. Chili Alexander is a sought-after campaign consultant who isn't prepared when her boss's daughter, Samantha Pellegrin, comes to work at the firm and shakes up Chili's life from the first day. (978-1-62639-222-9)

Advance: Exodus Book One by Gun Brooke. Admiral Dael Caydoc's mission to find a new homeworld for the Oconodian people is hazardous, but working with the infuriating Commander Aniwyn "Spinner" Seclan endangers her heart and soul. (978-1-62639-224-3)

UnCatholic Conduct by Stevie Mikayne. Jil Kidd goes undercover to investigate fraud at St. Marguerite's Catholic School, but life gets complicated when her student is killed—and she begins to fall for her prime target. (978-1-62639-304-2)

Season's Meetings by Amy Dunne. Catherine Birch reluctantly ventures on the festive road trip from hell with beautiful stranger Holly Daniels only to discover the road to true love has its own obstacles to maneuver. (978-1-62639-227-4)

Myth and Magic: Queer Fairy Tales edited by Radclyffe and Stacia Seaman. Myth, magic, and monsters—the stuff of childhood dreams (or nightmares) and adult fantasies. (978-1-62639-225-0)

Nine Nights on the Windy Tree by Martha Miller. Recovering drug addict, Bertha Brannon, is an attorney who is trying to stay clean when a murder sends her back to the bad end of town. (978-1-62639-179-6)

Driving Lessons by Annameekee Hesik. Dive into Abbey Brooks's sophomore year as she attempts to figure out the amazing, but sometimes complicated, life of a you-know-who girl at Gila High School. (978-1-62639-228-1)

Asher's Shot by Elizabeth Wheeler. Asher Price's candid photographs capture the truth, but when his success requires exposing an enemy, Asher discovers his only shot at happiness involves revealing secrets of his own. (978-1-62639-229-8)

Courtship by Carsen Taite. Love and justice—a lethal mix or a perfect match? (978-1-62639-210-6)

Against Doctor's Orders by Radclyffe. Corporate financier Presley Worth wants to shut down Argyle Community Hospital, but Dr. Harper Rivers will fight her every step of the way, if she can also fight their growing attraction. (978-1-62639-211-3)

A Spark of Heavenly Fire by Kathleen Knowles. Kerry and Beth are building their life together, but unexpected circumstances could destroy their happiness. (978-1-62639-212-0)

Never Too Late by Julie Blair. When Dr. Jamie Hammond is forced to hire a new office manager, she's shocked to come face to face with Carla Grant and memories from her past. (978-1-62639-213-7)

Widow by Martha Miller. Judge Bertha Brannon must solve the murder of her lover, a policewoman she thought she'd grow old with. As more bodies pile up, the murderer starts coming for her. (978-1-62639-214-4)

Twisted Echoes by Sheri Lewis Wohl. What's a woman to do when she realizes the voices in her head are real? (978-1-62639-215-1)

boldstrokesbooks.com
Bold Strokes Books
Quality and Diversity in LGBTQ Literature
victory
EDITIONS
Drama
MATINEE BOOKS
SCI-FI
E-BOOKS
MYSTERY
erotica
BSB
SOLILOQUY
EROTICA
YOUNG
ADULT
BOLD
STROKES
BOOKS
LIBERTY
EDITION
Romance
W·E·B·S·T·O·R·E
PRINT AND EBOOKS